ESCAPING THE CAVES

KRISTIN TALGØ

ESCAPING THE CAVES
Kristin Talgø

Science Fiction and Fantasy Publications

http://scififantasypublications.com
An imprint of DAOwen Publications

Copyright © 2015 by Kristin Talgø
All rights reserved

DAOwen Publications supports copyright. Copyright fuels creativity, encourages diverse voices, promotes free speech, and creates a vibrant culture. Thank you for buying an authorized edition of this book and for complying with copyright laws by not reproducing, scanning, or distributing any part of it in any form without permission. You are supporting writers and allowing DAOwen Publications to continue to publish books for every reader.

Escaping the Caves / Kristin Talgø
Edited by Douglas Owen and Holly Hunt

ISBN 978-1-928094-35-7
EISBN 978-1-92094-03-6

This is a work of fiction. Names, characters, places, and incidents either are the product of the author's imagination or are used fictitiously, and any resemblance to actual persons, living or dead, businesses, companies, events, or locales is entirely coincidental.
Jacket art: MMT Productions

10 9 8 7 6 5 4 3 2

To

My parents Tone and Steinar, for all your love and support. My sisters Heidi and Ingvild, for brightening up my day simply by being there. My friends Ingrid, Camilla, Stefania and Stine, for never failing to make me laugh even when I'm crying. And last, but always first, to my daughter Maia, for all that you are.

Forward

This is not the story of how the world ended. No one really knows how it ended. All that is certain is somehow, somewhere, someone fucked up.

Big time.

Now it is up to us, those unfortunate enough to be born at the edge of these god-forsaken caves, to prevent what is left of the world from being overrun by the monsters. Demons. Ghouls. Aliens. Whatever you choose to call them, they're not nice. They'll rip your head clean off. Trust me, I know.

I'm one of those unfortunate ones, born anonymously in the middle of the night.

This is my story.

Chapter 1

The day my world came to a crashing end started just like any other day. The hazy, grey pre-dawn light seeped in through the cracks between the blankets draped across the windows. This was my favorite time of the day. The night had not quite ended, and the day had not quite begun. It was my in-between time. For a precious half an hour, whatever deity existed took pity on me and hit the pause button on my life. For half an hour, time stood still.

It was the only time of day I could breathe. For the remaining twenty-three and a half hours, I held my breath, figuratively, of course. There was sleep, but it was tense, strained, as if my sub-conscious knew what the consequences would be if it relaxed and let its guard down.

Those pale, frail thirty minutes were filled with the only sense of peace I knew. There was no need for the abyss of alcohol, sex, gambling or incessant chatter to keep my thoughts and memories in check. The feeling of an imminent catastrophe, a shadow darkening my horizon, was, for the time being, asleep.

The world had not yet woken. Outside, the street was quiet. I turned over on my side, and scooted over to Kyle's side of the bed. My head found a familiar resting place just underneath his chin. I felt the steady beat of his heart against my palm. Despite being asleep, Kyle's arms wrapped around me and pulled me close. My fingers drew circles, meaningless patterns, across the skin on his chest.

His breathing shifted and I knew he was awake. Kyle's hands trailed patterns of their own up and down my arms and back. I responded to the silent signal and tilted my chin up.

Afterwards, Kyle lingered just long enough to catch his breath. I sat up, watched him dress. He never bothered to wash in the morning. No one did. We scraped the grime off in the evening. A bit of sweat hardly made a difference where we were going. The creatures we worked with could smell us out a mile off. No amount of soap or water could change that.

His muscles flexed as he pulled his hair back and tied it with a thin piece of rope. I watched him buckle his belt and button his shirt. It was strange to think that it was the same hands which dealt out so much death during the day that loved me at night.

Something in my eyes must have betrayed me, because Kyle laced up his boots without meeting them again. He opened up the door, and turned his face halfway toward me, not quite shutting me out, not quite inviting me in.

"See you later, yeah?"

He didn't kiss me goodbye.

I nodded at the closed door. The three words had barely been formed in my mouth before they died. They left a bitter aftertaste.

Escaping The Caves

To prolong the inevitable, I contemplated staying in bed, but our small room was getting hot. The morning sun cared nothing for my misgivings.

I pulled on one of Kyle's t-shirts and a pair of shorts that looked reasonably clean. At least there were no blood stains.

The heat and noise hit me like a fist the moment I opened the door. I blinked against the harsh glare of the sun, and made my way to the tap in the wall. The cool water helped marshal my thoughts. The people around me, family and friends as well as strangers, sometimes reminded me of robots, the kind I'd read about in Grandpa's books.

When I'd woken up half an hour earlier, all had been silent and everyone asleep. But at the exact stroke of six, it was as if an invisible hand had flicked a switch. There was no gradual build up to the hustle and bustle surrounding me. Everyone launched themselves into an almost hectic cheerfulness.

There was a grim set to most peoples' mouths, a tightening around the eyes noting my passage through town. But they were loud, like kids trying to out-do each other, to keep the boogey man away.

My flip-flops scraped across the dirt, sand sticking to my toes. I slid on a pair of sunglasses. Mom had always said the eyes were a window into a person's soul. I didn't want anyone sneaking a peek.

I greeted, nodded and wished a good morning to everyone who looked my way.

There was one man who decided whose turn it was to put their life on the line for this colony. That man was my father. Whenever a string was pulled in this town, you could be sure one of my father's fingers twitched. And his second-in-command was the man who claimed to be my husband.

3

Kristin Talgø

It was never official, no ceremony, but to all intents we were man and wife. He'd never actually come right out and asked me. It'd been a dusky afternoon, orange light spilling everywhere, warming even the coldest shadows. Sitting on a bench facing each other, he'd taken off one of his rings. He'd tried it on every one of my fingers until he found one it fit. He'd slid it down the middle finger on my left hand and there it'd stayed. When he started calling me his wife, everyone accepted it as just another fact of life. The sky is up, the earth is down. Kyle and Jess are married. End of discussion. No one questioned it. Least of all me.

The ring on my left hand made up for most of the unspoken words between us. Most, but not all. Kyle, a man of few words on his best day, would never understand all the things I wanted to say. Hell, I hardly understood them myself.

I felt around in my other pocket, but came up short. My usual packet of cigarettes was missing, undoubtedly finished last night, though I didn't remember smoking them.

Despite the early hour, the cafeteria was packed with people sitting down with their breakfast trays. I grabbed one of my own, seeking out familiar faces.

"Jess! Over here!" Trenton waved a piece of toast.

"You don't need those in here, darling." Jen pulled down my shades and gently folded them on the table.

I sipped my coffee and hoped the headache would go away. I'd preferred the world encased in shadows. It softened the sharp edges.

"Here, thinking you need those?" Trenton winked at me.

Grateful, I smiled and swallowed the pills he'd slipped me. I'd known Trenton since he was still in diapers. No one knew me like he did. Except maybe for Jen.

Escaping The Caves

"Why aren't you dressed?" She pretended to look at a make-believe watch on her wrist. "We're on the same shift, aren't we?"

"Sure, nine o'clock," I spoke through a mouthful of yoghurt. It tasted sour and by the time I swallowed, I could've sworn it'd grown to twice the size.

"And aren't we scheduled for our usual training and preparation at seven?" In another life Jen would've made an excellent school teacher.

"I'll change on the way there. You can do without me for five minutes."

Jen shrugged. "Kyle doesn't like it when we're late."

I thought of Kyle walking out the door, his sweat still cooling on my skin. Suddenly Kyle's likes and dislikes plummeted down the list of my priorities. Trenton watched me, chewing slowly.

I focused on my lack of appetite, and resisted the urge to put my sunglasses back on. In the caves and on the training field, Kyle was my ranking officer, but I never got to play favorite. On the contrary, he pushed me twice as hard as the rest of them. Maybe he had a point to prove, or maybe he really didn't want my head getting ripped off. Either way, sleeping with my boss didn't buy me any advantages.

Except one. The one and only thing I'd ever insisted on was to always, always be on the same team, running the same shift as Jen. Once we were in the caves, there was only so much I could do to keep her safe, but at least I was there. It was one of the few things Kyle and I hadn't argued about. He didn't comment on my protective streak towards my younger sister, but he didn't push me on it either. His silent acceptance of things was both the thing I loved and hated the most about him.

"Well, we should get going. You might have ways of

softening him, but I doubt he'd appreciate it if I tried some of those ways."

"Ugh, Trenton. Gross!" Jen pretended to slap his hand away, but giggled when he kissed her.

It was still a bit strange to see my best friend together with my sister. I'd never seen him as anything other than a brother, but if they had a falling out, it would put me in a very awkward position. However, two years on, they still looked at each other as if they couldn't believe their luck.

There was an odd twinge in my heart. I gave up on my breakfast and pushed away from the table.

Once outside, I could put my glasses back on. The world turned the preferable shade of muted grey again. Before leaving them, I put out my hand toward Trenton, raising my eyebrows.

He shook his head, slipping me a few cigarettes. "Thought you'd quit?"

"Do I strike you as a quitting woman?" I lit one up and inhaled deeply.

He eyed the crumbling cigarette. "Not now, not then, not ever."

"Glad to hear it. See you out there." I kissed Jen's cheek.

"Don't be too late!" Jen called after me.

I waved a hand over my shoulder without turning.

˅ ˄

The room had turned into a small furnace by the time I got back. I changed into my uniform as quickly as possible. I lighted a second smoke. Trenton knew me too well to give me just one. I clamped it between my teeth, scraping my hair back into a bun of some sort. Jen had smooth, chestnut colored hair, looking like something out of a shampoo ad, even after an entire shift in the caves. Jo had the same bright blonde hair as our mother, and where Julia received her mass of red hair from, no one knew or dared to say.

Mine was a strange mix of the three of them. Just like my heart, my hair seemed unable to make up its mind. I could count the times I'd bothered to pull a comb through it on one hand, so the only constant thing about my hair was messy. I killed beasts for a living. I wasn't exactly entering a beauty contest.

I headed towards the training field, wondering how Jo and Julia were doing. The former had a six-month-old girl balancing on one arm, and the latter had one kicking inside. Last I'd seen Julia, she'd resembled a medium-sized family cottage. That combined with her fiery hair and temperament, I'd thought it best to keep my observation to myself. Even pregnant, she was a force to be reckoned with. Especially pregnant.

In addition to her hair, Jo had inherited our mother's quiet, but determined, disposition. She offered a much-needed balance to Julia's intense personality. Both of them were off duty for the next three years.

I rubbed my stomach, feeling the puckered flesh of the scar through the fabric of my pants. The only thing growing in there was unease. I sucked down my third and last cigarette just as I entered the training grounds. Kyle didn't as much as look my way, but I could tell from his clenched jaw that he'd noticed my late entrance.

I smiled. It was the first smile of the day. There would be a chill wind in the air and snow at the top of the mountains before there was another.

Kristin Talgø

On the way up the rocky slope towards the caves, the vegetation slowly died down. Eventually it faded away altogether. Despite the dusty desert sand and stony hills surrounding this godforsaken place, there was life. Mostly consisting of cactuses, but some bushes braved the heat, shimmering like mirages.

I squinted up at the boiling sun, shielding my eyes with the back of my hand. Two dark shapes circled overhead, momentarily eclipsing the white orb. Vultures. Goosebumps raced up and down my spine. They left a nasty cold spot at the base of it. I focused on placing one foot in front of the other on the treacherous ground, but the greedy eyes above never left us.

The dark mound of the opening of the cave emitted a chill breath, but it did nothing to soothe our sweaty brows and clammy hearts. It stank. Reeked of blood, rotten flesh and that particular smell the monsters left behind. Moldy and dry at the same time. It was what I imagined the inside of a coffin must smell like.

Kyle turned toward his troop. Everyone present, including me, knew we could be facing our last minutes on this desolate earth, but you wouldn't have known it from our faces. Not a muscle twitched. Immovable. Impassive. Just the way Kyle liked us.

"This is a routine mission. We move in as one, but once inside, everyone for themselves. You fall behind and you get left behind, unless you're a better fighter than you think you are. No one will save you except yourself. If your time has come, there is only one thing I ask of you. Give them hell first."

Kyle searched every face in front of him, except mine. No one did silent treatment like him. This might be the last time we

Escaping The Caves

saw each other, but pride was at the core of his emotional make-up. Even the threat of death couldn't budge it. "We fight until our last breath. What is our motto?"

"Pain will not break me. Fear will not take me," we chorused back, like obedient schoolchildren.

Kyle nodded. "Then let's go."

Jen and Trenton walked side by side. Before the shadows erased their faces, I caught a glimpse of Trenton's eerie green eyes tattooing Jen's face on his mind. Grandpa had been fond of saying a picture was worth a thousand words, and if that was the case, a single look could speak untold millions. Unable to help myself, I wondered what it must feel like to be loved like that. I walked alone into the cave.

Kyle was right. Once inside we spread out, a spider casting its web hoping to get lucky. Despite our best efforts, footsteps bounced off the slimy walls. They echoed back to us. We might as well have rung a doorbell and announced our presence to the malicious hosts inhabiting these dark crevices.

But we were well-trained. Our feet never faltered. Our fingers never lost their steady grip on our firearms, and our ears strained to pick up even the slightest shuffling. Our eyes were next to useless in this darkness.

After a few minutes we were able to make out our surroundings, but only enough to navigate. There was hardly enough light to avoid stubbing our toes on protruding rocks or smashing our heads on the low ceiling, let alone spotting the enemy.

Our mission was to avoid being killed long enough to take them out. It would've been simple, really, if it hadn't been so terrifying.

We were brave, strong, but sweat poured down our bodies in

buckets. And the monsters smelt fear. Even if they'd been deaf, our scent brought them straight to us. A tiny twinge in my gut halted me. I sensed Kyle ahead doing the same. Jen and Trenton moved off to each side of the space available to us. The rest of our team fanned out, slowing their progress as well.

Water dripped somewhere off in the distance. These caves were huge, everyone knew that. The only thing we didn't know was how huge. I pictured a vast, sprawling labyrinth, with thousands of dark crouched forms moving in our direction. My breathing slowed, my heartbeat drummed against my skull. But it was steady, even, ready.

There was a familiar coppery taste in my mouth, but instead of ignoring it, I welcomed it. Fear will not be ignored. I let it wash over me, lash at my mind, my heart, my body. It met no resistance and gave up, dissolving like vile smoke on the wind. An empty, hollow feeling filled me up and I drew the strength I needed from it.

Then all hell broke loose.

One minute there was nothing. Then they were everywhere. Razor-sharp claws. Long, pointy fangs, all lashing out. Black, lidless eyes took in the trespassers, assessed the threat in a millisecond, then lunged into action. Mucus ran from noses shaped like slits, like that of snakes. Some slid forward on all fours, moving with the grace and rapidity of panthers. Others reared up on two feet, like some enormous deformed bear.

Scales ran down their bodies, as strong as steel. No weapon or ammunition known to us could penetrate that coat of armor.

But all living creatures have their weaknesses. These beings could only be killed with a shot to their brain through an eye or the mouth, or with a shot to the only vulnerable spot on their hideous body: the nape of the neck.

Escaping The Caves

The combination of the terror, the dark and their physical advantage... Killing these beasts took practice. Most of us never lived long enough to accomplish the feat. Safe to say, our job had a high turn-over rate.

I acted on instinct more than anything else, and aimed as well as possible. Fired six shots in rapid succession. The inhuman screams told me I'd hit my mark. I reloaded the rifle by the time the corpses hit the ground. A furious growl rose from the remaining creatures. They had, if not feelings, brains capable of understanding anger and loss.

Without pause, I took out the pissed off comrades. From what I could make out of the surrounding cacophony of snarls, human yells and gun fire, my comrades held their own.

How many more left? Half a dozen? Maybe as few as four? I took out one and then another. I hardly felt one of them scratch my arm. Another battle scar for my collection.

After the weapons ceased firing, the silence lay heavy on our minds. Did we dare hope we'd taken them all out this time? There were plenty more where they came from, but routine missions usually went like this. The beasts would present us with a welcoming committee and, if possible, we'd take them out, though often with casualties. This time, we were all present and accounted for.

I risked a shuddering breath, but it froze on the way out. A deep growling, sounding almost like an underground train, echoed through the caves. I tried to focus my weapon, but there was nothing to aim at. That cold spot started off goosebumps that ran down my arms.

"Everyone get out!" Kyle commanded.

No one had the least bit of interest in finding the source of the noise, and we were quick to obey. I felt, more than saw, someone trip and falter behind me. *You fall behind, you get left behind.* I knew the drill and though my mind screamed for Jen, my legs wouldn't obey at first. A pair of arms clamped around my waist.

"Move!"

"Let me go! Jen!" I screamed until hoarse.

"Jess!"

Relief surged through me.

"Get out, Jess! Trenton twisted his foot, but we'll be all right. Just get out!" Her voice broke on the last word. Not from emotion, but from the sheer strain of being heard above the noise.

The train, or whatever it was, was coming closer. The caves shuddered with the sound's force.

"I'm not leaving her!" I kicked and bit down as hard as I could. Blood flowed into my mouth.

The instant his grip loosened, I was off, but only for a moment. I was too preoccupied avoiding the boulders crashing down from the ceiling and never saw the fist coming. Stars exploded behind my eyes. Pain cut through my head like a parting knife. I remained conscious, but there was nothing I could do to avoid being slung over Kyle's shoulder. The darkness in the cave receded and the sun shone once again on our faces.

The last thing I saw before my own dark cave claimed me was the exit of the one behind us crashing shut. Rocks and boulders came together in one tremendous avalanche. When the dust settled, there was nothing left but a huge trembling mountain. It looked like it'd never been touched.

Escaping The Caves

I came to in the shade of a small tree. Kyle carried me part of the way to the compound, but a bullet in his left shoulder had slowed him down. In the dark it was easy to shoot each other. Even if we knew who was responsible, there would've been no repercussions. These things happened.

I touched my jaw and flinched. My fingers came away bloody. "Where is she?" My throat was sore and my voice didn't work properly. "Where is she?"

Kyle tightened the bandage around his wound with his teeth. Apart from the two vultures in the sky, we were alone. The rest of the team had crept back to the settlement. No one wanted to witness this.

"You don't need me to answer that for you." He tore off another piece of his shirt. There was a deep gash across his chest, but the blood was already clotted.

"Yes, I do." It hurt to speak, it hurt to clench my jaw like this, but I wanted to tear his guts out. "Where is she?" My yell ran up the hills and came back down again, repeating itself until it faded and died away.

Kyle folded a compression and tipped his water canister against it. "Either the mountain took her or the creatures did. Let's pray it was the mountain." He pressed the compression against my wound.

My reflexes had always been good. I pulled him towards me, and sunk my fingers deep into the red trenches on his chest. His cry of pain did nothing to numb the gaping hole in my heart. But it made me hungry for more. My fingernails dug deeper.

Murderous anger or not, Kyle was still physically stronger than me. He pushed me off him, and my head struck the ground with a sickening thud. Bile rose in my throat. I forced it down.

Kristin Talgø

To pass out was not an option. Kyle rose up above me. His shirt soaked in red.

"I will forget what you did. But don't you dare forget," he spit out the words, "that I just broke one of our commandments for you. You fall behind, you get left behind. I came back for you. So hate me if you must, but don't ever forget that."

The cracked soil eagerly licked up my tears. The vultures never stopped circling.

Chapter 2

The sun moved along the horizon and the shade followed it. I sat up, clutching my head. When I moved, it felt as if my brain was rolling around in there, a rotten egg yolk ready to burst. Unsteadily, I got my feet. There was a sticky maroon spot on the rock where I'd hit my head. The earth wasn't picky. Blood, water, didn't matter, it'd drink it anyway.

Kyle would've sent medical personnel for me by now. The man hadn't broken one of his precious commandments only to leave me to die of dehydration. I picked up the water bottle left for me under the tree. Despite sipping carefully, it came right back up. Leaning on my hands and knees, I retched. I wished the mountain had taken pity and buried me too.

Jen.

She couldn't be gone. If I refused to accept it, it wouldn't be true. Hundreds of images flashed across my mind.

Jen, age three, holding my hand as we looked for Father, waiting for him to visit.

Jen, six, messy pigtails and crying as I cleansed out her bleeding knee.

Jen, thirteen, I, fifteen, hiding underneath our blankets after lights out, whispering, giggling.

Jen, two and half years ago, nervously admitting she liked Trenton.

Jen, less than two hours ago, smiling, laughing, breathing, living.

I gagged. A door opened up inside of me. I slammed it shut. There was a cellar down there. Just as deep and dark as the caves up ahead, and filled with just as many monsters. The hinges creaked, resisting.

One of the unspoken commandments of our thinning tribe was to never come apart. You did what you did to move on, but you never, under any circumstances, fell apart. Breaking down was easy. Being strong took practice.

Pain was a part of life, but you kept it to yourself. And if, in the end, it all proved to be too much, you went out of this world the way you entered it. Bloody and screaming. Being killed in combat was a soldier's death, and soldiers were honored and remembered. Those who failed to abide by these simple rules were neither.

I lurched up the crumbling ground, and noticed the scratch I'd received earlier, a shallow red gash on the inside of my lower left arm. Compared to the mother of a headache breeding inside my skull, I filed it away as getting off lucky.

I had to stop every few minutes, resting hands on knees, willing myself not to throw up again.

She could still be in there, still alive. The exit was blocked, but the entrance might not be. Please, please, please.

Voices broke through my incessant chanting. I pushed on a

little faster. The ground rose up to meet me, but I avoided impact at the last second. I straightened and focused on the black pin-prick in the distance, marking my goal.

My body felt drunk. I tried to walk in an even line, but nonetheless, I zigzagged left and right. The cave came closer and I realized I'd left my firearm by the tree. A soldier's death was an honorable one, after all. At least it would prevent me from becoming an outcast.

This time around, the chill of the caves was welcoming. I was running a fever and the cold dampness was a mother's touch compared to the scorching heat outside. The voices shouted, but once inside the caves, they were swallowed up. Delirious, but far from suicidal, I closed my eyes, trying to get a feel of the place. Nothing moved. Panic reared up within me like a wounded animal.

I would've shouted her name, but it stuck in my throat. It couldn't get past the lump. Be here, just be here, please, be here.

Nothing.

No shoes, no weapons, no blood, no monsters, nothing. Either the cleaning crew had already been here, or the mountain had made the job redundant.

"Jen." I didn't recognize my own voice. It was the voice of an old woman. Trembling, hoarse, fragile. "Trenton."

A wall of sharp rocks and blunt boulders guarded the path ahead of me. I touched it. Dry and cold.

"They should be here." That creaky door within me swung open. Just a little. Just enough. "They should be here."

"Jess. Please, come with us." A warm hand. Red freckles. Michael. A surgeon and a dear friend. "There is nothing more you can do for them. You're putting your life at risk for nothing. All of our lives."

Two more pairs of eyes avoided my face, grateful for the shadows. I didn't know them. I didn't know anyone right then.

"Michael?"

"Yes, Jess. Now, please come with me. We can do this the easy way or the hard way, but you're coming with me."

I sat down on the ground and pushed at the door in my mind. Almost closed, but almost wasn't good enough.

Michael sighed. "You're the daughter of our commander and the wife of one our strongest soldiers. Don't let them see you being carried out of here like a child. Please."

He touched the three marks forever carved into my left cheekbone. Courage, integrity, honor. By these words we made our lives. "Remember who you are. You are a warrior. We grieve, but we do not cry."

He wiped my face, gently, and pulled me to my feet. "Remember them as they lived. Proud and strong."

His words meant nothing. That hollowness within me widened and the door opened up a little further. There was a gap between us where there previously had been none. We'd stood on the same side of the mountain, seeing the same sky and earth, hearing the same birds and animals. But now I found myself at the opposite side of a canyon, with no idea how to get back.

Pride. How little it mattered when your reason for existing was taken from you.

I allowed him to lead me out.

"I understand you disobeyed protocol. I would've expected more from you, Jess." My father stood with his back to me, facing the window. It overlooked the few green patches of grass there was around here. His office was neat, orderly to the point of sterility. Just like its owner.

"Jen was in danger. I had to save her."

"Yes, she was, but no, you didn't."

"She was your daughter!" I didn't realize I was shouting until my voice broke. I straightened the overturned chair, but remained standing.

Slowly, everything done with precision, my father turned toward me. He hadn't met my eyes in twenty years. I had my mother's eyes.

"I was there when each and every one of my daughters were born, so rest assured that I know very well Jen was my daughter." A muscle worked in his jaw. "Don't be so arrogant as to presume that your anger and grief are greater than mine."

I willed him to meet my gaze, but he looked everywhere else. My hair, my bruises, my scratches, his desk, the ceiling, the floor, the window once again.

"But you don't see me putting the lives of others at risk because of it, or acting like a madman." He held up his palms. "No, don't try to deny it. You might not like our rules, Jess, but they are our rules because of one very simple reason. Because they work."

"Work? Your youngest daughter was crushed to death. How well would you say those rules worked for her?" The back of the chair dug into the cuts in my hands.

The disdain on my father's face hurt more than any slap ever could. "How many of you were there when you entered the cave?"

"What does tha—"

"How many?"

"Seven. There were seven of us."

"And how many died in that cave?"

It was a terrible thing to hate your own father, but just then I did. "Two."

Father paced behind his desk, hands clasped at the small of his back. A teacher lecturing a rebellious pupil. "And how many came out of that cave, relatively unharmed?"

I concentrated on breathing evenly. "Five."

Father stopped his pacing. "Five." He sat down at his desk, stapling his fingers underneath his chin. "Two casualties, five alive to fight another day. I call that a success. You might have a different view on the matter, Jess, but I think you'll find yourself rather alone in that assessment."

"Are we done here?"

"Not quite. Because of your disobedience, you needlessly risked your own life, which prompted Kyle to put his life at risk. By the grace of whatever god exists, you two are still alive to tell the tale. But because of your blatant disregard of our rules, there could've been four deaths laid at my door today, instead of just two." Father never raised his voice. He didn't have to.

"Would you have preferred me to have lost two daughters today, instead of just one?"

"Are you telling me that if it'd been you in those caves with Jen, you would've kept going despite knowing she was being killed only meters away from you?" I always raised my voice. I had to.

"Yes." Not a pause or a blink of an eye. "I would've." He started shuffling some papers around. Case closed.

I opened my mouth, then closed it. There were some things I just couldn't say. I might as well have stuck a knife in his heart. I turned to leave.

Escaping The Caves

"I've already spoken with Kyle, and while he had my thanks for saving your life, I gave him the same speech as I've given you. He won't disobey the commandments a second time for you. Don't force him into that position again."

Father's voice drifted out to me through the closing door. "And for god's sake, Jess, I've already had one woman dishonor our family. Don't follow in her footsteps."

He didn't have to worry about that. Those footsteps had left far too large an imprint for me to ever have any hope of filling them.

Kyle wasn't in our room when I got back. I filled a bucket with water and poured it over me. I wrapped myself in a towel and sat down on the bed. The physical wounds were already healing, but the mental and emotional wounds hemorrhaged.

Nothing felt real anymore. Jen couldn't be dead. Not Jen. Not Trenton. Anyone else but them. At that moment, I would've preferred it being Kyle rather than my sister. The thought left me feeling even more alone and desperate. The door in my mind kept inching open, the cellar looming closer.

Kyle found me crying on the bed. I could see him through my fingers. He stood quite still, watching for a full minute. No emotion showed on his dark face. Then he turned around and left.

Warriors do not cry, warriors do not cry. Courage, integrity, honor. I chanted the words over and over, but the sobs kept on coming. Sometimes there's just no stopping a storm. You've just got to hold on, praying you'll make it through.

Kristin Talgø

We didn't do funerals, mostly for practical reasons. There was rarely anything to bury. In Jen and Trenton's case, there was nothing. The caves swallowed them whole and hadn't bothered to spit anything out.

To say the atmosphere between Kyle and I had been strained would be an understatement. He'd sneaked back into our room long after lights out. He'd slipped underneath the covers, and we lay there, both feigning sleep. When his hands sought out my waist, I accepted the shelter offered. Not because of any real need to feel close, but because resisting would be exhausting.

It was easier to simply go where he took me, let our lovemaking wash over me. I hoped the rhythmical waves would wash away the unbearable ache in my heart, leaving me clean and bare. But it had no impact. *He* had no impact.

An ocean of faces, some familiar, some not, filed past me and Father. The memorial service was brief and to the point. We still had a mission to fulfill and the time took our lunch break.

"From dust to dust…" The priest mumbled the words. His eyes curiously blank, his words disrespectful in their repetitiveness. He must have done this so many times that the ritual had long-since lost all meaning. The people he buried were of no more use. Once death claimed them, they lost their purpose. Why should he care?

Kyle's hand was warm and dry, but it gave me no comfort. He knew I still hadn't forgiven him for stopping me from going after Jen, but that wasn't the real root of our problem. The infestation ran much deeper.

My obvious grief was slowly poisoning our relationship, one

teardrop at the time. Our marriage had stood the test of time, as well as many mistakes on both sides. What my temper and his indiscretions had failed to do, my bone-deep sorrow had wiped out in seconds.

I hadn't revealed just how far the door leading into the cellar in my mind had opened. It took willpower to drag myself out of bed in the morning. The sun was too harsh, the noise too loud. I drank myself into a stupor at night and if I kept smoking so many cigarettes, there would be a severe cigarette shortage within weeks.

My nerve endings were raw and sizzled. They flinched as people shook my hand. Their hollow condolences infuriated me. They were an insult to Jen and Trenton's memory. Sleep deprivation made it hard to think coherently.

"Jess?" Kyle whispered. His eyes never left the crowd, but his voice probed me. "Are you all right?"

"Yes, I'm fine," I spoke through numb lips. There was a strange tingling in my left hand and the left side of my face. A glass wall had risen up between me and the other mourners. I was increasingly cut off from my surroundings. Trapped in a bubble that didn't exist.

So this is what it feels like to lose one's mind. The thought struck such terror in my heart as I'd never felt before. It made the nightmares in the caves seem like fuzzy maiden aunts.

So this is what it feels - what it feels - it feels - feels…

"Jess!" Kyle and my father shouted after me, but I paid them no heed.

Running away was the only thought getting through the fog and terror. If I could outrun this awful sensation, this sense of a wall coming down, a wall which should never have been approached in the first place, then maybe I could close the door

Kristin Talgø

again for good.

The cellar yawned. It flaunted black depths and haunted inhabitants. My legs pumped as fast as they'd ever done before. Sweat poured down my back, my fear manifesting itself, putting down roots.

I didn't stop until I'd reached a hill at the outskirts of our terrible town. From there, I could see the caves that stretched from one end and continued through the range of mountains, reaching as far as I could see.

A thin veil of clouds weakened the sunlight. The slight breeze ruffled my damp hair. I tried to focus on something real, something tangible. Eventually the black and white dots at the edges of my vision receded. The feeling of being wrapped in cotton was blown away in the wind.

I slid to the ground, dug my fingers into the stony earth, relished the dry pebbles scraping across my skin.

Reality.

It was a hard, cold uncaring bitch, but preferable to the frightening world I'd glimpsed in the cellar. Nothing certain, everything possible. And the feeling of going insane.

I shuddered. My mind still felt far too fragile, a trembling bubble threatening to burst at the slightest movement. But at least I had control of my body once more. The all-consuming terror had pulled back for the time being. But it left a smudge, a mark that hadn't been there before. It'd left a calling card and I knew it would return, sooner or later.

The thought made me want to curl up and die.

"You planning to be like this all evening?" I stood over Kyle, watching him do the laundry.

He worked the fabric, expertly washing it, rinsing. He twisted a shirt and tossed it onto the pile, ready to be hung to dry.

"Planning to be like what?" It'd been five minutes since I'd asked the question, but I wouldn't budge. Neither would he.

"Stonewalling me."

"I'm not."

"I couldn't help myself. It just…proved too much. I needed to get away."

"That is your right." He washed. Rinsed. Twisted.

"She was my sister. How can you not understand that?"

Yelling was the last thing I should have done. It would prick his pride, close him down completely.

That awful tightening of his jaw. His hands worked faster. Water splashed over the basin, sprinkled our feet.

"She was my sister and now she's gone. It's all I can do to hold on and I need you, I—"

"Except you're not and you don't." Kyle raising his voice wasn't a good sign. He never bothered unless truly provoked. "You're not holding on. Look at yourself." He made the most contemptuous sound, clicking his tongue and flicking his wrist, as if to shake off a bothersome fly.

His lack of understanding and obvious anger rattled me. What right did he have to be angry? "I am doing the best that I can." My teeth ached, I bit down so hard in an effort to control my temper.

He scoffed, shook his head. "Then try harder."

Grabbing hold of his coarse dreads, I pulled his head back, forcing him to look at me. He grabbed my wrist, twisted it like the discarded clothes. There was a moment when time stood still, when our life could be so easily destroyed, disintegrated by

Kristin Talgø

a few misspoken words and heated actions.

Then he released my hand, and pushed me away. He turned back to the laundry. Washed, rinsed, twisted. I'd almost preferred he strike me.

The cellar showed no mercy at night. It threw the door open and unleashed its unspoken contents upon my mind. I saw their faces.

Jen and Trenton.

So many more. All of those who'd been close to me, my beacons in the dark, and even those I'd barely known. Even those whose names shamed me to have forgotten. Their howls, cries of anguish, pierced my soul, clawed at my sanity.

Their eyes burned holes through my skin. They tore at my heartstrings, pulled at them, wanted them to unravel.

See us, hear us, remember us.

Jen was there and so was Trenton. Their love, unmarred by death, slapped me in the face. It reminded me of all I wanted and never would have. There was a craving for each other on their faces, plain for the entire world to see. No untimely temper, no hurtful indiscretions. A mutual understanding of each other that cut me to the core.

And so much blood. It poured in rivers down the streets. Their blood created pools of loss. An abandoned shoe floated on the murky surface. The sticky fluid penetrated the walls, the ceilings, the floors of all the houses. It would soon drown those of us left. There was only so much we could take, only so much we could ignore, before it caught up with us.

Courage, integrity, honor. Those badges of pride carved into

Escaping The Caves

our faces failed to shield us from the truth. We were doomed by one fact of life we could never hope to escape.

Our humanity.

Sooner or later, it would land the killing blow. My nervousness, my failing sanity could trigger a landslide. If I could tip over, be dragged down by the torn ghosts that floated among us, anyone could. Morale would weaken, and what would be left?

A wrecked town filled with madmen, killers and monsters. Once the first two had dispersed with each other, the latter would win. The steel ring of warriors meant to shield the rest of the world from reality would be no more. The monsters would be free to roam the Earth. To bring bloodshed and destruction. Leaving nothing but ashes scattered on the wind.

And so ends the world.

All because of my weakness, my haunted cellar, my ghosts. My lingering attachment to those already crossed over. Crossed out. Because I couldn't ignore the truth anymore.

My father looked down from above, his eyes clouded by the shadows that gathered on the horizon.

Kyle had long since turned his back on me.

Blinding light cut through my moaning. I bolted upright. The soaked sheets clung to my body. I blinked. The harsh glare of the light bulb dangling from the ceiling stabbed my eyes.

Kyle stood by the door, one hand still on the light switch. His face didn't betray any emotion, but on this rare occasion his eyes did. He was scared. Of me.

"Why did you turn on the light? Turn it off, it's hurting me."

Kristin Talgø

The nightmare still crawled over my skin, but oddly enough the dark soothed it. The light only enhanced my fear. And the look in Kyle's eyes was more than I could take on top of everything else.

He did as I bid, and came back to bed. Side by side, but not touching. "I turned on the light to get rid of your bad dreams. You screamed in your sleep." He shuddered.

"Just ghosts in my mind." The arms that held me, comforted me, pulled me close, never came.

"These ghosts will destroy you if you let them." His shape seemed so huge next to me. He could crush me if he wasn't careful.

"I won't let them, but they might not give me a choice. They won't be ignored any longer. I stopped listening to them. They're angry." I shivered.

"You have to kill them. It's the only way." His arms had found their way to me, but he didn't offer what I needed.

"You can't kill what is already dead." I buried my nose in his neck, inhaled his familiar scent. His skin, so dark, so smooth, was suddenly all I could see. My nightgown fluttered to the floor.

But the ghosts didn't leave. They stood quietly by the bed. They watched. Waited. Their time would come when they would claim what was theirs. They would be remembered.

I saw them, heard them and remembered them. I knew what I had to do. If it proved to be the end of me, then so be it.

See us, hear us, remember us.

Kyle moaned and shivered.

Chapter 3

When I walked through town, it was clear that the news of my departure had spread like wildfire through our community. No one looked in my direction, but everyone stopped talking. In theory, we were all entitled to exercise our right of freedom. We were warriors by choice. We weren't slaves. But for all intents and purposes, we might as well have been. Not by any cruel law or legal injustice, but by the strict set of rules our violent society operated by.

In reality, leaving was never an option. It was considered not only a betrayal to the tribe we belonged to, but a betrayal to the entire human race. We had all taken sacred vows to protect what remained of humanity from the monstrosities lurking in yonder caves. The marks etched into our faces were not only a reminder of our three founding pillars, courage, integrity and honor; they served another purpose as well.

Members of our community never traveled anywhere. Never journeyed further than the borders of our town or the edges of the caves. So if someone bearing the fateful three marks across their left cheekbone should wander into the outside world, people would know them for what they truly were.

Traitors. Oath breakers. Cowards. Weak.

Not worthy of your piss if you should come across one on fire.

People in the outside world knew what this meant. Outcasts were the lowest of the low. No one should offer these worms any words of comfort, gentle touches, nor water from their well or food from their table. Not even the dampest, dirtiest part of their stable should be offered as a resting place.

Those who left were doomed to live out a life in the shadows. They called us "the living dead". And I meant "us", because I would soon be joining this hated clan.

Apart from the obvious discomfort and unpleasantness this despised half-life consisted of, there would be a constant death sentence hung around my neck the moment I stepped across the point of no return. My life would be forfeit. I would not be officially executed, but anyone witnessing my shame and feeling compelled to right such a wrong, would be well within their right to do so.

They would not be charged with manslaughter. They didn't need to fear a trial or repercussions of any kind. Most likely they'd be voted citizen of the week. They'd be able to entertain their local pub with tales of their great bravery for many years to come.

So why leave? Needless to say, most didn't. Most people chose the caves and the greedy jaws of death within them. But though I was many things, I wasn't most people. To willingly hand over my life to the monsters I'd dedicated my whole life to destroy… That would be a defeat far greater than the disgrace

Escaping The Caves

of leaving. If I let them commit my suicide, I let them win. And I'd rather be damned a thousand times over than allow that to happen.

Traditional suicide was most peoples' second choice, usually by blowing their brains out. After all, there was no shortage or restrictions on firearms. But this second choice was hardly any better than leaving. You might not be around to witness the dishonor you brought upon yourself by pulling that trigger, but the ramifications were no less.

In the end, you proved yourself a weak coward. Your family would be guilty by association. They would not be ostracized from the community, but suspicion was a heavy shadow few were able to shake.

And with the gun cocked inside my mouth, one especially dark night, hands slippery with sweat, I had an epiphany. I wanted the ghosts gone, the horrors they kept showing me to disappear and their agonizing voices silenced, but I didn't wish to join them. Not yet anyway. Despite the tearing pain inside my chest, the rawness of my mind and the fragility of my nerves, I wanted to live. Really live.

I wanted to wake up in the morning without having to wonder if this was the day I got to witness Kyle being disemboweled in front of me. Or if this would be the day I joined all those headless skeletons littering the ground inside the caves.

I wanted to walk along the sandy beaches Grandpa had told me existed far west of this broken land. I wanted to see the ocean he described to me over and over again. See its dark blue waves come crashing toward me. Let it wash away all my tired thoughts, aches and feelings.

I wanted to sit on the beach, free to do nothing but

contemplate the vastness that my life had become. I wanted to embrace that vastness. Despite its painful consequences, the vastness could have been my salvation.

That vastness was freedom. It was my one chance at a new life. Away from all the death, the stench of blood and flesh torn to pieces. Away from the hard walls the people around me hid behind. And, most importantly, away from the ghosts.

I knew they'd travel alongside me wherever I went. But I'd never find a way of getting rid of them if I stayed. I'd go insane first. My sanity crumbled around me like quicksand. The more I struggled the deeper I sunk.

They all told me to be strong. To remember who I was, as if shaming me would bring my sanity back, when all I wanted was a bit of kindness. A bit of understanding. But I would never find that here.

In a world where survival was the only currency, mercy had no place. If you weren't part of the solution, you were part of the problem. To my friends, family and colleagues, I was a growing threat in need of neutralizing. I was the daughter of their commander and I was setting a bad example.

I was under no illusion that the kindness and understanding I craved would be found among strangers in the outside world. They'd hang me as soon as look at me. But maybe there was a world beyond the outside world? And if not, there were two people, if they were still alive, that I very much wanted to see again.

I knew all of this. But the hatred and sheer contempt my decision to leave triggered in those closest to me, shattered the vague sense of being loved.

Exercising power over another human being doesn't need to be violent. One of the most effective ways you can hurt someone is to ignore them. If no one acknowledges you, how can you be sure you even exist? You become just another ghost, without actually dying.

I walked through the cafeteria. Not one head turned to look at me, but my presence created ripples like the wind through the grass. Shockwaves that touched everyone present, but they kept their eyes on their plates and their minds on the conversation.

I squared my jaw, told myself I didn't need the approval of these people. What did it matter what they thought of me? But the people we surround ourselves with are mirrors, and we believe the reflections they throw back at us.

After a few degrading moments, I caught sight of the people whose acknowledgement, if not approval, I did need. Michael. Susan. Josh and Mary. I'd known these people since the cradle. Though many of those who used to crawl alongside us in the nursery were gone, we were still fighting for the right to breathe.

"What shift are you on?" Josh spoke through mouthfuls of scrambled eggs.

"Two o'clock." Michael tore his napkin in half.

"You?"

"Same." Mary wiped her lips with the back of her not-quite-steady hand.

Susan shook her head. "Doing the night shift. Lucky me." She bit down on her lip.

Josh frowned. Michael's napkin was already shredded into a pile of tiny, fluttering pieces. Susan rubbed the back of her head, her close cropped hair standing on end. Mary seemed extraordinarily fascinated by the red and white checkered tablecloth.

I stood so close to Michael I could discern between the red and brown strands of hair on his head. Still, he wouldn't look at me. These people I'd fought next to. Loved. We'd never really shared our true thoughts and feelings, but we knew each other as well as our world permitted us to. Their dislike hurt more than I thought it would. I turned to leave. An outcast I might be, but I wouldn't let them see me cry.

"I won't let you do this." My father's voice trembled at the edges. Not with tears, but anger. His lips were pressed so tight they disappeared, skin white around his nostrils.

"I don't see what you can do to stop me." I didn't want to have this conversation. I sat outside what used to be my room and smoked. There was a splintering headache where my brain used to be. The ghosts became more persistent by the day. I could see them now. Actually see them. They bled onto my sheets at night.

I rubbed my brow. I blinked hard, and was able to shake the hallucination standing behind my father. I didn't want Jen to be here. Scared of what she might look like. What did a person look like after having been crushed by an entire mountain?

Despite myself, I laughed. Nerves, most likely.

"If there is something amusing about this situation I fail to see it." Father spoke through gritted teeth. His fists were balled so tightly together, a thin line of blood dripped through his fingers. I looked away.

"There's nothing, nothing…" I forgot what I was about to say. Confused, I looked at the crumbling cigarette in my hand. There were too many people talking at once. I couldn't focus on all of them.

"Jess? Jess!"

Escaping The Caves

"What?"

Father fought to control himself. Even he knew my sanity couldn't be restored by banging my head against the wall. "I realize that Jen's death have taken a greater toll on you than any of us could have anticipated. I'm prepared to give you some time off to gather your wits about you again. You are one of my best soldiers."

He hesitated. "And you are my daughter." This was tantamount to him throwing his arms around me, to say he loved and couldn't bear the thought of losing me.

"Jess, don't do that." He averted his eyes.

I wiped at my tears. "I can't stay, father. I know you will never understand, but I can't... I don't want to live this life anymore."

The sound of skin on skin echoed off the walls around us. I rubbed my cheek, feeling the swelling already growing there.

"What makes you think anyone of us want to either?" Father's voice never rose above a level suitable for dinner conversation. "What makes you so special? Do you think the rest of us relish the massacres, the losses, the eternal fight to stay alive?" He pulled back a little. "Of course we don't. But a few must be sacrificed so the many can live. We are all that stand between the rest of humanity and those creatures up there." He pointed toward the caves. "We don't have the luxury of designing our own lives. Fate made that decision the day we were born into this hateful place."

It was disturbing to hear my father talk like this. I'd always presumed he considered it a great honor to lead our small battalion of fighters. He'd certainly made a great show of creating that illusion.

"But I can tell that my words have no effect whatsoever on

you. May God have mercy on you, because no one else will." His lips twisted. "You're just like your mother."

I knew he'd meant that last comment as a curse, but I pressed the words to my chest. A flimsy bandage against my dissected heart.

It took longer than I'd thought to gather up what courage I had left to face my sisters. Lucy, Jo's small daughter, gurgled happily on a soft carpet on the floor. To her, rolling around in the spot of sunshine that came in through the window, sucking on her own toes, life wasn't just good. It was perfect.

Her mother sat by the kitchen table, cradled a cup of tea, trying to calm down Julia. Her red hair seemed to hiss and crackle, like an open fire. Her anger was clearly directed at me. They both shut up the moment I entered the small cottage.

Jo's eyes brimmed with unshed tears, but underneath she was just as furious as her sister.

"Jess." She seemed to want to say more, but stopped.

"I'm glad someone here is still talking to me." My laughter wasn't quite right. Too high. Off-key.

Jo sighed. "What good would ignoring you do? You're our sister. You leaving doesn't change that."

"Speak for yourself," Julia spat. "How can you do this to us? After everything Mother put us through? I'm surprised Father hasn't died of shame yet. I know I would, if I'd bred such an ungrateful bi–"

"That's enough." Jo's voice was uncharacteristically sharp. Julia's mouth snapped shut, more out of surprise than anything else.

Escaping The Caves

"I'm sure Jess is well-aware of the consequences of her actions, and what that means both for her and us. She doesn't need another lecture. For God's sake, Julia, look at her."

I didn't like what I saw in their eyes. Not one bit.

"I just wanted to say goodbye." My fingers itched for a cigarette, but I couldn't very well light one up in front of my six-month-old niece. Jo would have my head off in one move if I tried.

"I know you did." Jo squeezed my fingers. This simple gesture spoke volumes and meant everything to me. It would both haunt and comfort me in equal measures for a long time to come.

"Why are you doing this?" Some of the anger had gone out of Julia. She sounded honestly curious and immensely tired at the same time.

"I'm in no shape to keep fighting. I'm hardly able to function on the most basic levels, I…" I rubbed my temple. Spots danced at the edges of my vision. Saying goodbye was more stressful than I'd anticipated.

"Shhh. You don't have to say." Jo looked slightly panicked.

"But why leave? Stay. You will get better. It was awful to lose Jen, for all of us, but leaving isn't going to bring her back. You're only causing more pain." Julia was winding herself up again.

"It's not just Jen, it's all of them. I hear them. They're all lodged in here." I pressed the sides of my skull. "And as long as I'm here, they'll never shut up."

My sisters had both gone white around the mouth. Jo picked up Lucy and walked to the other side of the table. She didn't sit down. I really didn't like them looking at me like that.

Julia winced as her baby kicked her in the ribs. Lucy, sensing

37

something in her perfect little world wasn't quite perfect, started crying.

"Just fucking leave then." Julia turned back to the kitchen counter.

I did as she asked.

No matter how painful and upsetting these encounters were, they did little to prepare me for my final visit. Despite his failings, I'd underestimated just how much I loved him.

Kyle sat on the threshold to our room, carving a small piece of wood. In less than a second, all my strength left. My heart pounded so hard I felt nauseous. He could be so cold and I so badly wanted him to prove me wrong. Just this once. Especially this once.

He bent the knife around the edges of the piece of wood, feeling for the shape locked within. He put my packed rucksack outside the door.

"I've come to say goodbye."

"Why?"

"Because I'm leaving and I wanted to see you one last time."

That contemptuous click of the tongue and flick of the wrist again. "Why? If you're leaving, just leave."

"Don't do this, Kyle. Please. I don't want us to part this way." I lit a cigarette, even though he hated the damn things. It took me three attempts.

He put down the knife along with the unfinished piece, and looked at me. His hands dangled loosely between his knees, his hair pulled back. He looked so achingly beautiful. I wasn't aware of my hand reaching out to touch him before he flinched. The

Escaping The Caves

disgust on his face was almost more than I could bear.

"No? Then how would you like us to part? How is a good way of saying goodbye for you? Will crying and kissing me make you feel better? Do you want me to say I love you? Should I hold you and tell you meaningless lies? How will any of this make it easier for you or me?"

"It might show me that you actually care."

He shook his head. "Well, that's too bad. You're leaving when you should be staying. There's nothing left to discuss. You've betrayed everyone. Including me. I don't want to comfort you. I can barely even look at you."

"Kyle, please…" There was a whining note in my voice I didn't much care for, but he was trying to find a way to get around me. I was losing him. Except for those awful moments in the caves when Jen fell behind, I'd never known such pure desperation before. There was a metallic taste in my mouth. Even if I lost him by leaving, I wanted him to love me. Despite how we ended.

"Kyle, please, don't go. Not yet. Just listen to me." I pushed against his chest, tried to halt him in his tracks. My pride and dignity had long since been left behind.

"Jess, let me be. Just take your things and go. There's nothing left to say."

"Nothing left to say?" I followed him into the street. "There's everything left to say."

People gave us a wide berth, but I could feel their ears stretching toward us.

Kyle kept on walking. I grabbed hold of his arm and he swiveled around to face me. "Did you ever love me?" How weak and pathetic that sounded. If you even had to ask such a question, the answer was probably no.

39

Kristin Talgø

Apart from one muscle jumping underneath the scars on his cheek, he remained impassive. "Why did you give me this?" I took the ring off my finger, and held it up. "Do you want it back?"

He shrugged. "If you don't want it anymore, I can take it. But keep it if you like. It doesn't matter to me."

I crushed the ring inside my fist and forced myself not to yell. The lack of emotion on his face made me want to punch him, tear his skin off with my fingernails. To shatter his heart the way he was shattering mine.

"What do you want, Jess?"

I want you to feel the extraordinary amount of pain that I do right now. To feel as if your insides are becoming your outsides, as if you're being torn apart, shredded the way Michael shredded his napkin. I want your heart to bleed so badly it feels as if you're choking on it. As if the mountains just came down on top of your chest.

I want you to shake, to howl, to cry over me, to beg, to grovel, to kiss me, to hate me. Most of all, I want you to love me the way I love you. To be as destroyed by the loss of us as I am. For you to know the pain of losing the one you love the most.

I looked at his blank face and sighed. How pointless it was to love someone who never loved you back. At least not the way you wanted to be loved.

"Everything, Kyle, I want everything."

He nodded, turned to leave, then stopped and did the last thing I'd expected him to do. He kissed me. With all the intensity and force I'd always wanted. All the same, it felt hollow, somehow. It didn't feel real. A beautiful wrapping without any substance inside. Despite his best efforts, there was no way he could fake love.

I broke off the kiss. "Goodbye then, Kyle."

He held on to my hand. "Last chance. Don't go. Stay. For us."

I would've laughed if I wasn't so tired. Maybe it was for the best that he'd never attempted any passionate decelerations of love. He wasn't very good at it. He sounded like an actor on a stage, a last line to hook the audience, of which we had many. Perhaps a desire for a last ego boost.

I couldn't look at him. It was embarrassing. "I can't."

That click of the tongue and, no doubt, flick of the wrist I didn't see. "Then to hell with you."

I walked back to get my rucksack. Somehow his last words hurt less than the kiss. At least they had been honest.

Chapter 4

Once I crossed the border of our town and into the desert of an unknown world, my followers turned around and left. I hadn't recognized them. Just two men with rifles ordered to witness my departure. No doubt they didn't want a lunatic dodging back at the last minute to look around for a throat to cut. They needn't have worried, though. I was dead-set on crossing over, and had enough bloodshed to last me a life time. Their throats were safe. At least from me.

So far, the outside world looked pretty much the same as the one left behind the electrical fence. The mountain range loomed to the right, the desert stretched to the left. A few dried up bushes dotted the path and a dozen or so cactuses spread around for decoration. And the vultures, of course. They'd be circling overhead, crossing their talons for my demise. I wasn't planning to give them that pleasure.

I took a sip from my water flask and looked at one of

Kristin Talgø

Grandpa's old maps. If this was accurate, or as accurate as anything could be in this desolate world, there should be a small settlement about 50 kilometers from here. Judging from the sun, it was around ten in the morning. Hopefully I could make it before sundown. It was hotter than hell right now, but come nightfall, it would be freezing. And the coyotes would come out to play.

The ghosts were ever-present companions, mirages at the edges of my vision, but the suffocating fear I'd been under for the past month wasn't as strong. With the town fading into a bad dream behind me, I could breathe a little easier. I hitched my rucksack higher onto my back and walked on.

Dusk had already fallen by the time I reached the settlement. Or what was left of it, in any case. The wind yawned underneath the awnings of the shambling houses. Despite the chill creeping into my bones, I couldn't help feeling some strange sense of awe.

This town, or village or whatever it had been, couldn't have been inhabited by people since before The Fall, which was how we referred to the fateful time when the monsters came into this world. Cities fell before their claws and snapping jaws, hence The Fall. It was as good a term as any. We were fighters, not poets.

In any case, this meant that this little place, hardly visible beneath the darkening sky, had been abandoned for the past seventy-five years. Or maybe it was seventy-six, or maybe seventy-four. Along with people and civilization, facts had been spread far and wide, and no one had ever been able to gather

Escaping The Caves

them altogether coherently.

Besides, this was all in the past. No one alive cared about the exact year things went haywire. The result remained the same.

The human race had been close to annihilation. And now it was up to one crumbling, dusty little town to keep the menace in check. The enormous responsibility I'd forsaken crept up on me, along with the shadows. I'd started to see a pattern, of sorts, where the ghosts were concerned. They seemed to draw strength and grow more solid whenever I was under great emotional stress.

To contemplate both the task I'd walked away from, and the horrible example I set for both the current and the next generation of warriors was both gruesome and mortifying.

What did my actions teach them? That it was okay to simply walk away when the pressure got too much? To be a selfish coward and turn away with your tail between legs? If every fighter started doing that, the monsters would soon be able to finish what they'd started seven decades ago.

Dust and weeds clung to my boots as I made my way through the settlement. Some of these houses must have been huge compared to what we now built, judging from the amount of concrete scattered around the fallen-down buildings. Rusty steel bars jutted like bones from half-decomposed carcasses.

But given my current state of mind, or rather lack of one, what was I to do? I kicked a rock. It hit something in the tall grass, which squeaked and skittered away. So much for dinner. It probably wasn't something I would've wanted to eat. Not that my stomach was particularly keen on a meal.

I kept coming back to the same dilemma. Leaving was a great betrayal and act of cowardice, but what would staying on have accomplished? My mental state was still about as sound and stable as the crumbling town around me. If I'd stayed, as the others expected me to, I would've lost it completely. Who's to say I wouldn't have ended up hurting someone?

At their most powerful, the hallucinations had seemed as real to me as the ground I walked on, more real than the world I actually lived in. What if I'd one day mistaken someone else for one of my ghosts? What if I'd killed someone in an attempt to rid myself of my tormentors?

The thought of such a scenario left me shaken and sick. I'd made the right choice, left while I was still sane enough to know how bad things were. Jo and Julia's white faces floated to the surface.

Stop it, I instructed. Just stop it. I was scared enough as it was. I ducked into what might have been a convenience store at one point, if the cans hiding behind a carpet of dust were anything to go by. I did a quick sweep, but there was nothing there that could harm me. Not even skeletons. Maybe the people in this town fled before the onslaught.

A little nudge prevented me from lighting a fire. It would get colder during the night, but a fire would attract coyotes and other predators. I knew little about the rest of the world I'd strived to protect. What had become of the people left to rebuild it? For all I knew, they were raving mad lunatics, the whole lot of them. I laughed shakily. If that was the case, I'd fit right in.

I risked lighting a cigarette. If the wrong animal or person looked in my direction they would've seen me. If so, let them come. I'd packed my favorite gun and several boxes of ammunition. It was clean, well-oiled and loaded.

Using it came as naturally to me as breathing did to others. I didn't want any trouble, but I wasn't afraid of some either. The last thing, or at least one of the last things, I wanted was more killing and bloodletting, but I would defend myself if needed. I wasn't suicidal.

My jacket was too thin and I tried to extract some warmth from the scratchy blanket I'd brought.

I inhaled the acrid smoke and thought about the fact that I wasn't suicidal.

My mind was a snake nest of accusations and misinterpretations. I was so sleep-deprived I could hardly see straight. My heart felt raw, swollen with grief and resentment, yet I didn't want to kill myself. I didn't know if this was a sign of some lingering sanity or the complete disintegration of it.

The ghosts were always at the back of my mind, even in my most lucid moments, but they were mercifully silent for now. I knew I should eat something, but with the dying cigarette between my fingers, my head slipped forward. I fell asleep with Jen next to me, holding my hand.

A wet slobbering noise woke me up. I slammed the back of my head against the wall, and uttered a string of curses that would've made my grandpa proud. Something yelped and ran away.

Rubbing my head, I walked to the entrance of the store, only to see a grey tail disappear around a corner. A wild dog. I guess I was lucky all it'd been doing was licking my hand, not chewing it.

The light was bright and clear, but the sky still had a faint flush. Just after sunrise, I guessed. My back popped as I stretched. Falling asleep like that had not been beneficial after a day of walking.

Every muscle and fiber was stiff and unresponsive. I forced myself to eat, and drank some water. It didn't take long to gather what little belongings there were. A few minutes later, I was back onto what used to be a street, but was now more an overgrown trail.

It was a beautiful day. Clear blue sky and a sunny day ahead. If only it could've been the same inside my head. I tied my jacket around my waist, and put the rucksack back on.

I walked through the long-lost town, trying to picture what it'd been like before The Fall, and came up pitifully short. What had life been like in the middle of the twenty-first century?

According to Grandpa, they had been very technologically and scientifically advanced, though you wouldn't know it from looking at this wreckage. Apparently there had been a lot of strife and war amongst the different religions of the time.

I shook my head. How stupid these people must have been, to fight amongst themselves about what superstition was the true one. If there was a God, I doubted he cared about what people called him, and I very much doubted he condoned acts of violence in his name. My tribe of warriors had enough problems on our plate without bringing the wrath of God into the mix. If anyone had any religious beliefs or budding faiths, they kept them to themselves.

My theological musings were cut short as I came over a hill. Down there among the grass, weeds and stony dust was a railroad track. I knew it was a railroad track because Grandpa read a book to me about a train once. Choo-choo something or other. Point being, those were railroad tracks.

I ran down the hill without toppling over and breaking my neck.

Escaping The Caves

Panting, I bent down on one knee and studied the tracks. There was a thin coating of desert sand, but nothing more than what the wind would've blown in during the night. If these tracks were unused, they would've been covered by the gritty grains.

My heart beat hard against my ribs. I squinted up ahead and caught sight of something that nearly sent my heart into cardiac arrest. A small, wooden platform with a sign hanging above it. A train station. The tracks started vibrating beneath my fingers. I looked behind me. There was a black dot speeding my way. I turned around, and ran, as Grandpa would've said, as if my ass was on fire.

I was just in time to swing onto the platform as the train thundered down the tracks where I'd stood only moments before. I waved my arms above my head, signaling it to stop. For one heart-stopping moment, I thought it would simply ignore me and thunder on its way, but just as I lost hope, it slowed and came to a shuddering halt.

A man opened the door at the front of the train and beckoned me over. I walked toward him, and let down my hair to cover the cheek scars. In my past life they'd been a brand of honor. In this new shady existence they were a badge of shame, and could very well get me killed, but that was nothing new.

The man tilted his cap, squinted to get a better look at me. His red jowls shook when he spoke. "What in God's name are you doing out here? No one lives out here. Hell, this station hasn't been open for nearly eighty years."

"Yeah, sorry about that. I... I've been camping you see.

And... and I got lost. Obviously. And so I was wondering if you could be so kind as to let me onboard your train? I've been walking for quite some time and I'd like to rest for a bit, if possible."

"Camping." He looked at me. "In the desert."

"Yes, sir. It's a, it's sort of a hobby of mine." I tried smiling. He didn't look convinced.

"Camping in the desert. And so where exactly are you from, Miss?"

I didn't care for the way he said 'Miss', but kept my opinions to myself. "A small town, some way from here. I've got a map, I can show you if you want." I reached for my rucksack, but he waved my suggestion away.

"Where you come from is no business of mine, I s'pect, but if you want to come along, you might want to know where we're goin'." He smiled. I wished he hadn't.

"I'm going to the west. To the ocean."

He laughed and it made his smile look pretty. "Well, that's specific. I can't help you with that, little darlin', where we're goin' there ain't no ocean for miles away, but you might be able to catch another train from there. And then another from wherever ass backwards place that train's goin' to."

His rheumy eyes swept along the platform. "But if you're comin', I'd suggest you do so fast. Cause what you're standing on, ain't gonna be here for much longer." He chewed something and spat.

A quick peek at the platform proved he told the truth. The wood was sickeningly soft and bouncy as I walked toward the open carriage door. I forced myself to walk slowly. The way the man, presumably the conductor, looked at me made me want to prove him wrong. I wasn't scared of the decaying platform, I

Escaping The Caves

wasn't scared of the train and I sure as hell wasn't scared of this unpleasant character.

The conductor closed the door behind me. He winked. "Welcome on board, Missy. Now let's find you a seat, shall we?"

Chapter 5

His hand was moist and soft, like the rotten platform I'd left behind, as he guided me through the carriage. There were less people there than I'd have thought, but plenty for me to feel self-conscious and ill at ease.

My hair offered a thin veil between the truth and those present, though no one seemed particularly interested in me. A young father sat with his daughter on his lap, reading her a story from a tattered children's book. Another man snored loudly, his face and head covered by his hat. A middle-aged couple quarreled quietly among themselves. The girl opposite them seemed to concentrate very hard on not eavesdropping.

The clammy conductor placed me next to an older lady. I immediately looked for an exit strategy, but the only one available at present was the window seat furthest away from the stranger with the pinched lips.

"All right?" The conductor smiled again, showing yellow

teeth.

I nodded, trying not to flinch as the train swayed a bit to the left, my hair swaying with it.

"Excellent. I'll be back to collect your fare."

I chewed my lip. How much could a train ticket cost? I'd had very little dealings with money. My community was more built on trade. We did our job out of duty and necessity, and someone in the outside world provided us with what we needed to survive, everything from food and clothing to medicine, alcohol and books, etc.

If we wanted something someone else had, we traded something they wanted for said item. Simple, but it worked. The only money I owned was in a small pouch Grandpa had left me.

My financial worries were interrupted by the lady next to me. "You really shouldn't bite your lip like that, dear, it'll ruin them." She sniffed.

"Okay..." I didn't know how to respond to that. Was this a normal conversational topic in the outside world, whether or not one should bite one's lips?

"They will dry out, you see."

I didn't.

"I always apply a generous amount of lip balm on my lips before going to bed every night. It keeps them young and full." She smacked her lips, but they didn't look very young and full to me.

On closer inspection, they seemed to be covered in some bright pink paint. How odd. I looked at the woman. In fact, her whole face seemed covered in some sticky substance or other, which made her appear almost orange.

Her eyes were circled with a black line, making them look unnaturally huge. I sneaked a peek at the rest of the female passengers, but if they wore paint on their faces too, I couldn't tell.

The lady noticed my look and smiled. "Yes, I know, I hardly look a day over forty, don't I?"

I would've guessed her age to be around sixty, but kept this to myself.

"Yes, I was a beautician in my younger days, you see, so I know all the tricks of the trade. You know, I even did Violet Evergreen's make-up once. It was only a small commercial, sure. This was before her breakthrough in 'Wildfire', but it was Violet Evergreen even then." She leaned closer and I got a whiff of cigarettes, and some heavy scent that made my eyes water. It was both sweet and spicy at the same time.

"Though, mind you, she was a bit more perky back then. She's looking a bit tired these days, but with three divorces behind her, you can hardly blame her." She laughed, reminding me of a crow cawing over some meager bones for picking.

I hadn't the faintest clue as to what this woman was talking about. I didn't know what a commercial was or make-up, but from the context I assumed the latter was the paint on her face. Neither did I know who this thrice-divorced Violet Evergreen was, but if this scarecrow beside me had painted her face once, my sympathies went out to her.

But I was curious as to what this 'Wildfire' was which had supposedly been Violet's breakthrough. It sounded dangerous. Maybe she'd been a fighter of some sort, like me. But why she'd need her face painted for it, I didn't know.

I smiled and nodded my way through another meaningless and confusing anecdote until the conductor returned. It was a testimony to how desperate I felt that his leering eyes and runny nose presented a welcome distraction.

Kristin Talgø

"That'll be five-fifty." He scribbled the sum on a stiff piece of paper, signed it with a squiggly mark and a stamp.

My head was starting to pound. Five-fifty what? I opened the pouch, but all I could see were a heap of coins and some crumpled paper. Aware of being watched, I squinted at the money. Fortunately, one of the small papers had the number five on it and after a bit of rummaging about, I found a coin with fifty on it. I handed it over, conscious of how sweaty my hands were.

"Thanks very much." The conductor pocketed the money and ceremoniously handed me the ticket. "Pleasure doing business with you, little darlin'. If there's anything you need of me, don't be too shy to ask." He did the winking thing again.

The woman sniffed. "Odious man. But what can you expect from a mere train conductor?" She applied some more paint to her lips. "Now, you have been very rude to me, dear."

"I- I have?"

"Yes, you've failed to present me with your name." She held out her orange hand, nails painted the same color as her lips. "I'm Edith Winterbottom, how do you do?"

"I'm fine. My name's Jess." I stammered, unsure of why she was suddenly asking me how I was. Did I look as strange to her as she did to me?

"Jess?" She twirled her hand.

"Jess, daughter of John."

Edith sniffed. "That's a very odd way of introducing yourself. What is your surname, dear?"

I was really beginning to detest the way she called me 'dear' every five seconds. "Where I come from, we don't really have surnames."

"No?" Edith raised her thin eyebrows. "And where exactly is

it you come from?"

Shit.

"Uhm…" My head turned into a quivering egg yolk again, but just as grey spots started distorting my vision, the little girl in the next aisle jumped over to us.

"Did you say your daddy's name's John? Because that's my daddy's name, too." She giggled as if this was the funniest thing she'd ever heard of.

I smiled, envying her innocence. "Really? What a coincidence."

She fixed her cornflower blue eyes on mine. "What's a coincidence?"

"Ehm…"

"I'm sorry. Eve, come here, love." The little girl's father smiled at me, and pulled his daughter back to their seats. "She's at a very curious age."

"I'm sure that can only be a good thing. My mother used to say that curiosity was a sign of intelligence." I smiled back, liking the way his sandy hair flopped into his eyes whenever he moved.

"Your mother must've been a smart woman." He pushed his hair away, but to no avail.

I couldn't stop smiling. They were the first two people I'd met so far that I liked. I'd been worried the conductor and the painted lady had been representative for the rest of the outside world's population.

"She was. Actually, she–" I stopped talking as the sniffing next to me became too much. "Excuse me." I turned to the flushing lady. "Did you have something you wanted to contribute to the conversation?"

Edith sniffed again. "No, dear, only that it is rather tiresome having you shout across me like that."

I thought of the gun in my rucksack and the image made me smile. Edith recoiled into her seat. "Of course, how terribly inconsiderate of me. Do you mind?" I nodded at the vacant seats opposite the father, whose name was apparently John.

John suppressed a grin. "Not at all."

"I don't believe you're supposed to move, dear, once you've been allocated a seat, you're supposed to remain in it until–" She shut up as I smiled at her again, still picturing my gun. "No manners whatsoever. Young people these days..." Edith muttered and sniffed, but it was easy to tune her out when I didn't have to sit next to her.

"Indeed, very rude behavior, young woman," John whispered, his grin wide and open.

I shrugged. "Well, I try my best."

"Is your name Jess?" Eve stood on her toes, trying to get a better look at me.

I touched the hair across my cheek. "Yes, it is."

"Is that short for Jessica?"

"No, it's just Jess."

"Oh." Eve's face fell. "My doll's called Jessica." She held up a raggedy doll with one eye missing, her smile once again radiant.

"That's a very pretty name for a very pretty doll," I said. Personally, the doll would've given me nightmares if I wasn't already suffering from them, but Eve hugged the doll to her bony chest with unconditional love.

"Yes, it is," Eve answered seriously. "My mother gave it to me. She doesn't live with my father and me anymore, but we're going to see her. That's why we're on this train. To visit Mother. Isn't that right, daddy?"

Escaping The Caves

"Ehm, yeah, sweetie, that's right." John cleared his throat, his ears turned the same shade of pink as Edith's lips.

"Sorry." He mouthed as Eve's attention was back with the doll.

I shook my head. "We've all got a past."

"Indeed. Some more than others." John stroked Eve's hair.

If you only knew...

"So, where are you off to? If you don't mind me asking?"

I did, but answered anyway. He looked so in need of a change of subject, something other than the topic of the runaway mother of his child.

"I'm going to the west, to the ocean." I looked at John, closely, mindful of how the conductor had laughed at me.

But while he appeared puzzled, he didn't laugh. "I see. So this is only one train out of many that you're planning to take?"

"I suppose it is."

"Do you have family there? In the west?"

I looked away. "Something like that."

John looked as if he was about to say something else, when Eve suddenly joined the conversation. "Even if you're name isn't as pretty as my doll's, I think you're very pretty. Your face. Even if you're a bit dusty. Why are you hiding it behind your hair?"

Before I could stop her, Eve reached out and pushed my hair aside. She looked at me, her innocent expression breaking what was left of my heart. "What is that? Did you hurt your face? I got scars to. On my knees. See?"

She pulled down her stockings, but I was busy cowering behind my curtain of hair again. Too late. All of John's good humor had vanished as if Eve had flicked a switch. His eyes didn't go cold and hard the way I'd expected them too, but they were guarded and watchful. He gathered Eve to him, and placed her on his lap.

"Daddy, did you see her scars? I've never seen anyone with scars like that before."

"Shhh, honey. Don't." John put a finger against his daughter's lips, but the damage was already done.

The atmosphere change in the carriage was palpable. The quiet conversations and relaxed murmurs had subsided. They left a silence I could feel on my skin. I closed my eyes, sighing. When I opened them, I looked straight into the multicolored face of Edith Winterbottom.

She pointed one trembling finger at me. "Shame. Shame on you."

I knew this had been bound to happen at some point as an outcast, but this was far sooner than anticipated. Slowly, I got out of my seat.

Edith jabbed her finger at me. "How dare you, to sit there, talking to that poor child, looking as if butter wouldn't melt in your mouth?"

I assumed the question was rhetorical, and held my tongue. Someone came up behind me. I swiveled around. The man, who'd been sleeping with his hat on his face, lifted his hands up. "Easy there, just wanted a chat."

I didn't blame him for covering his face while unconscious. His skin was pockmarked, purple scars stood out among fresh pimples.

"Really?" My hand crept into my rucksack. I found it a little easier to breathe once my fingers closed around the gun. That familiar headache built up behind my eyes.

"I can't imagine we would have much to talk about."

The pockmarked man took a step back. "You really gonna

Escaping The Caves

use that? Shoot me? In front of a kid?"

"I don't want to, but I will if you make me."

A pimple near his mouth stretched to the bursting point when he smiled, revealing uneven teeth. He opened his mouth to answer when the conductor came humming into the carriage. His eyes widened at the unexpected scene before him.

"What in the seven hells is going on here?" His chest puffed out like a toad.

Edith's finger still jabbed in my direction. "That woman, that- that- she called herself Jess, didn't tell me her surname, very odd I thought, she —"

"Hells bells, woman, will you just spit it out?"

"She's a traitor! One of the outcasts!" A small self-satisfied smile tugged at her pinched lips. This would undoubtedly make a much better story than Violet Evergreen's three divorces.

The conductor glanced at my cheek, and did a double take. "Well, I'll be damned... I've never seen an outcast before." At that moment he seemed more curious than angry.

"What's an outcast, Daddy?" Eve tugged at John's sleeve, but he shushed her.

"Did I get Jess into trouble? I didn't mean to, I only wanted to see her face." Her bottom lip wobbled.

"Of course not, darling. Everything's going to be okay." But John's eyes travelled from my gun to the faces of the people gathered around me.

I risked a quick look over my shoulder. The middle-aged couple and the girl sitting opposite them were still in their seats. Their mouths hung open in identical o's, but they didn't seem to harbor any immediate urges to attack me.

Good. That left Edith, the conductor and the pockmarked man.

"No, you didn't get her into trouble, dear, she managed to do that all by herself. Tell me, how do you sleep at night, knowing you've betrayed the entire human race?"

"Pretty well, actually. And I haven't betrayed anyone, not that you care about my side of the story."

"Damn right we don't." The conductor seemed to have found his anger. "You'd been appointed with the most important task anyone could've been given and you just walked away? To do what? Travel by train? See the ocean?" He snorted with laughter. "You make me sick."

"Don't worry, the feeling's mutual. Please, don't do that." I leveled the gun at the pockmarked man's chest again and he stopped. "Like I said, I would greatly prefer not to shoot you, but I will if you force my hand."

"Yeah?" He licked his lips. "I would greatly prefer it if you didn't shoot me either. But tell me something."

"What?"

"You're the first warrior I've come across, even if you're an outcast. Tell me, are all of the warriors as pretty as you? I mean, your clothes are a bit dirty and your hair's a bit mangy, but still... I've seen worse." He bared his teeth again.

My finger itched to pull the trigger. He really wasn't one to call anyone dirty and mangy. "Oh yes, if you like me now, I bet you would've just loved me when I'm all splattered in blood and gore, wouldn't you?"

"All right, that's it. I won't have any more of that filthy talk on my train." The conductor stepped closer. I shifted the gun to him.

He stepped back hastily. "Ma'am, I'm going to have to ask you to leave the train." No more little darlin'. Not that I minded.

Escaping The Caves

"That's okay. I'd just come to the conclusion that trains aren't really my thing." I kept a steady aim on them as I backed toward the door. "Tell them to stop the train."

The conductor hesitated. After a moment of dithering back and forth on his feet, he hurried toward the front of the train.

"Well, I've never." Edith sniffed. "To think of how you so shamelessly tried to pass yourself off as one of us."

"Yes, to think that I wanted to live a life without death and destruction every waking moment," I replied, pleasantly keeping the gun trained at her stiff blonde head.

Edith walked backward until she bumped her seat and fell onto it. Her face white underneath the orange taint.

"Tell me, what's it like –"

"You. Shut up and sit down." I waved the gun at the pockmarked man. His jaw worked. Eventually the weapon convinced him to find his seat again.

"Thank you." I exhaled. How long could it possibly take to stop this damn train? The headache was blinding. Grey butterflies distorted my vision. That panicky fear clawed at my lungs.

What had happened to me? Fear used to calm me, wrap me in a cool, cold blanket which protected me from unpleasant feelings such as this. I forced myself to ignore the urge to wipe sweaty hands on my pants.

"Jess?" It was Eve.

"Yes?" I kept my eyes firmly planted on the door at the end of the carriage.

"I'm sorry," she whispered.

I swallowed. "There's nothing to be sorry about."

"Yes, there is. You look so sad and scared. I wish you could come with me and Daddy. You could be part of the family, like

63

my doll."

I laughed. It was genuine, and it hurt all the more for it. "I would've liked that, Eve. But I'm afraid I have to go now." The train was, thank God if He existed, slowing down.

"Will you be safe?" Eve sounded upset.

"Of course I will." Liar, liar...

"I don't believe you."

"Eve," John reprimanded her.

"It's okay. Don't worry. I've dealt with far worse creatures than these." I indicated the people watching my every move with mingled curiosity and disgust.

"So it's true then?"

"What is?"

"That the monsters are real?"

"I'm afraid so."

"But if you're not there to stop them, what will happen to us?" Eve was crying now.

Stop the train, just stop the fucking train. "There are plenty more of me to stop the monsters. You have nothing to fear, Eve."

Finally the train shuddered to a stop. I didn't turn back, but spoke over my shoulder. "Take care of her, John. And good luck."

A beat of silence, then, "I will. And may luck be on your side as well."

Yeah, I wish. Opening the door, I rejoined the desert. It'd been patiently waiting for me.

Chapter 6

Dust swirled up around me as the train picked up speed, until it was nothing but a grey blob in the horizon. So much for resting my feet and mind a little. There was no use looking at the map. From the look of it, I was dumped approximately in the middle of nowhere, right on the border of no man's land. Perfect.

The only sensible thing would be to follow the train tracks, and although my mind was a little short on sense at that moment, it wasn't entirely lost. Fortunately, I had at least six hours of daylight left and intended to make the most of them. I put the gun back in the rucksack and swung it onto my shoulder.

The sun was scorching hot. I rolled up the sleeves of my shirt. Something caught my eye. My mouth went dry. I'd completely forgotten about the small scratch I suffered the day Jen and Trenton were killed. I'd once been partially disemboweled; a small scratch at my lower arm wasn't likely to get much attention from me. And now it looked as if this small

Kristin Talgø

wound could be my downfall.

An angry red line had appeared below the scratch. It snaked its way up the inside of my arm. I breathed deeply. There was nothing I could do about it. I had no medicine and I wasn't likely to get my hands on any, either. If I was meant to live I would live, and if I was meant to shuffle off into the afterlife then shuffle I would. It didn't do to worry about it.

Except I did worry. I didn't want to die; at least, I wanted to have truly lived a little before checking out permanently. To feel sane again. If I'd wanted to die, I would've stayed where I came from. But I'd risked everything on a wild gamble. That maybe, maybe, if given the chance, life could be good. Could be worth something more than just to kill and be killed.

I found an old pen at the bottom of my rucksack and put a black line just underneath the crook of my elbow. If the red line crossed the line I'd drawn, I'd get worried, and somehow get my hands on some medicine. Antibiotics, I think Michael called it.

Soothed by this small measure of control, I started walking again. If I survived this day, if I survived this heat, I could certainly survive blood poisoning. I imagined a white healing light. That it flowed through my body and washed away the poison running through my system. I imagined the ocean. Clear, blue water. And maybe someone waited there for me.

I walked.

By the time the sun set, I was done for. I'd reached the borders of some town, this one inhabited, but it was all I could do not to fall flat on my face. Blisters burned on my feet. My skin boiled from the sun and my lips and throat were as dry as

Escaping The Caves

the desert I'd just crossed.

I fell on my knees in front of a water pump. The water tasted of iron and was flecked with rust, but right then it was the sweetest thing I'd ever tasted. I drank 'til my stomach bulged, retched, then drank some more.

The cool water made it easier to think. I refilled my water canteen and mopped the water off my face with a handkerchief. Hunkered down by the pump, I tried to get a feel of the town. Sounds drifted out to me. Children laughed. Parents called them in and a dog barked. A generator rumbled in the distance. But where there were people, there were trouble, my fiasco of a train ride being the most recent evidence. I was so tired I could hardly see straight. The ghosts were always the most agitated whenever I was tired. The defenses in my mind weakened and they crept right in.

Still too rattled by the incident on the train, I didn't dare to ask for lodgings somewhere. But I needed a place to sleep for the night. I lumbered forward, keeping my head down, until I found a small abandoned shed not far from the water pump.

It was unlocked and held nothing more than a rusty bike, some shovels and other long-forgotten tools. There was a heavy layer of dust on the floor.

I wrapped an itchy blanket around me and used the rucksack as a pillow. Making sure the safety catch was on, I put the gun next to me. Despite the fatigue, I couldn't sleep. John's eyes wouldn't leave me. Eve's crying echoed through my skull. I pulled the gun closer and fell asleep with my finger wrapped around the trigger.

"Wakey, wakey."

Something cold and hard caressed my cheek. My mind was fuzzy and unreceptive. How long had I been asleep? Three hours? Four at the most. I flexed my fingers, searching for the gun, but when all I encountered was thin air, my eyes flew open.

Even in the hazy darkness I was able to make out the pockmarked face in front of me. I froze. It couldn't be. It didn't make any sense. What was he, of all people, doing here in the same small, abandoned shed in the same small, abandoned town that I'd just happened to walk into?

He sniggered. "Man, if you could see your face right now. Slowly," he warned as I sat up. "Now, correct me if I'm wrong, but shouldn't you have been a little more on your guard? I mean, falling asleep with your gun like that... Tut, tut." He wagged one finger at me.

He wasn't wrong. There'd been a time when no matter how deeply asleep I was, some hidden instinct would have woke me up in time to put a bullet in this creep's brain before he got a chance to say as much as boo. But that was before my sanity started falling down like a shaky house of cards.

I shrugged. "It's been a long day."

His smile widened. "I bet. It must've taken you all day to get here. Wonder how I found you?"

I shrugged again.

"Now, come on, Jess. I saw your face when you realized it was me. Priceless! Anyway, it wasn't that hard really. This was the next stop after you jumped off. I figured you'd make it here by nightfall. And considering the unfortunate debacle on the train, I didn't think it likely that you would venture very far into town." He fell silent, looked at me. "Penny for your thoughts."

"Nothing. I'm just not able to figure you out exactly."

He frowned. "What do you mean?"

"Well, no offence, but you look like you were born on the wrong side of a dumpster, but you sound educated. The way you look and the way you talk don't add up."

To my surprise, he threw back his head and laughed. He got himself under control, wiped a tear from his eye. "Yes, you have my father to thank for that. He's very rich, you know. Living a very important life on the east coast. The size of some of the cities there would blow your mind."

He inched closer. He smelt of sweat and onions. "I didn't like his very rich and important life and he didn't like my dislike for it. And a few years later, here we are. There's a bit more to the story than that, but I won't bore you with the details. Born on the wrong side of the dumpster." He laughed again. "Traitor or not, you got a sense of humor, Jess, I'll give you that." He stopped laughing as suddenly as he'd started. His eyes went cold and speculative.

"But now that we've established how I got here and the disparities between my appearance and verbal abilities, you must be wondering why I'm here. Don't you?"

Of course I did. But I had a feeling I knew where this was going. I didn't think both of us would make it out of this shed alive.

"What? No clever comeback? Aw, Jess, I'm disappointed in you." He leaned even closer and traced the scars on my cheek with the gun. "You see, as I'm sure you're aware of, you're fair game. Outcasts don't tend to last very long, but you're the first one I've come across that's pretty. Mostly because you're a woman. The rest of them have been male, smelly and bearded."

An icy fist pressed into my gut. "I thought you said I was the first outcast you'd come across."

He grinned. "Did I? How awfully rude of me to lie like that. No, you're definitely not the first one I've come across."

My mind raced ahead. It stumbled over questions and possibilities, disregarding most of them. "There aren't that many of us."

"More than you think. Some slink away in the middle of the night. I got a feeling that whoever's in charge of your little tribe of warriors covered their tracks whenever possible. Deserting like that wouldn't be good for morale, would it?"

I tried to think back. How many had left town? It couldn't be more than twelve. But trust my father to cover up deserters if he could.

The pock-marked man eyed me. It was obvious he took great pleasure from all of this. "For example, did you know someone named, what was it, Jake... Jack... no— Jackson." He snapped his fingers. "Yeah, Jackson. That was it. You knew him, didn't you? Yeah, I can tell you did."

That icy fist buried even deeper into my gut. Jackson had been my first boyfriend. I hadn't been more than sixteen at the time, he was a year older. It lasted for about eight months, but I still replayed the first kiss sometimes, if I felt particularly lonely.

"I knew a Jackson," I said cautiously. "But he died of pneumonia."

That obnoxious laugh again. It grated on my nerves, like nails on a blackboard. "Pneumonia. Is that what they told you? No, he snuck away in the middle of the night. Couldn't handle the pressure of the caves anymore. He thought he'd save his family some embarrassment by doing it while everyone was asleep."

"You're lying!"

He winced. "Please, don't shout like that. And no, I very much speak the truth. He... Was he a friend of yours? He told me about a Jess. Was that you? Don't think he ever got over you. He was so lonely and desperate for someone to listen; he told me quite a lot of interesting things."

"Jackson and I were just friends. But I don't think you knew my Jackson."

"My Jackson. Now that doesn't sound like something 'just a friend' would say. And yes, I knew him. God, am I saying this out loud?" He fixed his eyes on me. "He had a birthmark on the small of his back. A rather large one, I recall, sort of shaped like a leaf."

Twelve years ago, I knew the shape on that back better than my own. And Jackson's birthmark had resembled a leaf. "How do you know that?" I couldn't feel my lips anymore.

"There we go. She gets the message. I saw it as he tried to get away. Bit of a bastard, that one. Put up a hell of a fight. I'll give him that. But in the end, I won, he lost. They all do. You see, it would appear that becoming an outcast takes some of the fight out of you. Or maybe it's just that losing your marbles makes you less of a fighter."

He pushed a lock of hair out of my eyes. "In the end, I gutted him like a fish. I bet he wished he'd really died of pneumonia then. And you, pretty one, you're not playing with quite a full deck of cards either, are you?"

He pursed his lips, putting on a face of mock sympathy. "No, I don't think you are. I see the ghosts in your eyes, just like the others. That's what drives you away, isn't it? All that blood and mayhem finally gets to you. Strange. I find a bit of bloodshed oddly reviving."

I sat up straighter, and ignored the gun pressing into my neck. "So is that what you do, then? You go around hunting outcasts. Is that how you get your kicks?" I found the image of

Jackson, sweet Jackson, gutted and dying by the hands of this lunatic, infuriating.

"More or less. You see, no one misses you. You've already got an unofficial death sentence hanging over your head. I only carry out the deed. I expect some people would've thanked me if they knew what I've been doing."

"Except you don't do it out of some fucked-up sense of duty. You do it because you like it." My lips twisted like I'd tasted something bad.

He raised his hands in a what-can-you-do gesture. "Some people like drinking, some people like gambling. I like killing. But that's not really sociably acceptable. After so much drama involving that girl who used to work for my father, I thought it would be less messy to go after the untouchables. And that's where you come in."

He smiled and looked like he wanted me to congratulate him on being clever. If that was the case, he'd wait a long time. He still held onto the gun and I still reeled from everything he'd told me. I could take him, I would take him. No way in hell had I survived countless encounters with the beasts in the caves only to be slaughtered by this freak.

"What's your name?"

He raised his eyebrows. "Why do you want to know?"

"Just curious. And if you're going to kill me, there's no harm in telling me, is there?"

He exhaled through his nose. "I suppose not. Ethan. Ethan Charles Sampson, to be precise."

"I'm afraid I can't say it's nice to meet you, Ethan Charles Sampson, but it is going to be extremely nice to kill you."

Ethan laughed again, but he kept the gun wedged under my chin. "I'm sure you would like that, but sadly that's not on the menu tonight. You see, while killing is pleasing enough, there is something I haven't been able to do since that slutty secretary of my Father's."

"So, I'm your first female outcast?" I wanted to be sure on that point.

Ethan sighed, clearly annoyed with my slow up-take on his previous murders. "Yes. I told you."

Something that had been tightly wound up inside of me relaxed.

"You look relieved. Were you afraid I'd murdered another friend of yours? Don't worry. I'll get to her eventually, whoever she is. I always do."

He leaned over me, and pressed the gun into my belly. "I've been told a bullet to the stomach is one of the worst ways to go. You bleed out so painfully slow." He pushed me down onto the hard dusty floor. "So, if you're a very nice girl and do exactly like I say, I'll be a gentleman and put a bullet in your head by the end of it, okay?"

"Actually, there are two things you should know about me."

"Yeah, what's that?" He'd slid the gun underneath my shirt, tracing my jaw line with his tongue.

"First of all, I don't like being told what to do." I brought up my leg, smashed my knee into his balls, while simultaneously directing the gun at the ceiling. Pieces of wood and splinters showered down on us. "Secondly, I don't need a gun to kill you."

I kicked him in the gut and he doubled over again. "But let's make this an experiment." I pressed the gun into the soft flesh of his stomach. "You claim that a bullet to the stomach is one of the worst ways to go."

"No, no, you bitch, don't you dare," Ethan whimpered. His

scars and pimples stood out like exclamation marks on his pale skin.

"You bleed out so painfully slow, wasn't that it?" I mimicked his posh voice, ignoring his whimpers. "Let's put that to the test." I fired the gun.

Ethan howled as if possessed. "Bitch! Oh, you fucking bitch. I'll get you for this! You won't get away, I'll find you!"

I hunkered down next to him. With one hand, I pulled on his sweaty hair, yanked back his head. "No, you won't. Unless you find a way out of hell, this'll be the last time you see me. And let's be absolutely clear on this, I did this for Jackson. And all the others. I guess there are monsters in the outside world as well."

I picked up my rucksack and opened the door. Ethan tried to pull his way across the floor. Blood bubbled through his lips. He didn't have long left. I might not be playing with a full deck at the moment, but my aim was as true as ever.

"Hey, Jess," Ethan called out just as I was shutting the door behind me. "I'll save you a place in hell. Maybe we can finish what we started." His voice was wet and hoarse at the same time.

"Yeah, you do that. I'll enjoy killing you twice." I closed the door and didn't look back.

That was a lie. I hadn't even enjoyed killing him once. I'd done it for Jackson. And for all the others he'd killed and would've killed if I hadn't stopped him. But I'd taken no pleasure from it.

I knelt once more by the water pump and washed myself as

Escaping The Caves

best as I could. It dawned on me. He'd been the first human I'd killed. I threw up.

I lay on the ground, gazed up at the starless sky, and wondered if Ethan would become part of the ghosts I dragged with me wherever I went.

To steady my shaking body, I reloaded the gun. I would clean and oil it at the next stop. It was barely after midnight, but I didn't dare to linger in this wayward town. Someone might've heard the shot and come to investigate. In any case, the town didn't feel safe anymore. Not that it ever had.

Ethan had tainted my surroundings by sharing his black deeds with me. He'd tainted me by forcing me to kill him. Until him, a part of me had been allowed to remain innocent, undisturbed. I'd made my living by killing, yes, but only soulless, vicious monsters. That the creatures were intelligent, far more than I dared to contemplate, I was well aware of, but a keen, calculating mind didn't merit a soul.

Though Ethan made me wonder if maybe some people could be born soulless. Or maybe his had been broken or twisted in some way along the road. What it all came down to, no matter the reasons behind his actions, was that the darkness which had consumed him had rubbed off on me. Darkness like that was contagious. I felt absolutely no desire to kill another human being again. But regardless of how evil he'd been, I'd taken a human life. And that left a mark.

It chipped away at me. I'd crossed a line, and I knew that, if put on the spot like that again, I would kill. But a distinct feeling crept up my spine. That killing another person, even in self-defense, killed off a part of you as well.

No matter how many baths I took, the stain would stay with me forever. There was no point in dwelling on it. What was done was done, and I'd do it again. But knowing this didn't take the itchy feeling away.

Eventually the shaking subsided and my breathing evened out. I pulled on my jacket. But not without glancing at the inside of my left arm, instantly regretting it. That red line crept along. The black mark I'd drawn to halt its progress had done nothing.

I briefly considered finding the nearest apothecary, seeing if I could pilfer some much-needed antibiotics. But I figured I'd caused enough damage in this town already. If I'd been back in my own town, Michael would've set me right straight away. Even a passing thought of Michael brought on such an acute bout of homesickness, I nearly doubled over.

Maybe homesickness wasn't the right word for it. Maybe it was more a longing for human company. Companionship. An illusory sense of belonging somewhere. To someone. This left me feeling even more desolate and alone. I didn't belong anywhere or to anyone. The knowledge was like falling into a vast, deep abyss, without knowing if I'd ever emerge again.

My mind fixed firmly on a mental image of a crystal blue ocean. The warm sun sparkled off it. I put one foot in front of the other, leaving behind a corpse and a part of me I could never retrieve again.

・ ・

A small hollow beneath an outcropped rock about two kilometers from town became my refuge. As expected, the night was freezing. Even if the cold hadn't put me off, the howling of coyotes in the distance warned me against walking further into the desert after nightfall.

I shivered under my blanket. Wrapped in all the clothes I'd

brought with me, my mind drifted towards Jackson. The saddest part was that I couldn't remember his face anymore. I remembered the color of his hair and the way his eyes used to turn up at the corners when he smiled, but rest of his face had become hazy. Like an old photograph, my memories of him had paled and faded with time.

But while I couldn't remember exactly what he'd looked like or what he'd sounded like, I remembered down to the smallest detail how he'd made me feel. From what I did recall, we didn't do much except have sex, smoke, and have some more sex. And discuss whatever book we got our hands on. He was the only other person in our small community who was as avid a reader as I.

He made me laugh. A lot. To be curled up in his arms, talk, tease each other, smell the scent of one another on each other's skin, it was the happiest I could remember ever being.

For a short period of time, I had belonged somewhere. To someone. I had been his and he had been mine. With him I'd thought to myself, this is it. This is how it's meant to be. He'd known me better than I'd known myself. We'd finished each other's sentences. If something had weighed heavily on my mind, he'd understood without me ever having to utter a single word.

To be with him had felt as natural as breathing. Then one day we'd drifted apart, or rather he'd started to drift away from me. He'd never offered an explanation and I'd been too hurt and proud to ask for one. How pathetic to think I might have loved and lost my true love at the age of sixteen without knowing it.

Ten months after he slipped through my fingers, I was told he died of pneumonia. Who told me? Probably no one. Most likely I caught the drift of a rumor on the street. But I still remembered how it felt. To know he was gone. Dead.

Beneath the covers at night, I'd cried until it felt as if my eyes turned liquid and rolled down my cheeks. To lose Jen was worse, but to lose Jackson had been a hell all on its own.

It was possible I still remembered his dark brown hair. The way it almost touched his shoulders. How it curled up in the rain. If I concentrated really hard I might even remember his blue eyes, so light they seemed to pierce me to the core.

But it was easier to forget. What good would remembering him do? In the end it didn't matter if he'd sickened and died or if he'd been killed. I would never know why he'd left me or why he'd eventually left our town. Had he felt his mind slip through the cracks of reality like I had?

It was terrible to think of him lost and alone. So desperate that he would've accepted Ethan's outstretched hand. He must have been far gone indeed, not to see the dagger cloaked in the other one. Or the way something seemed to have been switched off inside the eyes of his self-appointed friend.

For the first time since Ethan woke me, I found some small shred of peace. I held on to it with all I had. Killing Ethan might've destroyed some part of me I could never get back, but he'd reminded me that even if I was an outcast, I had been loved.

The people I'd loved would always be lost to me, but at least I had loved and been loved. It was a strange feeling, but Jackson becoming part of my collection of ghosts didn't scare me. He'd always been there. I'd only chosen to ignore him. Remembering him hurt like hell, but beneath the hurt there was comfort.

How he'd looked at me when he thought I didn't notice. And I'd known he loved me. He'd never spoken the words, but

Escaping The Caves

it'd been in the way he waited for me at the end of a shift. The relief made him appear like a kid again. It'd been in all the thousand small things he'd done just to see me smile.

I turned over on my back and looked at the distance I would have to walk tomorrow. Was that why part of me had resented Kyle? Because he hadn't loved me the way Jackson used to? Or maybe because I'd known love once, I'd known deep down that Kyle wasn't capable of feeling like that. At least, not where I was concerned. Why he'd felt the need to claim me as his wife was just another thing I would never know.

Life was full of unanswered questions. The most important one was if I would be able to go on, move on with my life, without those answers. The only certain thing was that life would go on, with or without me. The only way I would find the answer to that most important question was to keep going. I'd place one foot in front of the other for as long as it took for me to find myself again. Maybe I'd been running to meet me from the moment I risked everything to live.

There was only one way to find out. I'd keep going.

Chapter 7

The days blurred together. I lost track of time as the fever raged through my body, until time, as a concept, ceased to matter. The red line had crept well past the hopeful mark I'd made on my arm. Without antibiotics to help it, my body fought the infection on its own. A fight it was increasingly likely to lose. Every day, the red line grew closer to its destination: my heart.

I didn't dare venture into any of the towns I passed on my way. If anyone recognized the scars on my face, I wouldn't be able to get myself out of trouble. It was a constant struggle to shuffle along. My canteen seemed to weigh a hundred kilos.

Even if the infection didn't kill me, the desert sun would soon finish the job. The heat added a fever of its own. It relentlessly beat down on my back. I was careful to rehydrate whenever possible, but the water left my body almost as swiftly as I consumed it.

During the day I thought I'd suffer from heatstroke, but the night offered no relief. My teeth chattered so loudly from the cold, that it attracted unwelcome attention from the coyotes that lurked in the surrounding hills. Eventually, I was forced to admit defeat and seek refuge in a small town.

A pack of coyotes had steadily tracked my progress through the desert. They could smell my sickness, and sickness meant one thing to them: weakness. A weakness they could exploit to their advantage. The night before, they'd come dangerously close to attacking, and I didn't trust my luck to ward them off any longer. I certainly didn't trust my trembling hands to shoot them, if it came to that.

The coyotes lingered at the edge of town, watching my every step. As quietly as possible, I crept along. I kept to abandoned streets and back alleys. Afraid I would pass out in the middle of the street for anyone to find me, I slid down underneath some dry bushes in a tiny, well-kept garden.

There were lights on in the house, but I couldn't see anyone moving inside. I was just about to nod off when a low growl woke me up. The hackles on my back stood on end. I slowly opened my eyes and looked into the suspicious face of a large, black dog. He growled again, revealing two neat rows of razor sharp teeth. His breath smelled of meat.

The back door of the house swung open, and the dog turned his head. I tried to scurry away, but the dog pounced almost before I'd moved. His paws crushed the breath out of me. I'd never known there could be some many possible unsavory ways of dying outside of the caves.

"Hey, what's going on out there? Watcha got there, boy? Eh?" Someone pulled the dog off me. Whoever it was shone a flashlight in my face.

Silence. The dog panted.

"Well, well, would you look at that…"

Escaping The Caves

"Could you... could you lower the light a bit please?" I dropped my hands as he did.

"I'm sorry for the unpleasant welcome, but Rufus here doesn't like strangers lurking around in our backyard after dark. Nor, for that matter, do I." The man stood there looking at me, one hand on the collar of the dog, the other holding the flashlight.

"I...I'm sorry. I didn't mean to b-b-bother you, I'm not we- we- we-"

"You're not well. Yeah, no shit. I've seen corpses looking more lively than you." He let go of the dog. "Stay. You best come in then. See if we can't put some color back in your cheeks."

He bent towards me and I turned my face away. He snorted. "Don't have to bother with that around me, girl. There's no point in hiding scars like that. Hey, take it easy. I ain't gonna hurt you. Okay? Now, come on. Put your arms around me. There we go. I might be gettin' on with my years, but I can still carry a damsel in distress when the situation calls for it."

Steadily he got back on his feet, holding me as carefully as Jo would've held her daughter. If this man wanted to hurt me, there was nothing I could do about it. Instead of fighting him the way my training dictated, I leaned into him. The man tightened his grip. He walked slowly back to the house, mindful of the rocks that hid in the grass.

His grey beard tickled. He smelled of pipe smoke, whiskey and something which must've been all his own. My father had never held me like this, not even as a kid, but this man smelled the way I'd always thought a father should smell like. He held me the way I'd always thought a father should.

"Hey there, what's the matter? Are you in pain? Did I jostle

83

you?" The stranger wiped my wet cheeks with a clean handkerchief.

I opened my mouth to reply, but only a great sob escaped. Mortified, I buried my head in a pillow.

"Told ya, you don't have to bother with that around here. Unlike some men, I don't find cryin' women particularly frightening. Now, you just stay there and I'll be right back. Okay?"

I nodded.

"Good." He patted my head. I heard him move around. He mumbled to himself, collected some things, discarded others.

I lifted my head. He'd placed me on a sofa in front of an empty fireplace. The living room was adjoined to the kitchen, where the man was opening cupboards. I saw the bedroom. It was a small house, but cozy. It wasn't just a house, it was a home.

Despite my dilapidated state, my heart beat a little faster at the sight of all the books. They filled bookcase after bookcase and when they ran out, books covered most of the available surfaces.

"You like readin'?" The man sat at the edge of the sofa. He moved some books, and cleared a space for the overflowing tray. The dog sniffed around, then settled at the feet of his master.

"Yeah."

"So I see. Your eyes looked almost alive there for a second." He winked. "Stupid question probably, but how you feelin'?"

I shrugged and winced.

"That great, eh? My name's Bill, by the way. I'm a retired physician. Even though no one ever retires in a town like this. During the cold season, I still have a line goin' all the way around my house. Eh." He shook his head.

I swallowed past the raw lump in my throat. "I'm Jess."

"Well, Jess, it's nice to make your acquaintance. Now, where're you hurt? It'd be a shame to have a lovely young woman such as yourself dying in my care." His voice was light, but his eyes were serious, assessing my condition as he spoke.

I pulled back the sleeve of my jacket and shirt. Bill whistled through his teeth. "I see. Then let's start by cleaning out that wound, eh?"

He worked carefully. His liver-spotted hands never wavered. My stomach turned as he literally had to scoop yellow puss out of the wound. I knew it'd festered, but I'd been too tired to clean it. Not my best decision.

When the wound was clean and wrapped, he held out two pills and a glass of water. "Antibiotics. Two of these four times a day and they should kill the infection. Even though, I gotta say, the infection has been allowed to spread for far too long."

He watched me swallow the medicine. "They might not be as strong as some you can get in the big cities on the east coast, but I reckon they should do the trick."

My head fell back on the pillow. Fever chills raced through my body. Bill put another blanket around me, then started to gently wipe the worst of the dust and muck off my face.

"Did you get this when you got hurt?" He indicated the blood stains on my jacket, which he'd draped across a chair.

"No. That's not my blood."

He only nodded and washed my hands. When he was finished, he cleared away the mess, washed his own hands in the kitchen sink. He sat back down next to me, and placed a cup of tea next to the glass of water.

"You should try and drink some of this, even if you don't

feel like it. Okay? All right." He tucked the corners of the blankets around me. "I'll let you get some sleep."

I didn't know if it was the fever or his kindness which prompted me to do the unthinkable, but nonetheless, I reached out my hand and pulled on his shirt tail. He turned back, white eyebrows raised.

"Would you stay with me? Please? Until I've fallen asleep. I'm so tired and I... I'm scared of the ghosts."

Bill stood there watching me and then sat down. A rough but warm thumb wiped away a single tear, which had escaped through my defenses. "You haven't had an easy time, have you?" He didn't seem to expect me to respond. I entwined my cold fingers through his warm ones.

"Yeah, none of you people have." My eyes had closed and my mind drifted, drifted down a soft, deep river. And so I didn't catch the meaning of this statement, something I would regret bitterly later on. Not that it would've changed anything.

Soft fingertips lightly touched the scars on my cheek. "Courage, integrity, honor," I whispered, a part of me bleeding without knowing why.

"Courage, integrity, honor," Bill repeated the words. He clicked his tongue. The sound stabbed at me, but I couldn't remember why I hated that noise.

"What bullshit they feed you to make you do the things you do," Bill said. The hard edge sounded out of place in his kind voice. "No one should be forced to live the kind of life you've been forced to live. They should've based it on volunteers. Though who in their right mind would volunteer for such madness?"

"There's- there's al- always someone who likes killing." The words were cotton in my mouth. I couldn't feel my body anymore. It was a pleasant sensation. I wanted to disconnect my mind in the same way.

"Yeah, I guess so. But you wouldn't trust any of them with such a task, would you?"

I heard Bill scratch his beard. The dog snored.

"No. Ethan would've- would've probably killed the people instead of the- the monsters." My tongue had gone numb. The words came out muffled, but Bill understood.

"Ethan. Who's Ethan?"

"A real b-b-bastard. He ki-killed my Jack-Jacks-Jackson…" I didn't know if I'd said the words out loud.

Bill remained silent for a while. A clock ticked somewhere deep inside the house, a metal heart marking the passage of time. "Was Jackson like you?"

The words were kind, but probed gently, the way his fingers cleaned my wound.

I sighed, my whole soul exhaled. "Yeah. I didn't-didn't even know he'd le-left."

"I see. Shush now. No more tears, Jess. I'm sorry, I shouldn't have asked. You just rest, and I'll be right here watching over you. I won't let anyone hurt you. You can stay for as long as you need to."

Sleep finally claimed me, but I struggled to get the words out. "Will-will you cha-chase the ghos-ghosts away?" Even as a child, I never asked such a naked, vulnerable question.

I heard the soft click of Bill's Adams apple when he swallowed. "I'll do my best, Jess. I'll do my best."

One night turned into another, and then another. As the

87

fever receded and the red line slowly lost the fight to the antibiotics, time took on meaning again. Bill said I could stay for as long as I liked, and I took him at his word. I think six weeks passed until I was forced to take my leave, but I can't be sure. Not that it's important.

Bill watched over me like a mother hen guarded her newly-hatched chicks. He wouldn't allow me to leave the house during the day, afraid people would notice the scars on my face. He needn't have worried though. As much as I hated it, Ethan had planted a deep rooted fear of anyone learning my past.

It wasn't my own life that worried me, even if I wanted to keep it. But I couldn't guarantee the safety of those who came looking for me. While I cleaned and oiled my gun with as much care as Jo bathed and dried her daughter, I didn't desire any more blood on my hands.

"You seem to have a rather strong attachment to that," Bill remarked one day as I rubbed down the weapon.

"It belonged to my grandpa." I never took my eyes off what I was doing.

"Ah," Bill said.

We got on remarkably well. Bill seemed to enjoy the company and I enjoyed his soothing, hoarse voice and calm, gentle way. He moved slowly, but efficiently. The dog never left his side.

Under Bill's careful nursing, my body healed and regained its former strength. My mind was still cracked and bruised, the ghosts and nightmares always just beneath the surface. But the voices and hallucinations gradually lost their power. My mental state was still fragile.

The physical wound healed, but my grief still festered. I grieved and raged at Jen, Trenton, Kyle, Jackson, my father, and friends in equal measure.

The night, my former enemy in the desert, had become my solace. After dark had fallen, Bill reluctantly allowed me to walk around and sit in his small garden. He would sit at the porch in a creaking rocking chair. He smoked and read, one eye and ear cocked toward the street.

I'd come to like the dark. It became easier to breathe, to think. The light smarted, jarred my senses, while the darkness soothed them. After having stretched my legs for a bit, I would sit underneath the apple trees, leaning against the rough trunks. I'd look at the sky, seeing the stars come out, one twinkling light at the time. The moon grew and waned while I sat there.

There was nothing in particular I thought about. I sent my mind off like a bird. Let it fly far away, and trusted it would come back when satisfied. The clenched fear in my chest dissipated. My neck pains and migraines faded into a distant memory.

I wasn't myself yet, whoever that was, but I found some measure of calm and peace that, up until now, had been complete strangers to me. If it hadn't been for that one evening, I don't know how long I might've stayed.

Bill and I were careful, but we forgot that eyes looking for trouble usually find it. Bill was a kind man, liked by most people, but there were those who had an old, shriveled bone to pick with him. One man in particular, the sheriff of this sleepy town, Jefferson, had been waiting a good long time for some dirt to come up which he could fling in Bill's face. The dirt turned out to be me.

An hour after dinner, there came a knock on the door. Bill stiffened. He motioned for me to hide in the bedroom and pressed a bandage into my hand. "Stay in here, but in case I have to call for you, put this across your cheek." He closed the door on my runaway heart.

It took three tries before I was able to make the bandage stick to my skin. The dog barked and Bill shushed it. I pressed my ear against the door. Voices drifted out from the hallway.

"Good evening, Bill." High, reedy.

"Evening, Jeff." Guarded, but calm. Always so calm. It was one of the many things I'd come to like about him. He was like Grandpa that way. "What can I do you for?"

"I'm afraid I'm here on town business, Bill." The man sounded as if he was constantly out of breath.

"Is that so? Can't imagine what I might've done. Unless you count smoking too much." Bill coughed. "But I don't reckon that's against the law, yet."

"You know why I'm here, Bill. You've been seen harboring and sheltering a fugitive."

"Have I?" Laughter. "News to me."

"Bill, I've seen it myself. A young woman, pretty." It came out sounding like 'purdy'. "But we both know where she came from."

"Do we?" I pictured Bill leaning against the doorframe, blocking the entrance.

A sigh. "She's an outcast, Bill."

"I'm afraid I beg to differ on that."

"Beg all you like, but I still need to take her into custody."

Bill scoffed. "Custody? For what? There's no law against being an outcast, not that there is one here."

"There might not be an official law against it." Angry now. "But we have a very strict unofficial law against it, which I take great pride in upholding."

"Yes, you do." The distaste was clear in Bill's voice. "But like

Escaping The Caves

I said, there's no outcast here."

Silence. From the open window I heard the crickets play their violins.

"But there is a woman here."

"Let me guess, having a woman in the house is against the unofficial laws as well?"

"Maybe not, but it would be in poor taste. I would've thought you had a greater respect for Eliza's memory."

"Don't push me, Jeff. You might be the sheriff of this dusty speck of a town, but I knew you when you were still a bed-wetter, so don't push me."

"Careful, Bill. Like you said, I am the sheriff."

Another silence. It stretched. And stretched.

"If she's not an outcast, might I see her then? To calm the minds of our fellow townsmen, like. Whoever this mystery woman is, if she's not an outcast, she has nothing to fear, has she?"

There was a coppery taste in my mouth. 'By blood shall you know me, in blood I deal.' Where had I read that? I couldn't remember. That sickening sense of vertigo in my stomach told me where this was going. I'd had the same feeling when Ethan woke me up. Somewhere on the dark streets outside, death waited. I closed my eyes.

The silence endured until I thought my teeth would splinter with the strain of it. Then, "Jess? Come out for a second, hon. Don't be frightened, it'll just be a moment." Bill sounded as calm as ever, but I wasn't fooled. I recognized fear in a man's voice when I heard it.

Even if I didn't believe in a god, I prayed when I opened the door. Bill stood in the doorway and barred the entrance like I'd imagined. Rufus stood silent watch by his side. His eyes never left the sheriff. The latter looked nothing like I'd pictured. I'd thought of him as either a very heavyset or very thin man due to his reedy, out of breath voice, but he looked disturbingly normal. Handsome even, despite his age, if it hadn't been for his cold eyes.

When he caught sight of my bandaged cheek, his lips twisted. "Really, Bill? Did you think a trick as cheap as that would fool me?" Again with that click of the tongue. How I detested that sound of disdain. He might as well have spit in Bill's face.

Bill didn't need to click his tongue to show disdain. It was etched as clearly onto his face as the scars hidden beneath my bandage. "Beg your pardon, Jeff, but I don't really give a rat's furry ass if you're fooled or not. The girl was severely injured when I found her. If the bandage feeds your paranoia…" Bill raised his hands.

"See, that's where you're wrong, my friend, my so-called paranoia is very much your problem." Jeff took a step forward. Rufus growled deep in his throat. The sheriff didn't glance at the dog.

"I know what's been going on in this house over the years. I looked the other way when Eliza was alive, out of respect for her, but I won't let you bring down the morale of our town out of some misguided sense of compassion."

Bill never lost his cool, but his voice did what the dog's had failed to do. Jeff stepped back. Apprehension briefly crossed his weather-beaten features. "Now you listen to me, Jefferson, and you listen good. I'm a physician. I've taken vows to heal the sick and ease the suffering of those hurtin', and I take my vows very seriously. And you stand there talkin' about Eliza, as if you've the right to speak her name."

The tip of Bill's nose nearly touched the sheriff's. Rufus'

growls increased in volume. None of the men paid him any attention. I remained lost in the shadows. I held my breath, one hand wrapped around the barrel of the gun behind my back.

"I've as much right to speak her name as you do, Bill. She was mine first, before you started meddlin', stealin' what wasn't yours."

Bill snorted and Jeff flinched as if struck. "She wasn't ever yours, Jeff. That's just a comfortin' lie you been tellin' yourself over the years to ease your hurtin' pride."

"She led me to believe we had somethin'." The look in Jeff's eyes confirmed what I'd already suspected. This man was a murderer.

Bill shook his head. "She didn't ever lead you to believe anything you didn't already want to believe. Eliza was one of those rare people who saw good, even where there was none. There wasn't anythin' bad in her, so she wasn't capable of believing there could be in anyone else, either."

Jeff's fists were white across the knuckles. "Why she ever chose such a weak man as you I'll never understand."

"Don't matter, Jeff. Cause she did."

"And yet, you couldn't save her. Could you? What good were your precious vows then? She died 'cause of you." Jeff took a step back, and savored the effect of his words.

All the color had drained from Bill's face, leaving only two red hectic spots in his cheeks. My finger tightened on the trigger. "Get out of here, Jeff. Ain't nothin' for you here. You ought to leave before I make you."

"Ah, but there is, Bill. I want the girl. She's an outcast and she'll have to pay the price." Jeff's hand came to rest on the butt of his gun. The smallest shake of Bill's head held me back.

"Leave her out if this. We both know this is between you and me. Ain't got nothin' to do with Jess. She'll stay on as long as she needs and then she'll move on. Nobody need ever know she was here."

Jeff smiled. His teeth were yellow, like that of a rat. "Tell ya what. Show me her cheek. If there's nothin' but a wound there, I'll graciously go on my way, though I ain't likely to forget your bad manners tonight, Bill."

"Ain't got to show you nothin', Jeff. Get out of my house. Last warning."

Jeff's smile broadened. We were playing right into his net, whatever it was made of.

"Sure thing, Bill. I'll do that." He tipped his hat in my direction, smiling all the while.

"Oh, just one more thing." He snapped his fingers as if he just remembered. "When you're on your knees later, cursin' my name, keep in mind that we could have disposed of her quietly."

Bill slammed the door closed so hard it shook. "Jess, I..." His eyes told me everything I needed to know. My time here was up. I could leave now, or not at all.

I swallowed. "I'll get my things."

Bill followed me around as I threw my belongings into the battered rucksack. "If I thought I could convince Jeff to stand down, I would tell you to stay. Permanently, if that's what you wanted. But in half an hour, he'll have rallied half the town. This ain't a safe place for you anymore."

"Yeah, I gathered as much." I stopped and looked at him. "I'm not the first outcast you've taken in, am I?"

Bill hunkered down to pat Rufus. "No, there've been others, but I'm afraid you might be the last. Jeff ain't gonna take his eyes off me from now on, I'll wager."

I studied his kind, worried eyes. "Will he hurt you? Or make

Escaping The Caves

others hurt you?"

"Naw. He'll be spitting mad once he sees you've gone, but other than dragging my name through the mud all over town, there ain't much he can do. And he's been doing that for years anyhow." But he didn't look up at me.

"Bill, I can't leave like this. You might not be able to protect me, but I can protect you."

Bill's back popped as he got up. "I'm sure you could, but I can look after myself. This town would turn on you like a pack of wild dogs, if not out of spite, then out of sheer boredom. But as much as it shames me to say this right now, I'm one of them. They won't harm me."

"After everything you've done for me—"

"The best thing you can do to repay me is leave. Right now. No ifs or buts about it."

"Bill—"

"Now, you listen to me, Jess." He grabbed hold of my arms, and squeezed painfully. "I know how well you must be able to fight, to have lasted as long as you did in those caves. I don't doubt that you could kill every man, woman and child in this town if it came to that, leaving nothing but a trail of blood and dust behind you. But is that really what you want? Killing those people to protect me? That ain't brave. That's just stupid."

He breathed deeply, but didn't let go of my arms. I resisted the urge to wince as his fingers dug deeper into my arms.

"My guess is that you left those caves so you wouldn't have to witness anymore carnage or have to smell the stench of death every day. What would the point in leaving be if death follows you everywhere you go? You ain't ever gonna be free from those caves. Cause they'll be in here." He tapped my forehead. "And they'll be here." He held my hands. "And they'll destroy this." He placed my right hand over my heart.

"The brave choice ain't always the one that would've made you look brave in front of those warriors you left behind. Stepping away from a fight is sometimes not only the brave choice, it's the right choice. It might not be an easy choice, but it's the right choice." He patted my hands. "Go now, Jess, before it's too late. That's the right choice."

I nodded, but my feet wouldn't budge. I looked long and hard at the tanned face, where deep furrows had marked the passage of time and he let me look. If there existed sufficient words to express how much his kindness, care and company had meant to me, I didn't know them. It wasn't just what he'd done for me. It was how he'd done it, as if it was the most natural thing in the world. Like there was nothing wrong with me, what I'd done or where I came from. He'd treated me like an equal.

"Jess..." Bill warned.

"Yeah, yeah, okay." But I still didn't walk away. I hesitated. My father's face hovered in front of me. I closed my eyes and embraced Bill. His old arms were surprisingly strong and his beard tickled my face the way it'd done the night he'd found me, half-dead, in his garden. I knew it wouldn't have mattered to him, but I wouldn't embarrass myself by crying.

"Thank you," I whispered, then pulled back.

He cupped my cheek with one hand, and my eyes spilled over anyway. "You're most welcome, Jess. And no matter what you might be thinking right now, you'll be fine. You're a fighter in more ways than one, so you'll be fine. Remember I told you that."

"Take care of yourself, Bill," I said. 'Don't get killed' is what I meant.

Escaping The Caves

Bill tipped an imaginary hat as he let me out the back door. They stood there and watched me, him and the dog. Two dark shadows against the light spilling out of the house. Something tugged at my heart as I turned my back on them.

I sneaked out of the town the same way I'd sneaked in. Silently and unnoticed, with nothing more going for me than the desire to live.

Jeff hadn't managed to raise half the town to its feet, but at least forty angry men and women trailed behind him. To my astonishment, they actually had both torches and pitchforks. Maybe it was mandatory equipment when assembling a mob of angry townspeople.

I almost turned back, but Bill's hard words steadied me. To leave wasn't the easy choice, it was fucking hard, but it was the right one. I got past the mob, without much of an effort really, and left town.

The ghosts followed.

Chapter 8

And so I returned to the frozen nights and scorched days. The coyotes stayed close, but never bothered me. Perhaps they sensed it would be a bad idea to pick a fight.

I almost wished they would. With so much pent up anger and frustration, I would've gladly emptied a couple of rounds into them. But they left me to my mental rage, only bothering to howl in the night, adding to my growing list of discomforts.

The train tracks became my route, mostly out of habit. Whenever I came to a town, I'd follow the same routine. I'd stock up on water, whatever food I could scavenge, and I'd seek one night of refuge from the cold desert. Then I'd move on, just as the sun touched the horizon in the morning. No one saw me coming or going, and if they did, they left me to my own devices.

There was no reason to complain. Thanks to Bill, I was once again fit and healthy, at least physically. Though the trek along the railroad was an ordeal, I never lacked in water, food or shelter. My mental state wouldn't pass a test anytime soon, but I'd learned to deal with, if not live with, the ghosts and the fear they brought with them.

The strain of keeping them out of my head tired me far more than the daily walk. The desert would one day come to an end, but the ghosts might stay with me forever. The thought left me weak and drained.

I had no way to mark time, other than the passage of days and nights, and soon gave up the attempt to keep track of the weeks. They didn't matter anyway. I was an outcast, and would live out my life on the fringe of society. I might as well live on the fringe of time as well.

Many things bothered me, but there was one thing in particular that stayed on my mind. The mountains which housed the caves I'd gone to such great lengths to get away from followed me. The mountain range stretched across the desert, keeping a parallel line to the train tracks.

I'd grown up with the sight of these mountains stretching into the distance, but I could never have imagined just how far the reach of these mountains was. Just like the ghosts, they refused to leave my side.

But after what could've been weeks, or months, I came to the end of the mountains. I stopped, wiping sweat off my brow. The bandanna went back into my pocket, and I pulled out a pair of binoculars.

There was a small town at the bottom of the mountains. The terrain looked different, lusher, livelier. Trees I'd never seen before, far greener than I knew existed, dotted the bottom of the mountains at this end. A small waterfall turned into a river, which flowed down one side of the mountain.

It was hard to tell from this distance, but even the town

Escaping The Caves

looked more robust and healthier, somehow, than the ones I'd passed on my way. The houses looked bigger, sturdier, and the streets looked cleaner. There was a neat look to the place. It looked like the kind of town people cared about. The kind of place where one might not just grow old in, but actually enjoy doing so.

I lowered the binoculars, and carefully put them back in my rucksack. Grandpa had been so proud when he gave me those. I took a swig from my water canteen and sloshed the water around in my mouth. No vultures circled above my head. The coyotes had lost interest in me a couple of nights ago.

I hunkered down and rested my back. My index finger drew circles in the sand. Sweat trickled down my spine. There was a new blister on my left heel.

The ocean was my destination. That hadn't changed. The picturesque town in front of me was probably the one the unpleasant conductor had mentioned. There would be other trains and other train tracks leading out of this place. Some might only go to sleepy, uninspired places, but some might also bring me to the ocean. Or at least part of the way there.

I couldn't trek all across this vast, inhospitable land on foot. If I ever made it to the ocean, I wouldn't have any feet left. But there was the small matter of me being an outcast. Or rather, the matter of my scars.

A rock the size of my fist lay next to me, as if it'd been there, waiting for me all along. I picked it up, and juggled it with one hand.

My body begged me to rest. To sleep in a bed without freezing my toes off, and to spend the day without my skin boiling off me. Most of all, I wanted to sit quietly in the shade for a while. Maybe the ghosts would eventually shut up if I

101

rested.

But I didn't want another Ethan to recognize me. It would be best if no one recognized me. One Bill to take the heat for me had been enough. I wanted to be me without anyone knowing who that was.

In the end it was easier than I thought it would be. Once the decision had been made, I didn't hesitate. Bill had been right. I was a fighter in more ways than one.

The rock smashed into my face.

～ ⁓

I came to. The blue sky was a vast endless expanse. For a moment it felt like I'd fallen right into it. I sat up, a sharp pain slicing my head in half. Gingerly, I touched my cheek and winced. There was no mirror to confirm my suspicion, but from the amount of blood and pain, I knew my cheek was smashed well and good.

I swayed on my feet, and deemed my mission successful. My scars needed to be obliterated, and I very much doubted anyone would be able to see them through the bleeding pulp my cheek had been reduced to. The ragged wound would eventually heal over and, hopefully, leave behind a new set of scars. No one need ever know what secrets lay buried beneath this wound. It was probably naïve as hell, but by destroying the visible marks of my past, I hoped to obliterate it completely.

On the way to the town at the bottom of the mountains, I pondered what story to tell people. If I intended to stay long enough to recuperate somewhat, I'd need a cover story. My head throbbed with every step I took and the fresh wound bled through the bandanna I pressed against it. I'd underestimated

Escaping The Caves

my own strength and determination.

In other words, my imagination didn't run full speed at that moment. I'd figure something out when the time came. The less I told people, the better. More details led to more complicated lies which would, sooner or later, be my downfall. As Ethan had so kindly pointed out to me, I wasn't exactly playing with a full deck. No need to add to the mental confusion.

I bent over and rested my hands on my knees. My gorge rose. I breathed through my nose and fought the nausea back down. In the process of wiping out my tribal scars, I'd given myself a concussion. If only I could've smashed the ghosts into obliteration as well. They took turns walking beside me. It was Jen's turn today. My eyes watered.

After what felt like an eternity, but couldn't have been more than a couple of hours, I crossed the border of the town. It really did look like something out of a fairytale. Even the people here looked clean and happy, though their smiles faded fast when I walked past them. A little girl in a blue dress and pig tails who was skipping rope tripped on her own feet as she saw me. She skinned her knee, cried out.

I half-turned in her direction, but saw the look on her mother's face and kept walking. Animated conversations ebbed out and people stepped back. They watched me from the corner of their eyes, never daring to face me head-on.

If my plan had been to blend in, I'd so far failed spectacularly. I wondered what I should look for first, an apothecary or a place to sleep, when my worn-out shoes snagged on a rock in the road. My palms tore open. Pebbles blended with my flesh. No one came to help me.

I staggered to my feet. The humiliation burned far worse than my ragged hands. I looked up and realized I'd fallen in

103

front of a small diner. Half a dozen guests gawked at me through the windows. I almost flipped them one, but figured that might send the wrong message.

A man, most likely the proprietor by the look of the apron around his waist, came to the window, urged the people back in their seats. The glare of the sun on the window pane rendered the man's face invisible, but I saw him freeze as he looked at me.

I turned away from the diner. Maybe if I found a place to clean up, I could risk coming back here for something to eat.

"Jess?"

The air was knocked out of me. Slowly, I turned back.

"John?"

"Jess?" He hadn't heard me. "Is that really you? What happened to your face?"

Carefully, he turned my face so he could get a better look at it. His hair still fell into his eyes. He shook it out, only to have it fall back again. I smiled.

"Shit, this is really bleeding. How did you manage this?"

"I tripped and fell." I just did it in front of his diner, if it was his. "I hit a rock."

"This doesn't look too good. You better come in." He hadn't seen me in months, and, even then, I'd been a stranger. An outcast no less.

I hesitated.

John looked at me. "Your secret's safe with me."

I nodded and followed him into the cool space within.

The conversation in the diner died down the moment I entered. It wasn't just my bleeding face, it was my whole appearance. The way I moved, the look in my eyes, the dust on my tired, faded clothes. I could bash my head in, but I'd remain something else until the day I'd die. And these people sensed that.

"Stop staring and concentrate on your food instead. There's nothing to see here," John said.

He stuck his head into a room behind the counter. "Dad, I need to go upstairs for a bit, can you come out here?"

"I'm busy," a gravelly voice called back.

"Playing solitaire doesn't qualify as busy. And put that smoke out, Dad. People are eating in here."

An old man came shuffling out. Grey, grizzly hair stood up on his head. "Don't tell me what I can and can't do in my diner, son. If I want to smoke in here, I damn well will." But he stubbed the cigarette out on a plate.

"Get rid of that? Please?" John nodded at the smoldering pile of ash.

His father didn't listen. His eyes were firmly glued on me. I shifted my feet and scratched my neck.

"Where the hell did you find that?"

John rolled his eyes. "Dad, this is Jess. She fell and hit her face on a rock. I need to help her get it cleaned. She might need stitches, in which case I'll have to get her over to Rosie. So I need you to handle the counter, okay? Think you can do that?"

His father bristled. "Boy, I was handling this counter long before you were even a thought in your mother's head. Don't insult your old man by asking such dumbass questions."

John held up his hands. "Okay. Just checking. It's just after that fire last week, I thought maybe —"

"Just go, will you?" His father flapped a hand at him, but he never took his eyes off me. "You do what you have to. But if you're determined to be the hero of the hour, you better step to it. That girl's bleeding all over my floor."

Kristin Talgø

I looked down. Two spots of red dotted the linoleum. I took a napkin from the counter and wiped it off.

"Hmprh," John's dad glowered and spat into the sink behind him.

"Don't mind him. He barks worse than he bites. Come on. Let's get you sorted out. Mind your step. The bottom one's a little loose." He led me up a rickety staircase. The boards creaked beneath our feet.

"Just sit here and I'll be right back." John left me on a beaten sofa. There was a bed at the other end of the room, a cluttered desk by the window. A picture of John and Eve stood by his bedside. A pile of books balanced on the table next to me.

I was just about to inspect it closer when John came back. Just like Bill had done that night so long ago, John carried an overflowing tray. It seemed I was destined to run into nice men determined to help me. Someone up there might like me, after all.

"Something funny?" John looked at me. He dipped a cloth in a bowl of water.

"Hmmm?"

"You're smiling. Not that there's anything wrong with that."

I shook my head, but stopped as the walls swiftly tilted in the wrong direction, though I doubted there could ever be a right direction for walls to tilt in.

"Yeah, you should probably not move your head too much. Hold still, this might hurt a bit." He pressed the cloth to my wound. Burning spikes shot through my face.

He dabbed at the wound. "You must have put a lot of force behind that rock." John rinsed the cloth. The water turned red.

"I...What?"

"Or maybe you just fell conveniently on your left cheek,

Escaping The Caves

without hurting the rest of your face?" John's face seemed very close where he sat, washing my wound clean of dust and grit.

"Why would I do something like that?" I kept my eyes on a spot to the right of his head.

"Maybe because of what happened on the train. Or maybe because of whatever you've been through on your way here. Christ, Jess, it's been three months. Did you walk all the way here?" He wrung the cloth. Water splashed over the edge of the bowl. He was angry, but I didn't know why.

Three months. No wonder my feet and back were sore.

"Did you?"

"What?"

He exhaled. "Walk here. All the way."

"Yeah. I followed the train tracks. I had a stop on the way though, for maybe around six weeks or so, but yeah. Mostly I walked. That's why I..." I waved a finger in the direction of my raw cheek.

"I saw this town and I just wanted to rest for a bit. But without the risk of being run out by an angry mob at night. It seemed like a good idea at the time." I gritted my teeth.

"Sorry. This stings, I know, but if I don't disinfect it, you'll get an infection."

I remembered the yellow, festering wound and red line running up my arm, and let John do his thing. The strong fumes of alcohol stung my eyes.

"How did you find water and food?" John placed a bandage over my cheek. "You got lucky, by the way. I don't think you'll need stitches."

"I just snuck into the towns I passed on the way. There was never a shortage of water and food," I answered. The way he looked made me want to squirm. It was like having my soul bared and examined.

"Did no one see you?"

"Don't think so. Or if they did, they let me be. I didn't stay very long."

"Except for that one place. You said you were there for six weeks?"

I shifted on the sofa. "More or less. I find it hard to keep track of time. It doesn't seem real to me anymore. It passes, but it doesn't mean anything."

"I see." John washed his hands and dried them slowly. "Jess…" He paused. "I don't know how to phrase this."

I got up. "If me being an outcast here bothers you, I'll find a train and get out of town tonight." His prejudices hurt more than I wanted to admit.

"What? No, Jess. That's not what I meant. Would you sit down? Please?" His hands fitted mine disturbingly well.

"I couldn't care less about you being an outcast. Personally, I think the whole concept as such a heap of hypocritical bullshit. I'd like to see any of those people last five minutes."

I snorted. "Trust me, they wouldn't last five seconds."

John's lips twitched. "See? Though you probably shouldn't go around telling them that."

"So, what is the problem?"

He took a deep breath. "Are you dangerous?"

Of all the questions I'd anticipated, this was not one of them. "Dangerous? What? You think I would hurt any of you?"

"Would you?"

"No!" I lowered my voice. "Of course not. Is that how you see me? As some trigger-happy lunatic?"

"No, I don't, but Jess… I am concerned. Especially since I have Eve to think about. Granted, you look better than when I saw you on the train, but you still... You still look like you're fighting some battles. In here." He tapped my brow the way Bill had the night I left him.

I flinched. "I'm not...I would never hurt Eve. Or anyone else, for that matter. The town I stayed in for some time, I left so I wouldn't hurt anyone when they discovered who I was. If I'd wanted to hurt people, I'd have ample opportunity." I looked at him. "I'm not that kind of crazy."

John held my gaze. The seconds ticked by. "All right. I believe you. But you're not...You can't, in all honesty, tell me everything's okay. I mean, if there'd been nothing wrong, you probably wouldn't be sitting here talking to me, would you? You'd still be making a living fighting in those caves."

I thought of the ghosts. The way I'd literally heard the ropes that held my sanity together creak. At least I'd stopped hearing voices.

"No, everything's not okay. I'm twenty-eight and I've been fighting in those caves since I was sixteen. That's twelve years of my life as a warrior. And the twelve years before that, I prepared myself for a life in combat. It's the only life I know."

I struggled. The words were hard and difficult to find. To talk about this was like pulling teeth without anesthetic. In other words, it was fucking painful.

"I'm a soldier. That's what I am. But I don't want to be. Growing up, they tell you it's the most honorable life anyone could wish for. People live their whole lives without knowing why they walk this earth, but we're born with a purpose. Our life, our destiny, has been decided from birth. We protect humanity. Without us there would be a second Falling."

John's close proximity made it even harder to dig for buried words. I walked over to the window. A tall, beautiful tree stood outside the window. It swayed in the wind. I didn't know its name.

"There needs to be soldiers. Someone has to keep the monsters confined to the caves. And I used to think I'd do it until I died, which could be any day of the week, really. I know that's true for everyone, but for us… We face death daily. Each day we get up and know it could be our last or the last for those around us. And each night we go to bed and know the next night could be spent in the ground."

"It must be a strained way of living."

I kept my back to him, but I heard him weigh his words carefully.

"It is. But that didn't bother me so much. At least, the thought that I could die, be killed…some days I thought it would be a relief. The great escape. The irony is that when that option should've been my choice, I didn't want to die anymore."

"I'm not sure I follow…"

"Yeah, me neither. My own death didn't frighten me, but… I think I got tired of watching the people I cared about dying. *Their* deaths frightened me. I didn't want to watch another friend of mine, another sister, another lover, be ripped to pieces in front of me. I got tired of washing their blood off my face every evening. I didn't want to go to sleep listening to their screams any longer."

I turned around. John still sat on the sofa. His skin was paler than when we started the conversation. "When my sister and her boyfriend, my best friend, were killed… It was as if their deaths snapped something in my mind. I think the break had been coming for some time, but their deaths pushed me over the edge."

I shrugged. I wasn't able to push any more words around the

Escaping The Caves

lump in my throat. "Or something like that. I suppose watching so much blood and death comes with a price. Or maybe I'm just weak. My father's in his fifties and he's avoided a nervous breakdown just fine."

All the digging around made me more tired than three months of walking. I sank down on the chair next to the desk. "I just want to rest for a while. I don't want to cause any trouble. If you don't feel safe with me around, I will leave, of course. Maybe I'm crazy, but I'm not dangerous. If I was, I'd spend another three months walking in the desert."

John cleared his throat. "Okay. I've got a suggestion. I'll be staying here longer than originally planned, and, well, you've seen my dad. I could do with an extra pair of hands around here. There's an extra bedroom down the hall, and if you're interested, you could stay. Here. I don't know how much I would be able to pay you, but you could stay for free and food's on the house. It might give you the breathing space you need. Give you time to figure things out."

I pulled at a loose thread on my shirt sleeve. "Why?"

"Sorry?"

"Why would you do that? I might not be dangerous, but we both know I'm not a hundred percent mentally sound at the moment. And while people might not know I'm an outcast, they will know something's different about me. A little off. There will be questions. Are you ready for that?"

He cocked an eyebrow. "Are you?"

"It's either that, board a train or start walking again. And to be honest, I've had my share of the last two for the time being."

John laughed. It made him look like a kid. "Yeah, that I believe. Why don't I show you the room and you can have a shower? When you're ready, come downstairs and I'll fix you

111

something to eat. Sound okay?"

"Sure." I wondered why the kindness of strangers should surprise me so much more than their pettiness.

The room was small and bare. A bed, a cupboard, a desk and a chair. But it would be mine, all on my own. And the view from the window was breathtaking. The snow at the top of the mountains glittered in the sun.

"I know it's not much, but–"

"What are those trees called?"

He came over to the window. "Oh, ehm, spruces."

"They're beautiful."

"Yeah, yeah, sure, guess they are…"

"Don't you think so?"

John scratched the back of his neck. "Don't think I've ever given them much thought."

"I've never seen anything like this before." For some reason their beauty made me want to cry. "Everything's so green and… vibrant here. Back where I, you know, all we have are cactuses, withered trees, dried-out bushes and sand. And then some more sand. And then some more. And rocks. Lots of them."

"This must be a welcome sight then."

I smiled at John's polite words. I would've staked my gun that he regretted his generous offer just then. "It is."

"The bathroom is the second door on the right, and there are towels and bed sheets in the cupboard. I'll see you in a bit then?"

"Yeah. Where's Eve, by the way?"

John paused by the door. His hair covered the eyes again, but his mouth became tight. They pressed down on his lips. "She's with her mother. Just for the day. She stays here."

"I see. Is that why you're staying longer than planned? So

Escaping The Caves

Eve can spend some more time with her mother?"

John's lips disappeared entirely. "Yes, no, my dad's also... Look, this isn't really something I want to discuss."

"Oh. Okay." I opened up my rucksack. My cheeks burned. "I'm sorry. I didn't mean to pry."

John sighed and rubbed a hand over his face. "No, I'm sorry. I asked you a lot of personal questions earlier, and you answered as best as you could. You deserve the same."

"It's okay. You don't have to explain. I was just curious."

"It's okay." John plucked at some peeled paint. "Things have been... strained between Eve's mother and I. Nobody understood when I took Eve and left, but I... I needed to get away. And Eve's mother... Wasn't as if she fought very hard for us to stay. I think she was relieved. Though she wouldn't have admitted that, even under torture."

"Really, John." I put a hand on his wrist. "You don't have to say."

"I know. But since you're staying you should at least know the basics. Makes it easier, I guess. I was only thinking of staying for a few weeks, but then I saw how it was with dad... You know, last week he almost burned down the place? Fell asleep with one of his damn cigarettes burning."

"Right..." I stashed one of my own packets out of sight.

"And he forgets things. Yesterday morning, I swear, for a moment there I don't think he remembered who I was. Though he got mad as hell when I asked him about it later. I worry about him. I don't know where he'll go if he can't hold on to this place. Someone's got to take care of him."

"He's got you."

John looked on the verge of tears. I plunged back into my now-empty rucksack. If this was how Kyle felt when he saw me

113

cry, I could almost forgive him for walking away.

"Yeah, sure, I'm here now. But I don't belong here anymore, Jess. I've made a life for myself elsewhere. Miles from here. A life for me and Eve, and I gotta tell you, that life does not include moving back into the same town as my demented, grouchy father and crazy-ass ex-wife." John leaned his head on the doorframe.

He looked up. The tears I thought I'd glimpsed were gone. I put away the rucksack.

"I'm sorry. I didn't mean to dump that all over you like that. The past few months have been a bit stressful for me, though I guess I've got no right to complain really, considering…"

He cleared his throat. "Right, anyway. So, I guess it's a good thing I told you that bit about dad. Like I said, he's grouchy, but his heart is in the right place, even if it's an old one. He forgets things he has no business forgetting, so keep an eye out for him, okay?"

"I'll do that."

"Okay, then I'll let you get to it. Just one more thing. When I said that nobody understood when I left… Dad did. Understand. So if he gives you a hard time when you're here, remember that he's old and his heart is not just in the right place. It's one of the best I know."

"I'll remember. You're lucky to have a father like that."

John nodded. "Yeah, I am. I'll have to keep it in mind the next time I catch him placing his slippers in the oven instead of the Sunday roast.

Chapter 9

And so my time as a waitress started. Put into comparison with the rest of my life, it was a brief career, and not one I ever excelled at, but I enjoyed the simplicity of it. Pour coffee, wipe off tables, scrub down the counter and wipe the floor at the end of the day. It gave my hands something to do, and left my mind free to wander. In the beginning, I thought it would've been a very comfortable job, if it hadn't been for the customers.

They were probably under strict instructions not to ask me any questions that weren't specifically waitress/customer related, because people were suspiciously easy-going around me. Don't get me wrong, their eyes kept tabs on my every move, gesture and spoken word, but most of them treated me with kindness and respect. Those who didn't treat me with respect didn't bother me much. I got the distinct impression that they didn't bestow much of either on anyone.

John was very evasive concerning what story he'd fed people. Eventually, he mumbled something about me running away from a violent relationship. He was right about me not jumping up and down at the idea of being painted the victim, but the story wasn't too far from the truth. I had run away, and the life I'd led had been violent.

It was also the kind of story people didn't question. It was too personal, too intimate for people to poke their nose into. They probably discussed it to pieces behind my back, but as long as they didn't do so within earshot, I didn't give a rat's ass, as Bill would've said.

The story gave me the necessary cover I needed to explain why something was a little off about me, why I was a bit raw around the edges. I didn't enjoy making eye contact with people, though John constantly reminded me a smile went a long way in this business. I replied that if he'd wanted a waitress of the sunny kind, he'd picked the wrong outcast.

It wasn't that I didn't want to smile; some of the customers, the regulars, I actually looked forward to seeing after a while. But I still wasn't fully there, somehow. My short-term memory made John's father's seem excellent. I was easily distracted. There were moments when grief hit me, a great wave, and I had to hold onto something to keep my knees from buckling. My mind played vivid, enraged mental conversations with everyone. From my father to Kyle to Jen to my friends who'd turned their back on me the moment I needed them the most.

So no, I didn't enjoy eye contact, and smiling didn't come easily to me. But it was something to do. I was surrounded by people with their hearts in the approximately-right neighborhood of where it should be. Best of all, I got to lay my head on the same pillow at night. And I never had to wonder if tomorrow would be the day everything would be torn apart.

There was a bitter comfort in losing everything and everyone you held dear. You had nothing left to lose. But it was also what chipped away at me, one piece of my heart at a time.

And there was Eve. I'd never been much of kid person before her. It wasn't that I disliked kids, I just never really saw what the fuss was about. But with Eve, I understood why people had children. I'd catch myself rubbing the scar on my lower belly, the one that had almost earned me a half-hour memorial service.

Eve possessed a special sort of light. There was such warmth and youthful enthusiasm about her that even a battle-hardened outcast such as me fell in love. She lit up her surroundings. Even the greyest day seemed bright with her around, and even the grumpiest people couldn't help smile if she crossed their path.

How her mother could've agreed to John taking their daughter, I would never know. But that was before I met her. Regardless, if Eve had been my daughter, I'd count my blessings every night before I went to sleep.

Eve was also very perceptive, despite her young age. She never betrayed my true identity by mentioning the incident on the train. She'd seemed to accept me suddenly appearing in her town, working as a waitress in her grandfather's diner, as naturally as the rest of us accepted the weather. It was a force of nature which she had no control over, and so she didn't question or waste her energy on trying to understand it.

But apart from this one aspect, she was the most curious creature I ever encountered. She'd follow me around the diner, asking me questions about everything from what my favorite color was to why I poured coffee with my right hand instead of my left. Eve was like a cheerful puppy. She bounced around me, yapping away, but somehow I was never annoyed.

Kristin Talgø

One night, as I listened to the crickets outside and watched the moon grow fat again, I finally understood why. She had a healing effect on me. Her innocence and good humor chased the ghosts away. Not for very long, but in her presence they lost some of their terrifying power. Her persistent curiosity drowned out their cries and harsh whispers. She softened the hard edges of reality, cushioning the sharp elbows.

Sometimes, when I polished glasses or re-filled ketchup bottles, she'd sneak up behind me and wrap her skinny arms around my knees. She never offered any explanation as to why she sought out my company, but the hugs made me momentarily forget what it'd been like to kill Ethan.

She did, however, have a tendency to find abandoned kittens and wounded birds. Maybe she had a sixth sense where broken and lost things were concerned. If that was the case, I certainly fit the profile.

This town might not be the center of the world, but it made the community I'd left behind look like some long forgotten age before the Falling. Up until then, my idea of a shower had been a bucket with water adjoined by a cup. In John's house, or technically his dad's, there was an actual shower.

At first I distrusted the huge faucet which rained warm water down on me in unimaginable quantities. But it didn't take long before I found the experience close to orgasmic after a long day working in a stifling, greasy diner. I'd never felt so clean. Most likely, I'd never been that clean, either.

Then there were the films. Back in my fighting days, we got shipments in twice a month. The first one would consist of food, drink, medicines, clothes, etc., whatever was necessary to keep up our physical strength. The second one, however, was dedicated to keeping our mental state more or less balanced.

Escaping The Caves

This included booze and cigarettes for those who were considered among the grownups, and toys of different functions and varieties for those who were not.

But what I looked forward to the most in the second shipment were the books. It didn't matter if they were old and tattered, what mattered was that they were, for the time being, unknown to me. They captured me, sucked me into an alternate reality. We were allowed to take out four books at the time and keep each for four weeks, not that I needed a month to finish a book. If pressed, I could've finished a book in four hours, depending on its length.

Kyle never understood why I sometimes preferred staying in, curled up with a book, when there was a perfectly good and raucous party going on just a few minutes away. But then again, he'd never been one to indulge in daydreams and fantasies.

He understood my need to escape from our chaotic world. The bit that puzzled him was why I'd choose a book, which to him, was only words upon pages. As long as there were booze and willing women, Kyle wasn't likely to pick up a book.

Not that I'd needed further proof to realize John was a very different man than the one I'd left behind. I only needed to peek into the living room. Three of the four walls in there were covered with shelves from floor to ceiling. They were crammed with books. Basically, it was my idea of heaven.

"You're welcome to use it any time you like," John had said, amused. "If there's any one in particular you like, ask me on a good day and you can keep it. I've got far too many books." He'd thought over this last statement. "Nope, I take that back. You can never have too many books."

Reverently, I'd walked up and down the shelves and trailed my fingers across the spines. My own spine tingled at the

119

Kristin Talgø

prospect of owning my own books.

I'd always been loath to return the books to the library. I acted the way with books the same way I acted if I slept with a man. I became attached. But unlike the men, I wanted to own the books and store them somewhere I could easily access again if I wanted to re-read them. Although, come to think of it, the last bit could be applied to men as well.

The living room, what I came to think of as the library, became my usual hide-out after work hours. I quickly became territorial about one huge, worn armchair. It was ideally placed next to a lamp and a small table.

I think it'd been Sam's, John's dad, favorite spot as well, but apart from gazing at it from the sofa, he never demanded it back. The gesture touched me, especially seeing as it came from a man who verbally abused me the moment he saw my face in the morning until I dived into my newest discovery from the shelves. Maybe deep down he enjoyed my presence. Or maybe he simply respected me as one reader to another. I never doubted where John had gotten his fondness of books from.

It ran in the family. Even Eve loved to read, and she had only just started to learn. She was the only person I tolerated to bother me once I'd inhabited the armchair, a book cradled in my hands like a long lost lover. But perceptive as she was, she would only sit next to my feet. She tried to read, carefully mouthing each word. Or she would draw or simply sit there, resting her small head against my leg. She fell asleep like that more than once.

It was on such an evening, after John tucked both Eve and Sam into their respective beds, that he introduced me to films. John knew how sacred the hours in the library were to me and never bothered me. Usually I would be so engrossed in a book, the roof could've caved in and I wouldn't have noticed.

But when John opened a cupboard and revealed a dark screen of some sort, my attention wandered.

"What's that?"

John smiled. "I thought I'd watch a film. Don't worry, I'll keep the sound down."

I closed the book. "What's a film?"

He raised his eyebrows. "You've never seen one?"

"Never seen one, never heard of one." I took a thin box from John's hands and turned it over. The title and names on the cover didn't mean a thing to me, but something tugged at the back of my mind. "Have you ever heard of someone called Violet Evergreen?"

John snorted. "Who hasn't? But please, don't insult my intelligence by assuming I watch the kind of films she makes."

I nodded, confused. To keep up with conversations like these was like trying to outrun the monsters. I would always be one step behind. "You remember the woman from the train? Ehm, Ethel something-or-other?"

"Edith? The charming woman with the orange face? Yeah, I remember her. Gave Eve nightmares for two days after she disembarked."

I giggled and slapped a hand across my mouth. That was an unusual sound coming from me. John didn't comment on it.

"Anyway, I remember Edith going on about her. She seemed to like her films, even though she tried to give every impression that she didn't."

John pushed a button on a slim, black machine and popped the shiny disc into it. I watched, half-fascinated, half-afraid, though I didn't know why.

"I'm sure she would. Those films are all about tall, dark,

muscly strangers sweeping swooning, busty damsels off their distressed feet. Lots of glitz and glamour. The industry pours an enormous amount of money into them, and gets back a tenfold profit. Not that it's ever done much for the quality of the productions, as far as I can tell. Think soft-core porn for women and you get the general idea."

"What's porn?"

John lowered the can of soda he'd raised to his lips. After watching me for a while, he asked, "What do you guys do for entertainment out there by the caves, when you're not ensuring the survival of the human species?"

"Weeell," I pulled at it, "we got books, but most people find booze, smoking, gambling and sex to be the preferable recreational activities."

John opened and closed his mouth. He shrugged. "I guess that goes for many people around here as well. But seriously, have you never seen a film before?"

I flushed. "Blame the government. They're the ones who kept us in the dark."

"You can say that again."

"What?"

"Nothing." John smiled. Wide and bright. It sent a pleasant tingly feeling through my stomach, but it didn't quite reach his eyes. "I did creative writing back in my delusional youth, when I believed I could make a living as a novelist, and one of the golden thumb rules were show, don't tell. But I think I'm going to override it this time."

I glanced up from browsing the other covers. They looked like books without pages. "You write?"

John's ears turned red. "Yeah, but mostly feature-stories for a magazine I work for. Or worked for, depending on whether or

Escaping The Caves

not I ever get out of this soul-killing town and back to the life I actually enjoy living."

He shook his head. "But the great novels seem to still be waiting for me. Some of them have been written, but none published so far. You never know though, the publishing business hasn't been up and running for more than a couple of decades since the Falling. A lot of them are still hesitant to take on new authors." The monotonous voice made me think this was a speech he'd given many people over the years, to explain his lack of success.

"Same with films, really. Which is why they're pumping out a new one with our friend Violet Evergreen every available season."

"To finance other films?" I turned over a cover with a black and white picture on it.

"Yeah, but most of the films you can get hold of are old ones from long before the Falling." John looked at me closely. "There's still a lot of technology missing which was as essential as bread and water back then, but they've recovered quite a lot of it. Probably a lot more than they want to admit back there on the east coast. And so they feed us these." He held up one of the films. "To keep us otherwise preoccupied."

The scar on the underside of my left arm itched. I thought of Bill scooping yellow puss out of it.

"Good books are also about leaving room enough left for the reader to read between the lines."

His eyes met mine.

"Is there anything between the lines you're trying to tell me?"

John cracked his knuckles, a gesture I came to associate with him stalling for time. "Maybe I am."

"If there's something you think I should know, why not just

come out and tell me?"

"Because I honestly don't know if you should know. Yet."

My mother used to say I was the most impatient girl she'd ever known. I'd been a month premature. I couldn't even wait for my own birth. To have a personal army of ghosts haunt me day and night hadn't improved my patience.

I caught myself doing that horrid clicking noise and flapped my hand. "It wouldn't be crime or mystery novels you write, is it? Because you're starting to sound like a mystery writer."

John laughed. It softened my irritation. "It is, actually."

"No wonder you're not getting published, if you only give out bits and clues, and never get around to writing a satisfactory ending."

He held up his hands. "Point taken. So, are you ready for the show part of this tutorial?"

I'd seen John distract Eve enough times when she wanted something he didn't think she should have, to know not to press him further. We'd come to the end of the conversational road. For now.

I leaned back against the sofa, and hugged a pillow to my chest. "Sure. Why not? If it's like a book, only with moving pictures, I might like it."

I was wrong. I loved it. The pictures, the sounds, the actors, the emotions and actions, I sucked it all up like the desert soaking up much-needed water.

The films silenced the ghosts in a way even the books hadn't been able to. Maybe the fast pace and loud noises helped drown them out, or maybe my mind wasn't able to focus on two things at the same time. Thankfully, the story on the screen won out over my mental scars for a short time.

I didn't stop reading, which was like breathing to me, but watching a film together became a daily ritual for John and I. After the diner had been closed and scrubbed clean, and the water tank depleted of hot water, we'd settle down in front of the TV, as John called it. Television. I'd never heard of that, either. Something in the way John looked at me made me feel as old and unknowing as Sam.

Eve would join us if we chose something appropriate. She always fell asleep on my lap. Those were the nights when the ache in my heart and mind spread to the scar on my lower belly. I grieved for what was lost and would never be.

No wonder I sought comfort and relief in the films. In the end, none of us can escape reality. It always comes back to bite us on the ass. But that didn't mean I couldn't give it one hell of a run for its money.

Chapter 10

The healing of my mind, like the breaking of it, was slow and painful. Jen once broke both her legs in the caves. The day the casts came off and she tried to walk again, she wobbled around like a newborn calf.

That's how I felt, mentally.

Everyday my mind tottered to its feet and felt around for safe purchase. I dreaded and expected the moment when the ground fell through. The moment never came, but it still left me shaky and scared.

The ghosts continued to demand their pay and I was still clueless as to what they wanted from me. Or I skittered away from the truth. I wanted them silenced, but didn't want them forgotten. Needless to say, that was a riddle I hadn't been able to solve. My own personal puzzle. I was still at least fifty pieces short.

One of the side-effects of trying not to lose your mind is that it turns you into a self-centered creature of unimaginable proportions. When I look back, it's impossible to pinpoint the moment my mind started to gather strength again. Eve's devotion certainly played a large part, but when I met Kelly, the balance finally tipped in my favor.

A cynical person might say it does me no credit, that it was another person's misery which saved my mind from going over the deep end completely. I have another, less pessimistic view on the matter. Maybe because it makes me sleep better at night, but there's some truth to it as well.

Though Bill had pointed it out, he didn't need to say I was a fighter. But what he needed to say was that I still needed someone to fight for. A cause to believe in. An injustice in need of correction. To scrub tables, pour coffee and bicker with customers somehow didn't seem to do it.

If you peeled back the various layers of my personality, what was left at the core, was a warrior. I was a warrior and hoped to die as one.

Kelly offered me an opportunity to continue my life as a warrior, but with less bloodshed. And Kelly cured me of any lingering fear of tears and emotions I might've dragged with me from the glorious upbringing of the caves.

The caves and my father. Bill probably would've been proud of me. My father would've been horrified. The thought gave me no small amount of pleasure.

The day I met Kelly, I was in a fouler mood than usual. I hadn't slept. The ghosts had kept me awake. The bastards turned the night into a competition about who could drive me insane the fastest.

My nerves, not the strongest at the best of times, were shot.

Escaping The Caves

My mind, not the sanest, was fried.

None of the frequent customers expected me to be all smiles and chatty comments, but I at least pretended to keep a civil tongue in my head. That was the day I proved them wrong. All of this led to John kicking me out of the diner on an early break, before he kicked me out of town on a permanent one.

I sat and smoked, already through half a packet. It wasn't even nine yet. There must've been chimneys with less soot in them than my lungs. Those were the days I contracted a rattling cough.

A young girl approached me.

She stared sullenly at my cigarette while mumbling testily if she could have one.

"Sorry?" I squinted at the girl through cigarette smoke.

"I said, can I have one of those?" She paused. "Please."

I eyed her small, round belly. The girl didn't look a day over fifteen, but whatever her age, she was old enough to get knocked up. "I don't think your tenant would thank me if I gave you one of these."

The girl wrapped her cardigan around her waist, but never broke off the sullen stare. "He can handle one. Mom smoked when she was pregnant with me. I turned out all right."

My grouchy tongue itched to release a snarky comeback, but my nicer side won out. The girl was clearly in enough trouble without me adding to it. Besides, with my murky past I really wasn't one to point any morale fingers. If I tried to get up on my high horse, I'd fall off pretty damn quick.

The girl's unwavering stare started to get on my nerves. I shrugged and handed her one. "Your call."

"Thanks." She took the cigarette. "You're that waitress I've heard about, aren't you?" A sly glance. "Dad says you're a class

'A' bitch."

I burst out laughing. "Was he in the diner today?"

"No."

"Then he ain't seen nothing yet." The laugh turned into a cough. Despite her rude stare and comment, there was something about this one I liked. I crumbled the cigarette butt under one foot, fished out a new one. The girl hadn't lit hers yet. She turned it over in small hands.

I blew smoke and held out my right hand. "I'm Jess."

"I'm Kelly."

We shook.

"So, you from here?" I really didn't care if she was or wasn't, but I tried to work on my conversational skills.

Kelly picked at the filter on the cigarette. "No, we're from the east coast. Or I am. My parents are from a small town to the south of here."

I nodded and used the smoke as an excuse not to answer. My heart suddenly beat a little faster. There was something familiar about this girl. Once I'd seen someone, I never forgot their face.

"Did you come here directly from the east coast?" My boots scraped across the dirt, tracing meaningless patterns the way I did when deep in thought. This girl, Kelly, where had I seen her before? The memory danced out of my grasp.

"Nope." Kelly lit the cigarette, but didn't take a drag. It hung from her fingers and looked as lonely and lost as the girl holding it. "First, we travelled to the town my parents grew up in. They thought it would be easier for them away from the big city, but when I... When this became apparent," She pointed at her stomach, "they chickened out. They decided it would be best if I had the baby in a town where no one knew us."

"Right." The ground was filled with deep circles and small

Escaping The Caves

trenches. "How did you travel? I mean, how did you get from A to B to C?"

Kelly raised an eyebrow. "The way anybody travels long-distance, I should imagine. By train. Though I heard you walked into town like one of those coyotes."

Train. The pieces clicked into place. The fucking train. Kelly had been the girl sitting beside the middle aged couple who argued. The second—or tenth, if you wanted to get technical about it—smoldering cigarette butt singed my fingers. I hardly felt it.

Kelly had been there when Ethan outed me as an outcast. Suddenly I was dizzy, but it had nothing to do with all the nicotine flowing through my veins. I could handle smoking too much. I didn't know if I could handle being kicked out of yet another town. I didn't have any plans to retire on this dusty speck, but did intend to stay for as long as it took for my sanity to come to grips with reality again.

Kelly gave me that look of disdain only teenagers are truly capable of. "Are you okay?"

"Yeah." I breathed, exhaled and coughed. "Yeah. I'm fine."

The knowledge that both Kelly and her dad had seen me and none of them seemed to remember me, calmed me somewhat. Maybe the extra layer of dirt and craziness on the train had been enough to mask my looks. I sure as hell hoped so.

"So, is it true?" Now that it was clear I wasn't about to faint, Kelly was back to picking on what was left of the cigarette.

"Is what true?" I leaned against the wall and resisted the urge to light another smoke. Without a cigarette between them, my fingers seemed big and fumbling.

"That you ran away from a violent husband and that's why you're a bit strange in the head?"

Now it was my turn to raise an eyebrow. "You don't beat about the bush much do you?"

"If I did, do you think I'd be in this mess?"

Fair enough. "Yeah, well, I guess." I chewed on a fingernail, studying my shoes. My past life had been violent, I'd run away from a husband, and couldn't deny the bit about being strange in the head. It wasn't an out and out lie. As long as I didn't embellish on the story, I was more or less in the ballpark of truth.

"'Cause you don't look it." Kelly tossed away the cigarette.

Her insistence made me forget I initially liked this girl. I wanted her to go away and leave me to my ghosts. "Look like what?"

"Like someone who'd stay with someone who treated her like their personal punching bag." This came out matter-of-factly, but Kelly's eyes betrayed her. Curiosity, but also a reluctant admiration she didn't know where to place. If I hadn't been so tired, I would've told her she shouldn't waste it on me.

"I didn't. I'm here, right?"

"Right." Kelly was about to ask me something else, but the look on my face convinced her now was not the time. She closed her mouth.

We sat there on the steps and watched the sun rise higher, making our shirts stick to our backs. My fingers itched for the pack of cigarettes. I wrapped my arms around my knees.

"So, aren't you going to ask me?"

"Ask you what?"

"How old I am, who the father is, etcetera? Everyone else does."

"Do I strike you as everyone else?"

"No."

Escaping The Caves

I pulled on the tight waistband of the skirt John forced me to wear. What I would have given to wear my own pair of worn-out jeans. Kelly pulled on her cardigan, her hair, and exhaled through her nose. I rolled my eyes. Some token curiosity was obviously called for.

"But while we're on the subject, and if you don't mind me asking, how old are you?"

Kelly raised her chin. "Fifteen. But I'll be sixteen by the time I have the baby."

Normally I would've left it at that. But something about this girl tugged at the part of me where I kept my hidden stash of empathy. "How do you feel about that?"

I doubted Kelly could've looked more surprised if I'd struck her. It seemed I was the first person to ask her how she felt about anything regarding her own pregnancy. My non-existing opinion of her parents dipped lower.

"How do I feel about that? Shit, I'm fucking fifteen, how do you think I fucking feel?" Kelly turned her head, wiped at her cheeks. "I'm supposed to be going on first dates, flunking algebra and wearing too much tacky make-up. I'm not supposed to be writing out a birth plan." Spittle flew from her lips. She wiped them with the back of her hand.

"A birth plan?"

"Whatever. It's this thing my doctor here, Rosie, is making me do. Where I want to give birth, if I want drugs, which is just stupid, because obviously I want to be stoned out of my skull when it happens. I mean, a human being is coming out of my vagina, for Chrissake."

"Seriously?" I was intrigued despite myself. Not about the bit about humans coming out of vaginas, I'd been there when Jo gave birth. I was pretty much up to speed on how births went.

It was the drugs bit that got my attention.

"You can get drugs when you give birth? Why?"

"You're kidding right? You've never heard about getting painkillers when you give birth? What cave have you been hiding out in?"

I knew this was rhetorically meant, yet the comment about the caves gave me a nasty jolt. "Nowhere you'd ever want to visit. I guess we do it differently where I come from."

"No shit," Kelly snorted. "Thankfully, we do painkillers around these parts. And I intend to be amped up to maximum effect when it all goes down."

She said this with a pride I found hard, if not impossible, to understand. Back around the caves, being able to endure pain was one of the true marks of the warriors. We didn't revel in it or seek it, but when forced to suffer, we did so silently and proudly.

To suffer wasn't a virtue, but painkillers were hard to get hold of. They were only doled out to those who really needed them. They poured me full of it when I nearly got disemboweled, but Jo had been offered none when she gave birth. A general thumb rule was this: Having your guts on display was a good reason for needing sedatives. Having your nether parts torn was not, no matter how much it hurt.

"Well, good for you then, I guess." A coppery taste flooded my mouth. I looked down. I'd bitten my nails down to the flesh.

"Not really, I still have to give birth."

I lit another cigarette, wanting to close the subject. The scar under my shirt itched. "You'll get through it. You're young and strong. And you're built for it. Even if it wouldn't have hurt you to be a little older."

"Do you have kids?"

Escaping The Caves

I scratched the scar, not quite able to keep the irritation out of my voice. "If I did, do you think I'd be here without them?"

"Sorry. Jeesh, dad was right. You are a bitch." Kelly got up from the steps, but to my disappointment she didn't leave. "You just talked as if you'd been through it."

"I was there when my oldest sister gave birth. Her husband didn't make it home in time."

"He got stuck at work?"

I thought of the dark and bloody caves. "Something like that." I didn't mention he hadn't made it home at all that day. My niece never got to see her father. Yet Jo hadn't taken to her bed for a single day. I'd always known she was made of stronger stuff than me.

"Was it horrible?" Kelly hid her true feelings behind a sullen mask, but she wasn't able to hide the fear in her voice.

"Messy, bloody and painful, but not horrible." I looked her straight in the eye. There was no point in sugarcoating it, but I also didn't see the point in making it sound like a horror film. John had shown me one. I didn't speak to him for a week afterwards.

"Awesome," Kelly said weakly.

"You'll be fine." I couldn't help to notice her narrow hips.

"Jess?" John stuck his head out of the back door. "Oh, hi, Kelly." He smiled, but it didn't entirely wipe the look of surprise off his face.

"Hey." Kelly took out a small pink tube and smeared a generous amount of the sticky contents on her lips. "I was just getting to know you're newest employee."

"So I see." John looked from Kelly to me and back again.

"I guess this means my break has come to an end." I got up and dusted off the back of my skirt. It might've been only

135

further proof of my failing sanity, but I could've sworn John's eyes strayed to my backside.

"If you're in the middle of something—"

Kelly cut him off. "Naw, we're okay. But I'll... Maybe I'll see you around?" Kelly couldn't have sounded more bored, but her fingers twisted the fabric of the cardigan.

"Sure, you know where I live and work, so anytime."

"Cool. All right. I'll see you guys later."

"Bye." John waved. He didn't turn to look at me until Kelly was well out of earshot.

"I don't know what I find the most newsworthy, you talking to her or her talking to you."

"What? I can be nice, you know." He stared at me. "Occasionally. When I feel like it. Stop it. Don't look at me like that."

"So I take this as insurance that it's safe to expose you to other humans again?"

"I won't bite and I won't bark."

"Is that a promise?"

"Yes, dear."

John rolled his eyes. "Well, you can write this off as a compliment. And a pretty big one too. Kelly hasn't exactly been a chatterbox since she came here. She was... Oh shit. She was on the train, the day you—"

"It's okay. She doesn't remember me."

"Are you sure?"

"Pretty sure. Her dad has been in the diner and he didn't recognize me either. Thought I was a bitch, though."

"No offence, darling, but you are a bitch."

"You sure know how to compliment a lady."

"That wasn't a compliment. If I wanted to give you a

compliment, I would've said you're the most intriguing woman I've ever met."

John's eyes were suddenly dangerous to look into. I almost got lost. The air was hot and heavy on my skin, but it had nothing to do with the sun.

"Not very original though, is it?" I cleared my throat and straightened my shirt. It gave me an excuse to break eye contact.

John snorted, but his ears were still red. "I'll work on it."

"You do that." I caught his shirt sleeve, mindful not to touch his skin. "But one thing. How much do you know about Kelly and her... situation?"

John let go of the door knob. "Not much. Just hearsay, really. I know her folks moved to the east coast some twenty-five years ago. Her father made it big in one of the cities. He and his wife climbed the social ladder, from what I've heard."

"Okay. But what does that gotta to do with Kelly?"

"From what I know, and please keep in mind it's based on loose rumors and nothing more, Kelly's parents provided her with a pretty extravagant lifestyle, but none of them spent much time with her."

"Which means she was left to her own devices."

"More or less. According to the small town telegraph, she met an older boy from an even richer family. Her parents encouraged the relationship for a while. Maybe they hoped it could further promote their social status."

"Bet they regret that now." I thought of the way they'd argued with hushed voices on the train, both of them ignored the source of the argument, who sat right in front of them.

"Oh yeah. They've been here for three months now, got off the train the same day as Eve and me. Every time they're together, they argue. Never loudly, but enough to make it clear their marriage is hanging on by a thread."

John shook his head. "Man, if it'd been Eve... God forbid." He spit three times over his shoulder.

"I didn't know you were superstitious." I didn't know why, but for some reason this annoyed me.

"If it keeps my daughter from getting knocked up at the age of fifteen, I'll be as superstitious as it takes."

"Probably better just to keep an eye on her when the time comes. I don't think spitting over your shoulder is going to help much."

John squinted. "Thought you said you were safe to expose other people to?"

"I am. I just don't understand how a relatively reasonable man like you can believe in old wives' tales." I pulled out a cigarette. John snatched it and the remaining packet out of my hands.

He rattled the packet in front of my nose. "This one was full when you came down this morning. You've had enough for now. And I don't believe in old wives' tales, but do I believe that there's something more between heaven and earth? Sure. Don't you?"

I tried to steal the packet back. After jumping up and down a couple of times, I gave up. My head hurt too much for this bullshit. "Fine. Have it your way. And just for the record, no, I don't."

John stashed the packet in the back pocket of his trousers. He knew full well I'd never put my hand there.

"Really? I would've thought, given your... history, that you might feel the need to be... Be open, you know, about there being something out there."

"Trust me. Fighting in the caves doesn't exactly strengthen

one's belief in a benign God."

"Maybe not."

"If there's something more you'd like to say, just say it."

John opened the door. "Uhuh. No way am I entering into a theological discussion with you when you're in this kinda of mood."

"I mean, what has God ever done for me?" I burst out, without any idea of where that came from.

John paused in the doorway. "You're still here, aren't you?"

I couldn't argue with that, but wasn't sure if that was by the grace of God or if it simply made me the butt of some cruel, cosmic joke.

Back inside the diner, John had me refill the ketchup bottles during the lull between breakfast and lunch. He didn't trust me around customers just yet.

"If you promise not to insult, yell or otherwise verbally abuse the people who pay my bills... Can you handle yourself alone for an hour or so?" John wiped off a ketchup stain that had slipped from one of the bottles.

Technically the place belonged to his dad. John said he couldn't wait to get back to his life as a journalist and failed author, but he treated the diner as if it was his own. He was meticulous about keeping it clean and neat.

I swept my eyes around the room. Sam read the morning paper and was still on his second cup of coffee. Other than him, there were two other customers, and they seemed equally submerged in their papers and coffee cups. "I can handle myself. Where are you off to? Playing truant?"

John snorted. "If only. I've to go over the books for this month, make sure everything's in order. Boring as hell, but it has to be done. I'll be upstairs if you need me." He squeezed my arm as he walked past. I didn't like how good it felt, the warm sensation that flooded me.

I brooded on my treacherous hormones and nearly jumped off the floor when a woman spoke into my ear. I say spoke, but she was loud enough to make even Sam look up from his table. And he wore hearing aids in both ears.

"I said, *excuse* me."

I swiveled around and came almost nose to nose with a pretty brunette. Her lips were pinched, her eyes hostile. I took a step back. "Sorry?"

The woman rolled her eyes. She attempted a smile. It wasn't a pleasant one. "I asked you if John was around. Is he?"

"Ehm, yeah, he's upstairs, going through the – hey!" I grabbed her arm, pulled her back from the stairs.

"Let go of me!"

I did, but I also made damn sure she didn't run up the stairs without my explicit permission. "I'll get him for you."

The woman gave me a look of such disdain I didn't think even Kelly could match it. "Please. You're embarrassing yourself. You clearly have no idea who I am."

"Clearly."

The woman inhaled through her nose. She tapped high heels on the linoleum. "I'm Marjorie."

"Good for you. I'll tell John that you're here." I went up the stairs before the woman made the mistake of trying to tackle me. A woman that skinny… I could have snapped her like a twig.

"John?" I knocked on the door to his room.

Escaping The Caves

"Yeah? Come in."

I did. John sat at his desk, a huge book and calculator lay in front of him. The sun filtered through the open window. The light played with his hair. I clenched my fist. It couldn't be a good sign that I wanted to brush that hair out of his eyes. I briefly wondered if it felt as thick as it looked.

"There's a wi - woman here to see you."

John frowned. He took off his glasses. "Who?"

"Someone called Marjorie?"

John closed his eyes and pinched the bridge of his nose. "Terrific. Just terrific."

The pieces clicked into place. "Is that her then."

John sighed. "The one and only. I guess I'd better deal with her. To leave her to wait and stew only makes her worse." But he didn't get up.

"I hope I haven't already done that. She wanted to come up here herself, and since I didn't know who she was, I stopped her. She seemed pretty pissed off, but she was pretty pissed off to begin with."

John rubbed a hand over his face. "She's always pissed off. When you said stopped, you didn't punch her, did you?"

"No!"

"Ah. Well, maybe next time." He tried a smile.

"Where's Eve?"

John got up, slowly. He seemed to have aged ten years since I came into the room. "With a friend. They have a play date, I believe it's called."

"Right. Well, that's good. At least she's not here to…" I bit my lip.

"Yeah, thank God for small favors, right?"

I only nodded.

141

John walked past me. "Well, in any case, God hates a coward, so let's get this over with."

Marjorie still stood where I'd left her. Pinched lips and tapping foot all present and accounted for. I wanted to make myself scarce, as in 'not there at all', but with customers still around, I busied myself by cleaning the already-spotless counter.

John pulled his fingers through his hair. The smile looked about as real as the one Marjorie balanced on her face.

"Marjorie, what can I do for you?"

"What you can do for me? I'll tell you what you can do for me. You can start by explaining to me why my daughter failed to show up at my house this morning, and when I asked around I was told she was with a friend."

This time all three customers looked up. John lowered his voice. "Why don't we talk about this upstairs?"

"Why? Am I embarrassing you? Well though luck, because you embarrassed me like hell this morning." Marjorie had turned a very unattractive shade of red.

Everyone present—myself included, I'm ashamed to say—leaned forward to listen. They could probably hear Marjorie over in the next town, but John kept his voice low.

"Eve didn't show up at your house this morning because she'd already agreed to spend the day at Maria's house. I told you this. Yesterday."

"You did no such thing! How dare you stand there and lie to me!"

"When I came to pick up Eve yesterday, I told you. But maybe you were too busy playing the role of the devoted mother in front of your new boyfriend to listen to what I had to say."

Marjorie's facial color deepened further. "Playing the role? I

Escaping The Caves

am a devoted mother, John! And don't make this about my boyfriend. What is this? Is this about jealousy? Is that it?"

John laughed. A genuine, amused laugh. There was nothing spiteful about it, but Marjorie flinched as if struck. "No, Marjorie, I can assure you this is not about jealousy. Who you date is no business of mine, as long as whoever is in the picture isn't a problem for my daughter."

Marjorie pounced on that last comment like a cat on a mouse. "*Excuse* me? Are you insinuating that I would allow someone harmful around my daughter?"

I'd noticed both of them referred to Eve as 'my daughter', never 'our' daughter, but I kept my nose well out of it.

"And what do you mean by 'whoever is in the picture'?" Marjorie made quotation marks in the air.

"Nothing, Marjorie, I meant nothing." This time they could probably hear John as well in the next town.

"No? If you didn't mean anything by it, why did you say it?"

"Oh, give me a break! It's not as if the previous ones lasted for very long, did they? Not even the one I found you in bed with while we were still married lasted more than two months. And you swore up and down the road that he was the one."

"How dare you bring that up where people can hear you?" Marjorie hissed. "Really, John, I thought you were better than this. Is that why you keep Eve away from me, to punish me for falling in love?"

John laughed again, but this time there was nothing amusing about it and a whole lot of spite. "Falling love? Yeah, no, never mind. Let's not go there. But you know damn well I don't keep Eve from you. You had every opportunity to be there for your daughter when we were together, and even after we broke up, but you were never very invested in being there, were you?"

143

Kristin Talgø

A muscle underneath Marjorie's left eye twitched. "How am I supposed to be there for my daughter when you took her away from me?"

"Took her? Oh, Marjorie, piss off. You begged me to take Eve with me. You 'needed time to find yourself without having to be there twenty-four-seven for someone'. Well, guess what? That's what being a parent means. Being there twenty-four-seven for someone, no matter what. And if you weren't ready for that, you really shouldn't have had a baby with me."

Marjorie's face was ashen. "You're right about one thing, at least. I should never have had a baby with you."

John nodded, his fists clenched at his sides. "Glad we can agree on something."

"But I do care about Eve—"

"Care about? You're not supposed to fucking care about her, you're supposed to love your daughter!" John shouted. "The only time you act like a mother is when there are other people around, people you want to give a good impression. But Eve isn't stupid, Marjorie. You might think you can get away with this because she's only four, but she can tell. She knows."

"I won't let you talk to me like this." Tears stood in her eyes, but whether they were for her or her daughter, was hard to tell.

John's jaw worked. In the end he finally swallowed what he wanted to say. "Fine. I'll leave it. For now. But keep in mind that I do care about Eve. I love her more than anyone or anything. My main priority is her well-being. If you keep on treating her like some accessory that goes well with your new image…" He took a step closer. "Let's just say that if I decide to keep Eve from you, you'll know it." Without looking around, he turned and went up the stairs. To his credit, he didn't run, but his hands remained clenched.

Escaping The Caves

Marjorie stood rooted to the spot for another five seconds. Then she turned and left. She did run.

Once both she and John were out of the diner, the rest of us released a collective breath.

Sam got shakily up from his chair.

"Guess I better…" He pointed up the stairs.

I nodded.

"I think that counter's as clean as it's ever gonna get," one of the customers remarked, a middle-aged woman whose name I couldn't remember. I dropped the cloth and bent to pick it up.

"Don't worry about it, sweetie. Wasn't as if any one of us could not hear what they were saying."

The woman patted my hand. I collected her empty cup and plate and saw she'd left a generous tip. Now I felt bad about forgetting her name.

The other two customers hadn't been as free with their money, but my mind was everywhere except on what I did. John had never talked to me about Eve's mother. From the bits and pieces I'd been able to gather from various one-sided conversations with Sam, their relationship had been of the stormy variety.

After having witnessed this argument, I was inclined to believe him. Even if he put salt in his coffee instead of sugar and called me Brenda, John's late mother, at least twice a day.

Sam tottered back down the stairs. "Brenda?" Strike one. "Maybe you should try talking to the boy? He won't listen to me."

"Sure, Sam. I'll do that." I took his elbow gently and helped him into a chair.

He squinted at me through his glasses. "Who are you again?"

"I'm Jess, Sam. I work as a waitress here."

"Right, yes, of course. Why are you telling me this? Silly girl, of course I know who you are." But the confused expression beneath the anger showed he didn't really know.

Without thinking about it, I kissed his cheek. Sam patted my hand. "We're lucky to have you. I hope you know that."

I only smiled. There was suddenly a lump in my throat that was hard to get words past.

I got to the stairs before he spoke again. "Brenda?" Strike two, and it wasn't even ten yet.

"Yes?"

"Go easy on him. He's been better."

"I will."

"Good, that's good…" His eyes drifted through the window. He looked frail and shriveled. I understood why John hadn't left yet.

The door to John's room was ajar, and this time I didn't bother to knock. Instead of sitting by the desk, I found him slumped on his bed. Back against the wall, his hair across his eyes. Nothing unusual there. The bottle of vodka in his right hand, however, stood out.

"I guess asking you how you're doing is kinda pointless right now?"

"You guess right." He sighed. "Never mind me, Jess. I'm just… in a bad mood."

I sat down next to him and he scooted over to make more room for me. "If it makes you feel any better, she didn't exactly brighten up my day either."

John's lips twitched. "Yeah, she has that effect on people."

He took a swig of the bottle. "Want some?"

I shrugged. The liquid burned my throat. "So that was Eve's mother?"

Escaping The Caves

"Yep."

"I didn't know you'd been married."

John grimaced and drank some more. "Yeah, well, it's not something I tend to bring up. Marrying her wasn't the best decision I ever made. Let's just leave it at that."

"But if you hadn't, you wouldn't have had Eve." I accepted the bottle, but didn't raise it to my lips.

John snorted. "Actually, it was the other way around. If there hadn't been Eve, we wouldn't have married. But don't get me wrong, I'd marry Marjorie a thousand times over if it ensured Eve's existence."

"So no matter how you turn it around, you and Marjorie... Something good, something great, came out of it, no matter how things ended between the two of you. You got Eve." I handed back the bottle, resting my hands on my stomach.

John sipped at the bottle, but with less vigor than before. "Yeah, I got Eve. And I wouldn't change her for anything."

"Of course you wouldn't. I don't know much about kids, next to nothing really, but she's amazing, John. Everyone loves her."

A shadow crossed his face and I could've bitten off my tongue. "Except her mother."

"I'm sure she—"

"Are you? Cause I'm not. There should be two people who would've gladly gone through hell and back for her, and I'm one of those two, but Marjorie... Fuck." He buried his face in his hands.

I won't lie to you, tears still made me want to run for the hills, but at least I fought the urge. After a few seconds, I placed an arm around his shoulders. When he didn't shake me off, I leaned my face against his slumped shoulders. He didn't make a

Kristin Talgø

sound, but wet drops dripped onto his trousers.

"I don't know how Marjorie thinks or feels. I don't know her. But I do know Eve's the luckiest kid alive to have a father like you. And if put on the spot, I think ninety-eight percent, if not a hundred percent, of this town would've gone to hell and back for her, if required." I chewed on my lips. "That's what I think. But what I know... is that I would've gone through hell and back for her. Gladly."

John squeezed my hand. Guilty about the electric sensation that sent through me, I changed track. "That probably does nothing to comfort you, coming from a crazy bitch like me, but–"

He tightened his grip on my hand. "It comforts me a great deal."

Unable to help myself, I wiped the wetness off his cheeks. As I drew my hand away, he took hold of it, and pressed it to his face. He kissed the palm.

Sometimes life presents us with an opportunity that's like a door. This door could be a chance for something truly great and we'd be a fool to pass it by. But it could also be a foolish mistake that we'd be wise to walk away from. The problem with these opportunities is that there is only one way to find out for sure. Open the door.

There was no way to predict how things would play out between John and me if we continued down this road, but fate intervened before we'd made a choice.

We existed for a few breathless seconds in that clichéd limbo were time seemed to stand still, eyes locked, hearts stuttering, lips slowly gravitated towards each other, invisible strings drawing them closer.

"John? Jess?"

Escaping The Caves

We flew apart. John knocked over the vodka bottle in the process.

"Shit!" He jumped out of bed, but the front of his trousers sported a large wet patch I couldn't take credit or be blamed for, depending on your point of view.

"I'm sorry to bother you," Sam craned his neck around the edge of the door. As a general rule, Sam never apologized. It was a long standing principle of his that he took great pride in, but both John and I were too flustered to notice.

Sam took a long look at the scene in front of him. His son's trousers, the vodka bottle in my hand and our flushed faces, looking at anything but each other.

He smiled. "I take it you're feeling better? Jess make you feel better?"

John's ears seemed to be two shades of red away from spontaneously combusting. "Dad, you play many roles around here, don't add pervert to your repertoire as well."

"Pervert? Who're you calling pervert? I'm not the one with a large wet patch on his crotch."

"It's vodka," John swiped the bottle from me.

"Sure it is, son, sure it is." Sam winked at me. For the first time since my mental meltdown, I actually wanted to die.

It didn't matter that we hadn't done anything noteworthy. Sam thought we had and there was no way he would let us live this down without relentless teasing and crude winks in front of customers. I'd known fourteen-year-old girls with less talent for gossip than Sam.

"Dad... No, it doesn't matter. You can think whatever you want. We were just talking and drinking, but if you want to... Stop looking at us like that! We're grown-ups; we don't have to explain ourselves to you."

149

"Two things, and then I'll leave you. One, if you're grown-ups, why are the two of you blushing harder than any thirteen-year-old I've ever seen? Two, you don't have to explain anything. I think your trousers do it for you."

I didn't look at John, but I think he was one second away from chucking the bottle at his old man.

"Oh, right." Sam stuck his grizzly, grey head back inside the room. "The reason I came up here was to tell you that the early lunch crowd has started." With one final smile and shake of the head, he shuffled down the hall. He left the door open.

"Right, so…" John cleared his throat.

"Yeah, you should probably change out of those trousers…" I risked a glance up at him. When our eyes met, we burst out in laughter. It might've been a bit high pitched, but at least it dispelled the horrid awkward atmosphere between us.

"You do realize this will be all over town by the time we get down there? Courtesy of my father." John wiped at his eyes. The tears of laughter suited him much better than the previous ones.

"At least it will give them something other than my shady past to talk about." I drew a shaky breath. The laughter still bubbled in my chest.

"Or maybe, if we're really lucky, they can discuss this rather than my less-than-impressive performance with Marjorie earlier." John tossed the bottle into the waste basket, even though it was still more than half-full.

"So, you'd rather have them think you were about to get busy with your waitress, than having a shouting match with your ex-wife?" I straightened my clothes and ignored the small glow inside. Ridiculous of course. And terribly girly.

"Absolutely." John opened a drawer and pulled out a new

Escaping The Caves

pair of boxers and jeans. "If nothing else, this is guaranteed to tickle Marjorie where she doesn't want to be tickled."

"Right. If nothing else." The laughter died without any effort on my part. "I'll let you get dressed."

"But, that being said." John grasped my hand before I left the room. "I wouldn't mind another chance to…" He searched for the right words.

"Get busy with your waitress?" I offered. I'd gone for a jokey tone, but it came out a lot more flirty than intended.

John laughed, but his ears flushed red again. "Something like that. Though I was angling for a more romantic way of phrasing it."

He entwined his fingers with mine, but the sounds coming from the diner downstairs made it clear romance was out of the question.

Hungry customers that were kept waiting were no joking matter. And hardly romantic background noise.

"Why don't we talk about it over a film tonight? When a war isn't about to break out downstairs?"

"Sure, we can do that."

Something told me to get down there before someone broke something, but our eyes and hands remained stubbornly fused together. I'd watched one of Violet Evergreen's films one evening after John had gone to bed, just to see what they were like. We were starting to act like one of those silly love-struck couples those films featured. Though love-struck might be taking it a bit far. But lust-struck? Oh, yes.

"Jess! John!" Sam roared up the stairs.

I winced and John gently pushed me out the door. "Two seconds. And I'll be right there to rescue you from the angry mob."

151

Kristin Talgø

"It's okay. It wouldn't be the first time I've dealt with an angry mob." I closed the door before John could say anything else.

It's my personal belief that we never really grow up, but remain more or less children trapped in the body of aging adults. We might learn to control our impulses and moderate our desires according to the codes dictated by the society we inhabit, but there are certain aspects of the human psyche which can bring out our inner children. And not in a good way. Hunger, I believe, is one of those aspects.

There's no need for me to draw you a picture of what waited for John and me downstairs: impatient, angry, hungry customers who fed each other's indignation. That wasn't one of those rare moments when I sort-of liked my job. John was a natural at calming people down. He brought out reluctant smiles where before there had only been curses and accusations.

I, on the other hand, wanted to punch the people hassling me about their orders. I stuck to my general rule and kept my head down, only occasionally offering a stiff smile to those who looked the least likely to bite my head off. I wasn't intimidated, I just didn't trust my fists.

Stress seemed to bring out the ghosts, and the ghosts brought on stress, and so the circle was complete. Someway, somehow, I got through it. John's intermittent smiles helped.

When the day was finally over, I leaned into the shower. Both John and I had been wrong. The customers had swapped gossip like ketchup bottles back and forth. Neither John's fight with Marjorie nor our supposedly rendezvous upstairs were given any rest. Both of the stories were openly discussed and dissected. You'd think they looked at a murder case, trying to see the crime from all possible angles. I'm pretty sure my shady past featured somewhere in the mix as well.

But the avid gossip of the townspeople wasn't on my mind right then. Not even the real events of my shady past or ghosts were present. I was preoccupied with far more guilty musings. No one could accuse me of being innocent and naïve about the ways of the world, but still, I wasn't entirely sure what John had in mind when he suggested we watch a film and talk things over. Though obviously there wouldn't be much film watching, and the talking would probably end up being kept to the bare minimum.

My stomach flipped over. I steadied my hands on the wall in the shower. The something between John and I had been pretty well-established, but I didn't know exactly what it was. Even on the train, with me covered in desert sand and craziness up to the eyeballs, there had been a spark of something between us.

The question was whether or not it would be a spectacularly bad idea to pursue it. I was still trying to get my sanity up and running again, and John was still getting over his ex-wife. He would probably swear up and down that he was well and truly over her, but I wouldn't kid myself.

His lingering feelings for her made it easy for Marjorie to pick a fight with him. Her lack of maternal instincts toward Eve didn't just cut him as a father. It cut him as a man as well. More precisely, as Marjorie's former husband. She had no problem walking away, or allowing them to walk away from their life as a family. John was still dealing with the pain of that.

Or so I thought. But then again, I could barely discern between my own feelings. Maybe I shouldn't try to take on

John's as well. And even if John was still hurt by Marjorie's rejection of him and Eve, he did feel something toward me.

Or so I thought in any case. I turned off the shower, grabbed a towel and buried my face in it. Who was I kidding? I didn't know how I felt, let alone how he felt. My heart was still a raw, open wound, grappling with so many perceived losses and betrayals that it was hard to keep count. Kyle certainly featured somewhere in there.

But I did want John. I enjoyed his company out of bed and it'd become more and more apparent that I wouldn't be averse to enjoying his company in bed as well. The sensible thing would, of course, be to take things slow. We'd start out with making up for the kiss we got cheated out of this morning. And then we'd take it from there.

Sadly, in the matters between lust-struck couples, there is rarely room for sensible.

⁂

"I don't know, maybe I overdid it?" John eyed me uncertainly. "I thought we could make a date out of it."

Since my tongue was still glued to the roof of my mouth, I only nodded. He'd pushed the table away from the sofa, and placed a carpet on the floor. Red wine, two glasses and at least a dozen lit candles decorated the scene. It looked soft and cozy. And very romantic.

I swallowed.

"You think it's cheesy, don't you?" John moved to blow out the candles.

"No!" I croaked. "Leave them. Please. I… I think it's kinda perfect actually."

"You do?" A small smile. Hopeful.

"Yeah. I don't think I've ever actually been on a proper date before. Not if this is what dates are supposed to be like." I sat down on the carpet. That small glow inside of me was back. He'd done this for me.

John sat down next to me. "I'm not sure this is customary for first dates or not, but surely you've been on a date." He frowned. "Come to think about it, you've never mentioned anyone before."

He knew how private I was about my previous life. He would never have come straight out and asked me, but I could tell he was curious. I accepted a glass of wine and swirled the liquid around. "No, I haven't, have I?"

"Apart from that talk we had the day you arrived, you haven't mentioned any part of your life before coming here." He took a sip of his own glass. "But if you'd like we can change the subject. We don't have to talk about it if you're uncomfortable."

And he meant it. Maybe that was why my tongue moved more easily than usual. "What do you want to know?"

John raised his eyebrows. "I don't know. Have you… are you married?"

He offered me a way out and I was the one who'd plunged ahead, but the question still pierced my heart.

"Yes. No. I mean, I was married. Sort of. I suppose."

I took a big sip of the wine.

John smiled. "You were sort of married. Isn't that usually the kind of thing you would know about?"

"Usually, maybe, but most things don't go by usual around the caves."

"All right…" John peered at me above the rim of his glass.

"We... we'd been together for some time, not very long really, but he gave me a ring and... after that we considered ourselves to be husband and wife. And so did everybody else." I shrugged. It sounded lame. Not at all descriptive of how much that ring had meant to me.

"That's it?" John couldn't hide the incredulity in his voice. "Didn't he ever ask you if you wanted to be his wife?"

"Not in so many words... He was, is, a man of few words." I contemplated the red liquid.

"That's a... Forgive me, but from where I'm standing, that seems a bit presumptuous."

I looked up. "If I didn't want to be his wife I would've told him so. But as I did, I wasn't about to argue with him about his approach to marriage."

John held up his hands. "I'm sorry. You're right. I don't know anything about him or you. It's not my place to judge."

"No. It's not."

The candles flickered around us.

"You loved him."

"Yes, I did."

"And still do."

I met his gaze head on. "You still love Marjorie."

John's lips twisted. "I guess discussing our ex-spouses was a bad conversation starter on our first date."

"Probably not the best one, no." I smiled.

"Okay. What's your family like then? Or is that a bad conversational topic as well?"

"What makes you think that?"

"Because at the word 'family', your face twisted as if you'd bitten on a lemon."

I laughed, but it didn't dispel the ghosts. "It's not a bad topic,

Escaping The Caves

it's just... Everyone and everything in my past life are interconnected. If I talk about one thing we'll bump into other things I'd rather leave buried."

John put down his glass. It clinked against the half-full bottle of wine. "But they're not buried, are they? That's what bothers you. You want them to be, but they're a lot closer to the surface than you want."

Goosebumps broke out on my body. He had no idea how close to the surface. They were around us now, even as we spoke.

"I guess we better leave them be then." I drained my glass, wanting to pour myself another, but my hands shook too much. A few drops spilled on the carpet. In the dim light, the wine resembled blood.

John straightened my glass. He clasped my hand. I tried to pull away, but he held on, gently, but firmly. "I know it's none of my business, but these... memories, the people you love and the people you've lost... They're always going to be there, hurting you if you keep pushing them away. I will never try and force you to talk about any of it, but I really do think you should talk to someone about it."

"Someone?" His warm hand comforted me, but didn't diminish the icy fist in my stomach. How could I talk about things that made me want to run screaming in the other direction?

"Well, you could talk to Rosie, the doctor here, if you wanted to. She's not a psychiatrist, but she's a very bright, perceptive and, not to mention, kind woman."

"You're forgetting one thing though."

"What?"

"You're the only one who knows I'm an outcast."

With that I threw myself at him. I know people say they threw themselves at their lover and it's all for dramatic effect and artistic embellishment, but I really did. Our lips crashed together so hard our teeth drew blood.

"Whoa," John pulled back, but didn't let go of me. "What was that about?"

"It was the only thing I could think of to make you shut up."

"Consider the message received." He wiped a drop of blood off my lips with his thumb. It lingered at the corner of my mouth. "Would you like to try again?"

I did.

Like I mentioned earlier, sensible is, more often than not, squeezed off the premises the moment lust enters the room. The second kiss, a bit less forceful and a lot more enjoyable, turned into a third, turned into a fourth, and… well, you get the picture.

John was a very different man than Kyle in many ways, something he kept proving over and over again. What struck me first was that he was in no hurry. He took his own sweet time and I was happy to let him. I was, after all, the lucky recipient of his affectionate ways.

Love wasn't part of the equation yet, but there was more than lust between us that first time. Maybe it was due to a mutual respect for each other, maybe it was that we truly enjoyed each other's company with our clothes on as well. Or maybe there was a small grain of love, even then.

Whatever the case, that night earned a special place in my heart. I won't diminish it by trying to describe what happened.

Escaping The Caves

Some things are beyond words. And if that's not true, then it would take a storyteller far more skilled than I to do that night credit.

Even though my mind was addled like Sam's, I hoped I could hold on to the memory of that night. There were other nights, days and stolen moments, and though they were special in their own way, none of them could ever compare to that first time.

It wasn't just the scent of his skin and the feel of it close to mine. Nor was it the taste of him and the intense warmth spreading between us. Maybe the candles added an extra touch, the thought behind them certainly did. Mostly, I think what did it was the look in John's eyes.

He saw me. Really saw me. He'd seen me at my worst and he still wanted me. Despite knowing what he did about me, though you might say that wasn't a whole lot, he thought I was someone worth caring about. What we did wasn't just about him. It was just as much about me. About us.

He genuinely cared about me and enjoyed my company. There's no faking love. Maybe that's why I was able to go wherever our bodies took us. I wasn't able to open up verbally yet, but I was able to give him a part of me I'd never really given to anyone. Not completely.

There were no restrained feelings or self-consciousness, no awkwardness. If I didn't know for a fact that this was the first time between us, I would've thought we'd done this a hundred times before. It came naturally, easy, with an edge of fervor heightening the sensations.

Afterward, I rested in his arms, my muscles pleasantly tired, sweat cooling on our skin. Just before I fell asleep, I had one clear moment when I realized the ghosts had disappeared for the first time. I was about to tell John there was no need for talking when there were acts like this, but then I knew no more.

"Jess?" Light, butterfly kisses across my back and shoulders. I arched my back, leaning into his embrace.

"Jess, it's five in the morning. We should probably move before we're caught naked on the living room floor."

More kisses, my neck, my throat. Hands caressed my stomach. Heat flared up there, and trailed downwards. So did his hands.

"Well, that would certainly give the townspeople something new to talk about." I twisted my arm. My hand searched for a part of him.

"Yes, it certainly would," John gasped as I found what I'd been looking for.

I turned around in his arms, smiling. "Five o'clock you say?"

"Mhm…" John pressed closer.

"Then we have time for an encore, don't we?"

I bit down on his lip.

He kissed me. Properly and thoroughly. My muscles weren't tired anymore. In fact, I couldn't feel them at all.

"Yeah, I say we have the time." He flipped me onto my back. There was no more talking.

"Okay, now we really have to get up, as much as I hate to say it." John nuzzled my hair.

I tightened my grip on him and looked at the treacherous

clock on the windowsill. Six fifteen. Yeah, we really had to get going. Both Eve and Sam would wake up soon. Forty-five minutes from now, customers would start to appear. John should've gotten started on the diner right around when he woke me up the first time. I considered his time better spent here with me.

I raised myself up on one elbow. The blanket fell down around my waist. John reached out and I slapped him away. "If you start that, we're never getting up from this floor."

He smiled. "Maybe that wouldn't be such a bad thing. I've never truly appreciated this floor before, but I do now. That might have something to do with the company." He reached out again and this time I let him.

"I'd really like you to take that exploration further, but the idea of your dad walking in on us, for real this time, puts a bit of a damper on things."

John groaned, but released my nipple. It almost hurt to be this close and not touch him.

"But," He leaned in for a kiss, "I will take a rain-check. If it pleases you."

"Oh, don't you worry about that. It pleases me." I inhaled him, memorizing the feel of his lips on mine. "It pleases me a great deal."

Chapter 11

Our daily film nights were postponed, and even my reading took a backseat. For the first time in my life, I preferred to spend my evenings curled up with a person instead of a book. Reality was suddenly better than an imaginary one. It both exhilarated and frightened me.

The ghosts were still present, but John's presence seemed to calm them for the time being. I knew it wouldn't last. The rest of my life wouldn't be spent wrapped up in his arms. This wasn't for keeps.

During weak moments, I thought, why not? Just why the hell not? But every night, just before I fell asleep, there was a tiny sensation of vertigo in my stomach.

I had the same feeling the day Jen died.

The memory of that dark feeling eluded me the moment I woke up. I slept deeply and soundly. No more tossing and turning. John stopped pestering me about the importance of talking about my past life. Nonetheless, he watched me. He always kept an eye on me in the same way he always kept an eye on Eve when she was around, making sure she didn't suddenly do something to hurt herself.

If people knew we were more than just co-workers and friends, they kept it to themselves. Sam gave us the occasional wink and nudge, but on bad days he was just as likely to fry his shoes for supper instead of hamburgers. The way I saw it, the man had to take his pleasures and amusements where he could find them.

I didn't see Kelly until three weeks after the day she'd asked me for a cigarette, about two weeks after John and I started our nightly exercise regime. I preferred to think of it that way. It sounded less likely as a recipe for heartache.

"Long time, no see," John said. I looked up from the coffee pot.

He stood next to a table where a middle aged man and a teenage girl had just sat down.

"Yeah, we've been… busy." The man shook John's hand, but his smile was strained.

"Busy, yeah, keeping your only daughter locked up at the house tends to keep you busy," Kelly snorted. She had sarcasm down to an art. The ice cubes rattled inside the glass as she took a sip of water.

Her father's strained smile disappeared altogether. "Kelly, do not start with me. You wanted to come here, we're here. Now, drop it."

"It's okay, Peter–" John started, but Peter waved him away.

"No, it's not, but we are where we are. Just leave us with the menus. We'll need a few minutes to decide." Peter buried his nose in the menu. He'd been here almost every day. I thought he knew pretty well what this diner had to offer.

Escaping The Caves

But John only smiled. "Of course."

Kelly looked around until she caught sight of me. I raised a hand. She returned the wave.

Her father looked up. His eyes narrowed. "Why don't you let them do their job and focus on figuring out what you want to eat?"

Kelly slammed the laminated menu down on the table top. "I know what I'm having. I'm having what I always have, just like you will." She pushed away from the table.

"Hey, where do you think you're going?" Peter called after her.

Kelly didn't slow down. "I need to pee. I'm knocked up. Remember? And in case you didn't already know, pregnant women have to pee a lot."

Her father's hollow cheeks turned purple. He sat down, hard, once again burying his nose in the menu.

"I need to talk to you." Kelly's voice was barely audible above the chatter in the diner as she passed me.

I waited a few moments, then followed after her. She sat on the steps by the backdoor when I came out. The sun played with her auburn hair, turning it copper. Her small, upturned nose was wrinkled against the harsh light, her green eyes squeezed half-shut. There were dark patches under her them.

"So, how've you been doing?" I resisted the urge to light a cigarette. John alternated between begging me to stop and trying to scare me out of the habit. He told me about all the calamities that would happen if I continued with my 'slow suicide', none of which worked. Even so, I thought I should at least try to be a good role model.

Kelly rubbed her cheek. Her white, unblemished skin was dotted with tiny freckles. She looked like the very personification of innocence. "How I been doing? Now, let's see…" She ticked off on her fingers. "One. My lunatic parents seem to be under the illusion that if people don't see me so often they'll stop talking. Two. My lunatic parents are delusional enough to think that they can convince me to give up my child for adoption. Three. My lunatic parents are, generally speaking, making my life a living hell."

"Right, ehm, I'm sorry." I chewed on my already-abused fingernails. That cigarette would've been really good right about now. What was I supposed to say to this?

"Sorry?" Kelly turned to me. "That's all you got for me?"

"Ok-ay… Let's take one thing at a time then." Kelly still looked like a cat ready to lash out with her claws at any moment. I pressed on. "They can't really think people will forget about you if they don't see you?"

Kelly stuck out her bottom lip. "Maybe not, but they sure find it easier. They don't have to answer so many questions that way."

"What kind of questions?"

Kelly gave a look that made me feel even more stupid and out of my depth than I already did. "Like, who's the father? Why did we leave the city? Are we going to stay here? Am I going to stay here?"

"Does the father know?" I didn't know if this was putting my nose where it didn't belong, but Kelly wanted to talk, that much I sensed. The fact I was more or less a stranger probably made it easier. Plus, apart from John, Eve and Sam, I didn't have any friends in this town. Who would I tell?

Kelly rested her hands on her protruding stomach. "You've seen him, actually."

Hackles rose up on my neck, but I didn't have a clue what

Escaping The Caves

she was talking about. "What? Is he here?"

"Of course he isn't. But he was on the train."

The sun was too hot and the air stifling. I opened the top buttons on my shirt. "What do you mean?" But I thought I knew all too well who she meant.

Kelly met my eyes, her green ones so young and clueless. "The man who revealed your identity. Ethan. He's the father."

The world completed a three-hundred-and-sixty degree turn. I was sitting down, but still had to hold on to keep from toppling over. "Ethan…" I breathed. Thank God I wasn't much of a breakfast person, otherwise I'd have been looking at it.

"Jess?" Kelly put a hand on my arm. "Are you all right?"

"Yeah, I'm… just confused. I don't understand. Why didn't your parents recognize him? What was he doing there in any case?"

"Following me, I suspect. As for my parents, please. They wouldn't recognize the President if he suddenly came strolling up next to them. Dad didn't recognize you from the train either."

I'd been so floored by Ethan being the father of Kelly's baby, I missed the main point. Kelly knew. About me. Who I really was.

"What? Seriously, you didn't really think I didn't know it was you, did you?" Kelly's green eyes glinted in the sun. There was quite a bit about her that reminded me of a cat. She was sneaky, for starters.

I closed my mouth. "You know I'm an outcast. You've known this whole time."

Kelly shrugged. "I don't care. I mean, I'm dying to know what it was like back there. What's it like fighting in the caves and all that, but I don't think you're like, a stain on society or

167

whatever people say about outcasts."

"Right, okay. But you haven't told anyone?"

Kelly rolled her eyes. "Give me some credit. If I wanted to tell someone, I would've done it right away."

"So why did you pretend you didn't know who I was?"

"I didn't want to scare you."

Smart girl. I shaded my eyes against the sun and looked at the end of the mountain range in the distance. A lone bird circled the tall spruce trees at the bottom of it.

"Kelly, do you want us to be friends?" I looked at her for confirmation and she nodded. "I need you to tell me everything about Ethan. About how you and he met. About your life in the city. I need you to be honest with me."

Kelly frowned. "Why? Why's it so important to you?"

I turned to the mountains again. They looked peaceful, serene almost if you could say that about mountains. The morning haze floated around them. It grazed the waterfall flowing down the sides.

"I just need you to. And I'll tell you about my life around the caves. I think we both could do with a friend right now."

"All right. Will you be as honest with me?"

I thought about all the blood, guts and heartache. "I'll tell you as much as I'm able to."

Kelly smiled. "Fair enough." She held out her hand. "Friends?"

I took it. So small yet so strong. "Friends."

"So where do you want to start?"

I looked back into the diner. If John needed help, he knew where to find me. "Your dad's gonna think you've fallen into the toilet or done a runner."

Kelly laughed. "I'm guessing he's enjoying the respite from

Escaping The Caves

me. He'll come looking when he wants to."

"If you say so." I lit a cigarette, careful about blowing the smoke away from Kelly. What the hell. I'd wanted to set a good example, but we were supposed to be honest with each other. Be honest about who we really were.

"Why don't you start with Ethan." Just saying his name brought chills out on my arms and the nape of my neck.

"Sure." Kelly studied her shoes for a moment as if conjuring up his face. I shivered.

"Okay. I'm sure John has already told you a bit about my parents. About how they made it big in the city, climbing the social ladder and all that?"

"Some of it, yeah," I coincided.

"Okay, so to cut a long story short, my folks weren't stinking rich, but they didn't exactly lack in means and funds. And they were continually brown-nosing other richer couples, trying to climb another few rings up that ladder."

I thought of her father. Thin, hollow cheeks and a five o'clock shadow. I hadn't spent much time around rich folks, but he didn't look the way I would've imagined him.

"One of those couples had a son. Ethan. His father is one of the riches and, not to mention, most powerful men in the city. You've never seen anything like him. You can practically smell the power coming off him like special cologne."

I thought of my own father and lit another cigarette.

"Ethan loathed him. I don't know why, exactly. Maybe he sensed it was really the other way around and he just wanted to get one over his old man."

"Ethan's father didn't like him."

Kelly nodded. "No, but it wasn't anything you could put your finger on, exactly. George, Ethan's dad, was never openly dismissive of his son. But he was never openly warm and friendly toward him either. He treated him pretty much the way he treated everyone else. Coolly polite."

"Like a stranger, in other words. So what makes you think George didn't care for Ethan? Maybe he just wasn't a very warm and friendly person." Again, I thought of my own father. I tapped some ash on the ground.

Kelly gave me a look. "You never met him. I did. George… His dislike for Ethan… It was like cigar fumes coming off him or something. It leaked from his pores, slowly contaminating his son."

I bent to tie my shoelaces that didn't need re-tying. "What do you mean 'contaminated'?"

For the first time since Kelly had walked into the diner this morning, she avoided my eyes. "Ethan… I don't know. There was something about him. At first, I thought he was the best or - at least the most exciting - thing that had ever happened to me. He was the son of the most powerful and richest man in the city. He was older, and in the right light and clothes he could be handsome."

"So far, so good." I didn't try to catch Kelly's eye either. I imagined Ethan's face when he pressed my gun into my neck, fumbled with my clothes.

A smile tugged at her lips. "Yeah… But he could be moody. Irrational. He can't take a joke, but he loves to make jokes at other people's expense. At parties, he would always have one drink too many. He'd become downright rude after a while. No one ever hit him, though. Everyone detested him. But they knew who his father was."

I stepped on my cigarette butt. "This might be a stupid question, but—"

Escaping The Caves

"Why did I bother with him?"

"Yeah. No offence, but he doesn't sound very appealing to me." In my mind, I heard Ethan's voice tell me about how he'd stabbed and gutted Jackson.

Kelly pulled at her tight and revealing t-shirt. "Honestly? I was flattered. I mean, he made it very clear that he wasn't much of a people person, but even so, he singled me out. He chose me, and I guess... I liked it. I felt special, or some stupid bullshit. I also got disturbingly good at coming up with half-assed excuses for his crappy behavior."

She swiped at her bangs. "I sound really pathetic, don't I? I have to be, right? Why else would I waste my time with a total asshole?"

Ethan's face was replaced with Kyle's. "You're not pathetic. He must've had some qualities that made you stick around?"

"He did, actually. Ethan could be really sweet sometimes. He told me things about his childhood I don't think he'd told anyone. And he knew things about his father... Well, let's just say George wouldn't sleep so easy at night if he knew what his son knew about him."

I thought there was a lot about Ethan that would've kept George awake for a long time if he'd known.

"Anyway, he could be funny. He's very smart, almost scarily so. And he didn't have many friends. None, actually, that I knew about. He confided in me and I liked feeling important. So when things started happening, I kinda closed my eyes and pretended not to see anything wrong with him."

I watched the trees sway in the breeze. Their creaking soothed me. I took what comfort I could. There was nothing comforting about where this story was headed. That something 'not quite right' about Ethan... I knew all too well what that had been.

The question was, how much did Kelly know? And if she didn't know everything, should I tell her?

I glanced at her expanding stomach, knowing there was a small piece of Ethan growing in there.

"What kind of things?" I asked.

"There was a woman, I think, a secretary working for George, she was found raped and murdered in the office building where George worked. She was found in his office, actually. Obviously, the police worked pretty hard at getting a confession out of him, but George had a whole army of lawyers dealing with them. The police couldn't touch him. Didn't help his case though, when they discovered the surveillance tapes from that night were missing.

"Like I said, the police couldn't do anything. But they leaned pretty heavy on him. It even went so far that George admitted he'd been having an affair with his secretary. I think his angle was that if he'd already been sleeping with the woman, why would he have raped and murdered her? In his office no less." Kelly sounded like she shared his view on the matter.

"Why indeed... But those missing tapes... They could've exonerated him. Why would he hide them?" I knew why, but did Kelly?

Kelly opened her mouth. And closed it again. Sweat had broken out on her brow, but it was far from that hot in the morning sun. "I'm not feeling very well... Maybe we should continue this conversation another day."

She moved to get up, but I grabbed hold of her hand. Her eyes widened. I relaxed my grip. "Kelly, I need to know."

"Why?" She pulled on her hand and I let go.

Why? I didn't know why. Maybe I was still looking for

closure about Ethan, about killing him. Or maybe I wanted to know because Kelly was pregnant with his child and she wanted to be my friend. Or maybe something else, something that was still hidden from me in the dark.

I settled for the friendship version. Kelly eyed me for a moment. She sat back down again. "I don't think that's the real reason, but I'll let it go for now."

She fidgeted with her hands before resuming her story. Her words came slower now, as if she had to drag them out. "I think that George hid those tapes because they revealed who Amanda's killer was. Amanda, that was the secretary. I didn't know her, but I read about her in the papers. Anyway, George destroyed the evidence so the police would have no sure way of proving who did it."

"It must've been someone he cared about, if he was willing to go to such lengths to protect him." I didn't dare light another cigarette, afraid to break Kelly's concentration.

Kelly snorted. "The only one George Sampson cares about is George Sampson. He hid those tapes because it would reflect badly on him and his companies if the killer's identity became public knowledge. He didn't want his corporate fingers stained by the association."

"But weren't his fingers pretty stained by the incident in any case? I mean, a woman was raped and murdered in his office, for God's sake!" I'd been trying to keep my anger in check, but it scorched a hole through my chest.

"Jess, take it easy."

"Easy? The man covered up a murder, Kelly. Didn't George ever think about Amanda's family? That they would want, would need, justice for their daughter?"

"I don't think he cared much, one way or another. They were

heavily compensated. Financially."

"Right, because enough money makes everything all right, doesn't it?"

"No, it doesn't, but calm down. Jess, I'm not George, so stop yelling at me."

My fingernails cut into my palms. "I'm sorry. But don't you see? By letting the killer go, he was free to do it again. To someone else."

Kelly had gone white around the mouth. "Don't you think I know that? But I didn't have any proof, and with George Sampson covering it up, there wasn't much I could do about it."

"I know that, Kelly. I'm sorry, I just—"

"Jess, what are you not telling me? And don't fob me off this time. I swear, I'll walk away and you won't ever hear the end of this story." She looked long and hard at my face. "Or maybe you know how it ends. What you're missing are the pieces in between."

I weighed my options. "You're a very perceptive girl, do you know that? When you want to be."

Kelly laughed, but it was hard and brittle. "You mean when I'm not sleeping with a sadistic killer?"

"You think Ethan killed Amanda?"

"Jess, stop bullshitting me. I know he did. I might not have admitted it to myself when I ran the risk of running into him, but I knew. The moment I heard what had happened, I knew. And I know that you know. I don't know how you know about this, but somehow you do."

"Did Ethan ever hurt you? Or try to?"

"If you answer another one of my questions with a question, the same thing applies. I'll walk away." She breathed deeply. "But no, he didn't. Like I said, moody, evasive and irrational.

But he was never cruel. Not to me. And after Amanda was killed, I didn't see him again until that day on the train."

"But you said you knew he'd been following you?"

Kelly's small mouth twisted. "I found out I was pregnant three days after they found Amanda. It was my idea to get out of the city. Just like his father, Ethan could be discreet. He never approached me, but he kept tabs on me."

"And your parents never realized this?" I shook my head.

"You saw them on the train. They saw you. Yet none of them have blown the whistle on you, have they? And my mother is an excellent whistleblower. You haven't met her, but she's seen you around town. Put it this way: my parents only see what they think will benefit them. When I started seeing Ethan, they only saw a potential gigantic leap up that golden ladder, not a potential danger to their only daughter."

"In other words, they didn't see Ethan following you or recognize him when he confronted me on the train, because they simply didn't want to." I found this hard to believe, but I didn't have any other explanation.

"They have selective blindness. Mind over body, and all that. It's amazing, or disturbing, depending on your point of view, what the mind can convince you of, if it puts enough energy into it." Kelly looked across the valley in front of us, across the river where the mountains rose up.

I tried to force the images of both my father and Kyle out of my mind. "I suppose. And they never connected the dots between Amanda and Ethan?"

"I think the news of my pregnancy drowned out anything else. The second Falling could've been imminent, and they would still have fretted about which town they should exile us to."

I really hoped we could find a better way to deal with all of this. Bitterness didn't suit Kelly's young face.

"But enough about my parents. When I told you the name of the father of my child, when I told you it was Ethan, the man who got you thrown off the train, I thought you were gonna faint right in front of me. I've never seen anyone actually turn as white as a sheet. But you did."

There were no avoiding Kelly's green eyes this time. They wouldn't let me go.

"You know something about him. Did you meet later? Ethan got off at the next stop. Did you meet him then? You walked through the entire desert. To walk into the nearest town wouldn't have been much of a challenge for you. Look at me! I don't know what's going on, but I know you're gonna tell me. Sharing goes both ways, Jess. So start sharing."

Facing a rightly-pissed off fifteen-year-old is daunting enough, but a pregnant one adds another dimension to it. Especially when you killed the father of her unborn child. Even if he was a pathological murderer.

When pressed into a corner, unsure of which lie to take, the truth can sometimes be a welcome option. "Ethan knew I'd reach the next town by sundown. He also suspected, quite rightly, that I'd find somewhere on the outskirts of town to spend the night. He waited until I was asleep before he woke me up."

Kelly twirled her fingers, but she'd gone very pale.

"When I did wake up, he had me at gunpoint. That was embarrassing. I'm a soldier. I shouldn't have been caught off guard like that."

"You were sleeping. I don't think you can blame yourself for that."

Escaping The Caves

"Even so, I shouldn't have been caught off guard. Under normal circumstances, it never would've happened, but as you know, those weren't normal circumstances. My mind wasn't—still isn't really—exactly as it should be." Jen, Jackson, Trenton, Kyle, my father all blended together. I shook my head.

"Ethan told me he'd followed me. And he had more or less the same plans for me as he'd had for every other outcast he met."

"He'd met others like you before?" Kelly's lips barely moved.

"He… He mentioned the… the incident with his father's secretary. Seems he didn't enjoy the publicity any more than his father. So he tracked down outcasts, since there's an open season on us."

"If he didn't like the publicity, he shouldn't have raped and murdered her in his father's office." Kelly's voice was a high-pitched, jagged sound.

"Kelly, are you sure you want me to go on?" I put a hand on her arm. To touch people didn't come naturally to me, but she looked so pale and frail. Almost transparent. Breakable, like glass.

"No, but I need you to. The truth can't be worse than what I'm already imagining."

I wouldn't have bet on that, but I continued. "All right. To cut a long, unpleasant story short, Ethan tried to do to me what he did to Amanda. Obviously, he didn't succeed."

A heavy silence drifted down on us. The air felt thick and stifling, but in reality it was clear and windy for once. A lone crow circled overhead, calling for its mate.

"You killed him."

"Yes."

"Did you have to?"

"Depends on how you look at it."

"How do you look at it, then?"

"If you're asking me if I had to kill him, in the sense that he would've killed me that night if I hadn't, then no. I didn't have to. I could've incapacitated him and then escaped. But if I'd done that, he would've come after me. And even if he didn't bother with me, he would've killed someone else. Raped them too, if it'd been a girl. I couldn't let that happen."

"That's not all of it."

"No. He'd... He killed someone I cared about. Very much cared about."

Kelly exhaled slowly. She nodded. "Thank you for telling me." Her lack of emotion both frightened and impressed me. My father would've been proud. She would've made a good warrior. She *was* a good warrior, in her own way.

"Of course." I glanced at my wrist watch. It felt like we'd been out here for hours. Instead, only twenty minutes had passed. Still, I should've been back in the diner fifteen minutes ago.

Kelly caught the motion. "John will be looking for you."

"Yeah, but—"

"I'll be fine, Jess. Really."

"Are you sure about that? That was... It must have been... It can't be easy knowing all of this about Ethan." I stumbled over the words. What would I have thought and felt if I'd been in her shoes?

"No. It's not. I knew Ethan was a disturbed boy, but I sure as hell didn't suspect him of being this disturbed. Shit." She buried her face in her hands, but when she looked up again, her cheeks were dry. Yes. My father would've been very proud indeed.

Escaping The Caves

"Why do you think he did it?"

"Honestly? I haven't got a clue, Kelly. Maybe he got off on it, somehow. Or maybe hurting others lessened the hurt inside of him." I swallowed and wanted something to wash away the bad taste in my mouth.

Kelly rubbed her stomach, slow circles. "Do you think Amanda was his first?"

I thought about it. "Yes. I think she was a way of getting back at his father for some insult, real or imagined."

"Try eighteen years of cold detachment," Kelly said.

"Whatever the case, Ethan wanted to destroy his father. And Amanda became the unfortunate pawn in his twisted game." I couldn't help adding, "A lot people grow up with emotionally-absent parents. Doesn't mean they run around killing people."

Kelly looked at me. "Who was he?"

I itched for my cigarettes. "Who?"

"The man Ethan killed. The other outcast."

"A friend." I got up. "I hate to leave you after all of this, but John needs me in the diner."

Kelly didn't get up. I stood there for a moment, and then sat down. "Are there many others like you out there?" she asked, as if I'd never tried to leave.

I shrugged. "Your guess is as good as mine. I didn't even know Jackson was an outcast until Ethan told me. I was told he died of pneumonia. Apparently, my father has made a habit of covering up desertions whenever possible."

"Why?" Kelly frowned.

"Wouldn't be good for morale."

"Is that why they put so much energy into hating outcasts? To keep you in line?"

"I guess that sums it up. Kelly, I don't want to be rude or

insensitive–"

"But you've got to get back inside. Yeah, I know." She rubbed her eyes, reminding me of a tired kid at the end of a long day.

I knew I would regret this when alone with John later, but I asked nonetheless. "Do you want to come over this evening? Watch a film or something?"

Kelly brightened. "Yeah, sure. That'd be great. I really don't want to spend any more time than I have to around my parents, and now… knowing what I do about Ethan… Yeah, I'd like to come over."

"Okay. Cool. I'll let John know." I got up, and this time Kelly followed.

"Is he okay with that, do you think? Me coming over? I'm not interrupting some alone time or something, am I?" Kelly's eyes had regained some of their usual impishness, but not nearly enough to placate my concern for her.

I pretended to slap the back of her head. "No, nosey, you're not. And keep those insinuations to yourself."

"Someone's got their panties in a twist." Kelly winked at me. She ducked under my arm and went back to her father.

Peter looked up. Only two seconds ago, his face had been smooth and serene. But when he saw Kelly, his face shriveled like a grape left out in the sun.

"And where have you been, young lady? That was a very long trip to the restroom, if you don't mind me saying."

"Actually, I do." Cheerfully, Kelly bit into her toast, which had to be cold and chewy by now.

Peter folded his newspaper. It shook slightly. "Then where were you, exactly?"

"I was just outside, talking to Jess."

Escaping The Caves

Peter's eyes pinned me down. I hid behind John on the pretense of getting more coffee. "I see. Have you been talking a lot to Jess lately?" The way he said my name made it sound like a profanity.

"No." Kelly brushed crumbs off her t-shirt.

"Oh." Peter's high color subsided.

"But she invited me to come over to watch a film this evening. I'm really looking forward to it. It'll be good for you and Mom too. You'll have the house to yourself."

Peter's high color returned. "Are you out of your mind? You don't know this woman!"

John took the coffeepot from me and poured Peter another cup. "But you know me. Think about it, Peter. It might be good for Kelly to do something else. And you and Jane can focus on the two of you, for a change. It's a win-win. I'll make sure she gets home safe."

It wasn't so much what John said, as the way he said it. He used the same voice when he tried to talk to me about my past. While it didn't elicit any stories from me, Peter's face resumed its normal skin tone.

"Fine. But I want her home by ten. Sharp."

"Perfect." John sent a smile my way when Peter bent to examine the bill. I turned around, hiding my face. If Kelly had to be home by ten, John and I would have plenty of time to... exercise.

"Keep the change." Peter got up from the table. He looked at his daughter. "Are you coming, or do you intend to stay here until closing time?" The tilt at the end of the question sounded half-hopeful.

Kelly saw straight through her father. Her eyes twinkled. "Naw." She stretched and yawned. "I'm coming back with you.

181

I feel like a nap. Pregnant women need their rest, you know."

Peter's face changed color at an impressive rate. Without saying goodbye to John or casting so much as a glance in my direction, he fled the diner. More than one pair of eyes followed him out.

Kelly smiled. "That never gets old." She waved at me. "See you later."

I raised a hand, picking up someone's meager attempt at a tip with the other. Kelly turned in the doorway. "Hey, John, you don't have any of those films with Violet Evergreen in them, have you?"

John groaned. "We are watching those films over my dead body."

"Ah, but you do have some?"

"Only those Marjorie left behind, and I suspect she did that because she knew how much I hate them." John's fingers lightly brushed against my lower back as he passed me. I didn't bother to suppress the shiver. It felt too good.

Kelly put on her best doe-eyed, pouty-mouthed expression. "So you won't even reconsider for me?"

"Nope."

"Not even if I play the pregnancy card?"

John sighed. A smart man knew when he was beaten, and John was a smart man. "Okay." He raised a finger, "But, you can only play that card on a very select-few occasions. Are you sure you want to waste one on a Violet Evergreen film?"

Kelly flashed her perfect, white teeth. "Very sure. Catch you guys later." Her auburn hair swished behind her as the door closed.

John shook his head. "Good thing I've got you to look forward to later, then, otherwise I don't think I would survive."

Escaping The Caves

His breath tickled my ear.

I smiled, but my eyes followed Kelly until she'd passed out of sight. No one knew better than me how to divert unwanted attention or how to put on a mask to hide the crumbling face beneath.

But Kelly wasn't the only perceptive one. She might've been smiling and joking on the outside, but on the inside… On the inside she'd been howling. How could I know that? I saw the look hiding behind her eyes every time I looked in a mirror.

Chapter 12

The film evening with Kelly became more or less a daily ritual. Kelly's father still insisted on the ten o'clock curfew, but none of us wanted to change anything on that account. Kelly tired more easily as the baby grew. The girl became more weary and silent. But everything was perfectly normal, according to Rosie, the town's doctor.

John gently leaned on me, trying to get me to talk to her. "Sooner or later, the nightmares will come back," he said one night, kissing the top of my head.

I started. "How do you know about them?"

John gave me a level look. "The walls around here are paper-thin. Besides, the way you were going on at your worst, I'm surprised you didn't wake up the whole town."

"Eve must have been so scared." I was both embarrassed and annoyed. Sam wouldn't have had a problem with my shouting. He took out his hearing-aid when he went to bed. Nothing short of an earthquake could wake him up

"Surprisingly enough, you didn't. She'd come into my room, but was more worried about you than scared."

I traced his cheek with one finger. He caught it, and kissed it. "You got really lucky with her."

"I did. And I got really lucky with you."

And that finished the conversation for the rest of the night.

Even if I didn't want to admit it, John was right. Sooner or later, the nightmares would return. I was stubborn, not stupid. The question was more how to prevent them. As long as the ghosts continued to haunt me, my mind would never fully recover.

It'd be like the wound the old man Bill had cleaned out for me. Without his help, the wound would've been free to fester. And, sooner rather than later, it would've consumed me completely.

My mind and heart were still infected, but I refused to give into the infection. I would fight it to my last breath. But if the infection were to be expelled, my mind needed a thorough clean up before it could heal.

This brought me back to square one. I still had no idea what it would take to purge my mind of the ghosts. To leave the caves behind had helped a little. Meeting Ethan had not. But coming here, to this little town with all its curious characters and melodrama, had.

John helped. Eve helped. Kelly helped. Sam helped. Even the most irritating and impatient customers helped. But, and how wretched and ungrateful this admission made me feel, they weren't enough. Not even Eve's innocent adoration or John's

Escaping The Caves

kindness and passion were enough to heal the gap in my mind and heart.

I still felt its hollow pull. There were voices inside that darkness. My thoughts were never allowed to stray in that direction. I'd been there once before, and I'd rather die than go there again. Therein lay madness.

But have you ever tried to control your mind? Told yourself not to think of some unpleasant business, an argument with a friend or a heart still aching? If you don't believe me, try not to think of a pink elephant and see where it gets you. You might succeed for a while, but sooner or later the thoughts you try to ignore circle back like the coyotes tracking me through the desert.

Things swept under a mental rug have a way of creeping back out again, most likely in the witching hour between three and four in the morning when your defenses are at their weakest. Sometimes they ambush you in the middle of the day while you make pancakes or do the laundry. Their absolutely-terrifying effect is not diminished by the daylight.

I tried to fight the ghosts, ignore them, not pay attention to them, and I tried to simply give in to them. None of these worked, they were still ever present. John wanted me to talk to someone, but this only proved how little he understood me at the end of the day, despite his best intentions and efforts.

How could I talk about something I couldn't even bring myself to think of?

Despite the ghosts' presence, my mind was sounder than it'd been in a long time. Years even. Life in this little town had taken on a comfortable routine. I worked in the diner, bickered good-naturedly with Sam and the customers, played with Eve and gossiped with Kelly. Loved, talked and laughed with John. It all

Kristin Talgø

blended into one soothing balm, which took the edge off the scary gap in my mind. And despite John's warning and my own fears, the nightmares stayed away.

If fate, or circumstances, hadn't changed my course of direction, I think I could've quite happily lived out the rest of my days in that town with those people. My mind might not have become what it once was, but I might not have been any worse for it. Maybe with time I would've told John about all the things he still didn't know about me.

And maybe he was right. Maybe it would've helped to tell him everything. About my mom and Jenna, whom I hadn't even mentioned to him yet, my other sisters, my father, my ex-husband, the child we lost before we had a chance to see her.

To tell him about the lost child would've lead to telling him about how I'd gotten the ugly scar on my lower belly. How having my guts literally ripped out hadn't hurt nearly as much as Michael telling me I'd lost the child.

It would've led to telling him about my life in the caves, the horrors, the blood and the downright massacres. But it would also have led to telling him about that calm coolness that allowed me to function within the caves, as if I'd left all of my emotions behind, leaving only raw instinct.

I could've told him about my friends, Jackson, Michael, Susan and all the rest of them. The strangeness of how close we were, bound by the same bloody fate and death sentence, yet so far apart from each other. Maybe we thought if we kept each other at arm's length, it wouldn't hurt so much when one of us was ripped to pieces.

Maybe I would've told him about Grandpa. The only man I knew of who had lasted until age seventy. All the books he showed me, which housed so many worlds and lives I would

Escaping The Caves

never get a chance to see. He was the one who said to me just before he died, in his bed, "If you ever decide to go after them, go to the ocean in the west. Your mother always wanted to see the ocean before she died."

I might've told him about my fear of not being able to recognize Jenna if I ever saw her again. She'd only been three years when Mom packed their things and left. There'd been a long letter of goodbye, but what her explanations were, I would never know unless I found the woman herself. My father had burned the letter before anyone could read it. Maybe he'd hoped to blame pneumonia for their absence as well, to bury his shame along with them.

So much to tell and, with time, I might've told him all of it, bit by bit. But like I said, the winds changed, and my peaceful existence in that sleepy town surrounded by pines, spruces, birds and waterfalls was not to last.

This little haven was so far from the dangerous caves I'd left behind. But it was also the next-door neighbor to the end of the mountain range, which originated where my story all began. This town, Havensfield (a fitting name, don't you think?), and its inhabitants earned their way through life by three main sources.

There were those like Sam and John, who earned the food on their table and roof over their heads by selling what other people needed.

Then there was timber, which was shipped out of town by huge trucks every month.

And then there was mining, which brings me around to the changing wind.

Part of my comfortable routine in Havensfield was to go for walks every Sunday. Long ones. John would sometimes come with me, but he preferred to spend his free time with Eve, and he knew I secretly preferred my own company on those walks.

The surrounding forest and hills were perfect for hiking. I'd pack my new rucksack with lunch and water bottles, walk until my body was satisfied and then turn back. My trips started after breakfast and I returned around dinnertime, just as the sun touched the horizon.

These walks helped my mind as well. The breeze cleared the passages in my brain. The clean air rejuvenated me, and the green trees and birdsong calmed me. I was more myself on those walks than at any other point during my time in Havensfield. The nature had a healing effect on me that the town, for all its qualities and people, lacked.

There was no one to see me there. I was free to take off my mask and let my real face breathe. In the beginning, I cried, on occasions so loudly, that birds would take flight from the treetops, startled by my sobs. I still cried now, the grief catching me unaware at the oddest times.

One moment I could be walking along, merry as a young girl newly in love, and the next I would have to sit down, grief and heartache smashing into my gut like a fist. I didn't bother to fight it anymore. When it happened, I let it. I rode the waves of pain as best as I could. Eventually they would taper off, and I'd resume my walk again.

If John noticed my red eyes, he didn't mention them. I smiled more, touched him more and was generally much less of a bitch when I returned from my walks, so he left me to it.

I explored most of the tracks and roads my feet could find through the surrounding landscape. The mines, from whence precious metal ores were brought up, never held any interest to me. The unsightly machines they used to perform the

Escaping The Caves

excavations intruded on the nature I'd come to love and cherish. There was nothing I could do to prevent them from blowing off bits and pieces of rock, digging ever deeper into the mountain, destroying the hillside as they went along. Instead I turned my eyes on more pleasing views.

But fate isn't just a fickle friend, it's also unmindful of what its subjects find pleasing or not. On this particular Sunday, fate was determined that I should take a closer look at the mines I generally avoided.

To this day, I still can't quite put my finger on what made me climb that hill leading up to the mines. A slight nudge inside my gut, maybe. Something fluttering at the back of mind, the same kind that disturbed my sleep at night. Instinct then, maybe. Or a good old fashioned hunch.

Or maybe I still hadn't forgotten their scent. Even if I couldn't possibly have smelled them down in the peaceful valley far away from their foul and secret nesting places, maybe my gut was still able to pick up the stench of the monsters which had destroyed so many good people over the years.

Whatever the case, I decided on a whim or by a discreetly guided hand, to take a closer look at the mines. The hike up the hills leading toward them was a more arduous one than I'd assumed. Assume makes an ass out of both you and me, Jen used to run around saying when she was a kid. I've no idea where she picked that up, but both our parents tried unsuccessfully to weed the saying out of her.

But in this case, assuming the hike would be an easy one certainly made an ass out of me. The workers who worked in the mines used a broad, hard-packed dirt road that led through the forest back into Havensfield. When I decided to take a look at the mines, I'd been down in a small valley looking up at them through the dense foliage of the trees.

Now I cursed my decision. For the first time since I started with my Sunday walks, I greatly resented the steep hillside. Normally I would take the various trails through the forest, but if I'd done that in order to get to the mines, I would've had to retrace my steps so often that there would hardly have been any daylight left to view them. That would've rendered the whole trip pointless in the first place.

This led me to take the quicker, but a great deal more vexing, route straight up one of the hills, through the densely-packed tree trunks and undergrowth. Apart from sprouting wings and flying over the hillside, this was the fastest way to go about it, despite the obstacles in my way.

Branches scraped my arms and twigs snagged at my hair. Some of them slapped my face for good measure. I'd never worried about snakes on my walks before, but walking ankle deep in grass and bushes, I certainly did now.

After a strained half an hour, I brushed aside an especially-stubborn branch belonging to an old pine, and stopped. I shielded my eyes against the sun, which faced me almost directly. A small gust of wind tugged at my sweaty clothes and hair. I looked at the mines, and they stared right back at me.

One of the things I appreciated the most on my walks was the incredibly beautiful birdsongs composed by various kinds of birds. I hadn't been able to enjoy it on the way up here, due to the fear of snakes and a general fear of tripping and breaking my neck, but there had been plenty of birds chorusing alongside my panting.

But here, in the presence of the mines, there was nothing. Not one small robin chirped, not a single woodpecker pecked. The silence was even more invading after the concert below. I

Escaping The Caves

wondered if the workers who came here ever noticed, and if they did, what they made of it.

I can't claim that the hairs rose at my arms and neck. There was no one watching me, not right then, but there was a presence here. And not a warm and fuzzy kind either.

I stood at the top of the hill, and took in the mines and their surroundings, catching my breath. I sipped water from my canteen and looked at the entrance to the mines. Nothing particularly noteworthy there. It was tall, broad and dark. From what I knew about the mines, there was a track leading some distance into the mountain. Then the workers had to take an elevator down to the mine shafts where the metal was excavated.

There were no accidents that I knew of, so far, even if the dynamite they used could bring the whole mountain down if not used correctly.

"Go, Jess! I'll be fine!"

"I'm not leaving her behind!"

I took another sip of water, wanting to get rid of the sudden taste of copper in my mouth. The entrance to the mines resembled the entrance to the caves too much for my liking. Jen had been dead close to eight months now. Still, I could hear her voice as clearly as the birds in the forest. It'd had happened too fast for Trenton and her to have felt any pain. There was that to be said about being crushed by a mountain, but even so. The idea of her slim, lithe body buried by sharp rocks and blunt boulders wasn't a pleasant one.

I shook my head, not liking how fast my heart suddenly pounded. My palms were sweaty as I walked closer to the caves. Mines, I corrected myself, they're just mines, for God sake, get a grip.

Kristin Talgø

But what my head knew and my instincts told me were two very different things. Five meters from the mines and I couldn't physically bring myself to go any further. The idea of approaching the mines any closer triggered the same kind of revulsion that the notion of touching a snake did.

The mines exhaled. At least, that's what it felt like. A stale, chill gust of air slipped past me. This time, my hair did rise up at my arms and neck. That gust of air wasn't just stale and chill. There was a hint of something horribly familiar in it. A stench that sneaked into my nightmares. It was vague here, almost unrecognizable if you didn't already know it for what it was. But once you've smelled death, you can't miss it.

It was only by exercising every ounce of my self-discipline as an ex-soldier that I was able to stand my ground. Every fiber of my being wanted to bolt and run, like a startled deer catching the scent of a predator. I wiped my brow and nearly poked my own eye out with a finger, my hands shook that badly.

That rumble the day the caves came down on us… did we ever find out what caused it? I searched back, but could find no recollection of anyone even asking. Nothing like that had ever happened before. Shouldn't we at least have been curious enough about it to avoid another rockslide like that? Maybe, but I knew enough about the cave-mentality to know people had enough problems as it were, without initiating an investigation which would be all but impossible to pursue.

In order to find out why part of the caves collapsed, we'd have to go into them. And once inside, your number one priority quickly became killing as many monsters as you could before getting the hell out of there before they killed you. To inspect loose rocks and a possibly eroded and crumbling ceiling above, wouldn't just be all but impossible, it would be

Escaping The Caves

downright insulting to suggest. Anyone thinking it could be done had clearly not been in the caves. They would've been treated with nearly as much disdain as an outcast.

I sweated, even as cold chills rippled through me. But I was in a safe enough position to think about why the caves had suddenly caved in. The entrance to the mines offered no explanation, but I thought the answer lay within them, nonetheless.

Just before the ceiling of the caves came down on us, there'd been a great, loud rumbling noise, as if a train were five seconds away from sweeping through the mountain. Even the monsters had responded, if not with fear, than apprehension, at the noise. And the noise had shaken the caves and triggered the collapse. But what had been the source of the disturbance?

Earthquake, I remembered, that's what we assumed had triggered the rocks to come down on us. Assumption makes an ass out of both you and me. How Jen had laughed when she said that, adding to our parents' discomfort. You weren't supposed to say 'ass', even if your father said far worse things when the mood took him.

But seventy-five years, give or take, and not once had our community around the caves been troubled by earthquakes. Why now? I turned around and looked at the machines and crates of dynamite stacked neatly under cover so it wouldn't get wet and spoiled by the rain. The circle complete, I ended up facing the mines again.

Dynamite. They used dynamite to bury even deeper into the mountain. I'd overheard some of the workers from the mines at the diner one time. They'd discussed the pros and cons of using it in the search for their precious metal.

Sure, they could blast away rocks at an impressive rate, one had said, but by doing so, you were blasting away the very metal you were trying to retrieve.

Yeah, but that don't matter, another chipped in, cause the deeper you dig, the more metal you find. And more metal means more money, my friend. You know the saying: money talks, bullshit walks.

So we keep on blasting. The first had raised his beer in a toast.

So we keep on blasting, the second had clinked his glass against the other, and we'll keep on blasting 'til we get to the other side, I reckon.

'Til we get to the other side. The chills really gripped me, then. They ripped through my body like a high wind through sheets hung out to dry. How far and deep into the mountains had these money-loving bosses ordered their workers to use the dynamite?

Far enough to trigger a rockslide in the caves that housed the monsters? Far enough to release the monsters on this side? Or just far enough to make that a very real and very frightening possibility?

Suddenly it wasn't just the hair on my arms and neck that stood on end. My whole body was on red-alert. It felt as if my scalp rose several inches above my skull. *You're not being watched. This is you letting your imagination get the better of you. You're imagining the monsters and your mind believes the monsters have come to Havensfield.*

But even so, I turned around slowly. I walked just as slowly back from the mines. Looked around, inspecting what I'd found there, as if nothing but the mines held any interest to me.

I bent down and pretended to re-tie my shoelaces, and glanced up. The surrounding hills were supposedly empty. I stretched, this way and that, as if preparing for the walk home.

Escaping The Caves

It gave me an excuse to sweep my eyes thoroughly over my surroundings.

Maybe the creature would've let me go if it hadn't noticed my eyes picking the shape out among the rocks directly above the mines. My instincts had been dulled by my fragile sanity, but they sure as hell weren't so dull that I didn't notice a three meter-tall monster spying on me.

But it didn't matter. The scaly being hadn't been there before, but it was there now. Maybe I would've been allowed to go on my way, but probably not. My blood scent and fear triggered the lust for hunting and killing, just as the dynamite had triggered the rockslide.

The monster noticed my widening eyes and gave up all pretenses. It rose up to its full height. In broad daylight, the creature looked even more surreal. Black, scaly, either not of this Earth or from deep, deep within. The pit-like eyes peered down at me, and I swear to God, it smiled.

Part of me had suspected the creatures capable of some form of intelligence. But to have it confirmed was quite a different matter. This demon smiling down at me had been out scouting. When it saw me on the way back, the monster waited, watching my every move. And now it smiled at me, mocking me and relishing the idea of shredding me.

That's all I had time to think before the smile disappeared. I made my move. My erratic state of mind might've dulled my senses, but when faced with a monster from the caves, my old, cool and collected mind took over.

Old habits die hard. After growing up as a soldier, and after what happened with Ethan, I never left the diner without my gun. To leave the house without it would've been like leaving the house without clothes. Not something I was prone to do.

Kristin Talgø

The first bullet took the monster in mid-air. The rest I emptied into it as the body hit the ground. I loaded the gun and emptied another round. The gunshots rolled across the hills and back again. I was out of ammunition, but there was no need of any. The creature was dead. I didn't bother checking. If the monster had been alive it would've been busy tearing my throat out.

I re-holstered my gun. The entrance to the caves was still empty, but it wouldn't be for long. Where there was one, there would be others. When this one didn't return, there would be a search party. The fact that the monsters had penetrated the mines all through the vast mountain range and had not attacked yet, even with the mines crawling with tender, delicious blood-filled humans, told me something.

They had a plan.

This time my restraints stood no chance.

I bolted.

Chapter 13

Despite my walks every Sunday, my stamina wasn't even close to what it'd been when I fought in the caves. It wasn't just the fighting itself which had kept me in shape. If you wanted even half a chance at making it past your seventeenth birthday, rigorous, daily training was needed. I had to give Kyle this, he'd kept me fit. Since coming to Havensfield, there'd been no Kyle to maintain my daily training regime.

I'd enjoyed my weekly hiking trips for more than one reason. They'd given me the opportunity to enjoy exercise simply for the sake of exercise. Not as a crucial key to survival.

This was all well and good when there were no monsters about, but unfortunately for all of us, there were now. I didn't waste time convincing myself I was as good as I used to be when fighting was all I knew how to do. The only reason I ran at full speed through the forest instead of being torn to pieces was because of one thing and one thing only. The element of surprise.

Kristin Talgø

The monster had assumed that I would be unarmed. It'd given me time to blow its brains out. I wouldn't have stood a chance if the monster had known I was armed. If what I suspected about the mountain range between the mines and caves was true, then some serious whipping-into-shape was required. And I would need a hell of a lot of back-up.

* *

It was Sunday and the door of the diner was duly closed, but I forgot and almost ran straight into it. I cursed, sweated and panted as I jogged around to the back, letting myself in by the private entrance. The stairs groaned under my frantic climb upstairs.

"Where's the fire?" Sam stuck out his grizzly head as I tore past him, but I was too out of breath to reply.

John had apparently heard me. He waited inside the living room. Worry and curiosity battled over his face. When he saw my wild look, the first won out.

"Jess, what the hell's going on? Sit down. Christ, you look ready to drop." He guided me over to the sofa. Gratefully, I sank down on the worn surface and accepted a glass of water. Sam shuffled into the room. He put on his spectacles.

"Where's Eve?" I managed to get out.

"With Marjorie." He looked at his watch. "They should be back in about an hour. Why?"

"I don't want her to hear this."

"Hear what?" John sat down next to me. Sam pulled up the armchair I'd claimed so many months ago.

I tried to speak, unsuccessfully.

"Take deep breaths. We're not going anywhere." John

replaced the empty glass with a new one.

After a couple of minutes, my heart didn't feel so close to bursting and I was able to tell them what had happened at the mines. Father and son grew pale as I talked. There wasn't a shadow of a doubt on their faces, but there was plenty of fear.

"Jesus." John rubbed his jaw, his hand not quite steady.

"I'm not a believer myself, but I might start now." Sam's voice shook as badly as John's hands.

I put down my glass. The water was heavy in my stomach. I thought there was a good chance of it staying where it was, but it could just as easily go the other way. I knew what was required of me. But even with all that was at stake, I was loath to do it.

"I have to go back." I pulled my fingers through my tangled hair. I released a twig from its imprisonment. "I have no idea how we're going to deal with this, but I have to warn the others." I swallowed. "I have to talk to my father."

John entwined his fingers through mine. He knew as well as I did that outcasts didn't just return from exile.

"Is he an important man, your father?" Sam wondered. It eased my heart a little to no longer hear the previous tremble.

"Where I come from, he's the important man. He's our Commander. We have a democratic system of sorts, but what he says goes. Most of the time." I added, thinking of Mom and Jenna.

"I see." Sam stroked his scruffy chin.

"Dad, I'm not sure–" John started, but Sam waved away his interruptions.

I looked from Sam to John, back to Sam again. There was obviously a silent discussion going on between them that I wasn't privy to.

201

"Do you mind including me as to what's going on here? John, I need you to find me a schedule for the next train back in the direction of the caves. The other creatures will know they've been sighted. There's no telling when the attack will come. We have no time to lose."

John tore his eyes away from his father's, but he was still trapped in his own musings.

"John!" I snapped my fingers. "I don't have time for this! What's wrong with you two?"

"I'm afraid you're going to have to make the time for this, Jess. Whether or not we really have it." Sam lit his pipe.

"I hate it when you do that in here," John said, but his voice lacked conviction. Whatever was on his mind, it took up most of his mental capacity.

"I'll air the room out before Eve gets here." Sam puffed. Smoke rings floated up to the ceiling. "I need to think and this helps me."

"John..." I warned, my patience running dangerously low.

John shook his head. "Sorry, Jess. It's just... I'm trying to put the pieces together here, but I don't have all of them. Most of what I know, I know only from hearsay. Bits and pieces from different people. Town-gossip mostly."

"What the hell are you talking about? I've told you the monsters have been able to tunnel through the entire mountain range from the caves to the very mines where half of your town's employed, and you're talking gibberish."

"I know patience isn't a specialty of yours, Jess, but for once, would you just keep silent and let me gather my thoughts," John snapped.

I bit back a nasty retort, but managed to do as he asked. Sam continued to puff on his pipe. One of the books that Grandpa had given me, which I'd enjoyed the most, had been one from long ago before the Falling. I thought Sam would've made an excellent hobbit. Not that it lessened my irritation with him or his son.

John gazed at his father's smoke rings for a full minute. "You've been told that your presence around the caves is vital to the survival of the human race, yeah? You've been brought up to believe that if it wasn't for you fighting the monsters, keeping their numbers at bay and confined to the caves, then they would once again overrun the earth. Destroy us completely. Is that right?"

I wanted to hit him. And not just bitch slap him either. I wanted to punch him full on the nose where it hurt the most.

"That isn't just what I've been told. It's a fact of life. It's not a life any one of us would've chosen, but someone's got to do it. My great-grandfather was one of the first people the task fell to. Since then the job has been passed down through the generations. If we suddenly took this up for vote, based it on people's desire to voluntarily give up their own lives and the lives of those they loved, we'd be pretty short of volunteers pretty fast." I breathed through my nose and clenched my fists. I might not always like the man, but I was still my father's daughter.

John put a hand on my arm, but I shook it off. "I know the history, Jess and I know that's how it used to be-"

"Used to be? It's how it fucking is! Why do you think I had a mental breakdown? Because it got boring in the caves? We're not doing it for fun, you know."

John didn't try to touch me again, but his voice was infuriatingly calm. "Jess, listen, please. I know that's how it is, but just suppose, just suppose there was a different way to kill the monsters? A weapon that would enable us to destroy the monsters completely. Wipe them off the face of the Earth once and for all. Do you think your father, the Commander and the rest of them, would agree to that?"

My mouth fell open. I closed it so hard, my teeth crashed painfully together. "Of course they would. But if there was such a weapon, they wouldn't still be fighting in the caves, now would they? And I sure as hell wouldn't have shot one just shy of five kilometers from here."

"You see, that's the pieces that just won't fit the puzzle." John slammed a fist on his thigh.

"Just tell her what Peter told you that night, son. We'll take it from there." Sam had switched from hobbit to being all wise and Gandalf-like. I was starting to want to punch Sam too.

"Peter was drunk that night, Dad. We can't trust what he said–"

"Peter? As in Peter, Kelly's father?" I dug my fingers into John's arm. He winced.

"Yeah. Let up, Jess. And breathe, for God's sake. I'll tell you what we know. Then maybe, if we put all of our heads together, it might make sense by the end of it." He looked at the time. "And I'll tell it to you quickly. I don't want us discussing monsters when Eve comes home."

John took a deep breath and started. "Peter came by here one evening just before closing time, a couple of days after our encounter with you on the train. He didn't say much, but I got the distinct impression he'd had another row with Jane, his wife, about Kelly. Truth be told, I think she's the one causing the

Escaping The Caves

most trouble. Too afraid about what others might say about them. Furious about losing their social status in the city. Too concerned about her looks."

My fingers tapped out an impatient rhythm on the tabletop next to me.

"Sorry, that's beside the point. Anyway, so Peter came in here, looking like he carried the whole world's problems on his shoulders. He ordered a scotch, neat, no ice, then another. And another. When I told him he might think about slowing down a bit, he was quick to tell me his drinking fed my daughter. In other words, my drinking ain't none of your business, but pouring my drinks are.

"Not wanting to get into an argument, I held my tongue this time and poured. By the table next to him, there were a couple of women, Macy and Ruth. I don't know if you've seen them around?"

I thought about it. "Are those the ones always yapping away, gossiping about everyone in town?"

"Yeah. Both of them love talking about others, but hate people talking about them. Both of them on sort of friendly terms with Jane.

"That evening, with Peter sitting at the next table, they were gossiping as loudly as ever, about you. Probably in an effort to draw the attention away from her pregnant fifteen year old, Jane had spread the word about the outcast on the train. From the way she told it, you were about to blast all of our heads off."

Jane didn't know the outcast had been me. She could say whatever she wanted. But I still didn't like that I'd been part of the gossip around here.

John waited for my attention to return before he continued. "In any case, Macy and Ruth went on about what a disgrace

205

outcasts are, traitors to humanity, should all be lynched, yadayadayada, you know the speech. I didn't pay much attention to them other than thinking to myself that they were lucky not to have been born around the cave. Otherwise they would've become outcasts themselves pretty soon."

"Doubt they'd have lasted long enough to become outcasts."

"Probably not. In any case, I listened with half an ear because only someone completely deaf would've been able to shut out the chatter of those women. Peter seemed to be doing a pretty good job at it, though. He sank further and further into his scotch. But when he spoke up, it was clear he'd soaked up every word they'd said.

"He turned around, asked the two of them to kindly shut the hell up. Macy and Ruth both dropped their jaws, for once both speechless at the same time."

"First time in all their lives I'm sure," I mumbled.

John ignored me. He was on a roll. "Peter told the two women they hadn't the slightest inkling of what those so-called traitors had been through. Said he'd have liked to see any one of them give the caves a try.

"Ruth was the first one to regain her ability to talk. Wanted to know how Peter knew so much about outcasts." I straightened. He had my attention now.

"Peter snorted and downed the rest of his scotch in one go. Said he probably didn't know any more than Ruth, but at least he had enough sense in his head not to blindly accept all the propaganda against outcasts."

I wasn't familiar with the term 'propaganda', but didn't want to interrupt John, so I let it pass.

"This made Macy speak up. Told Peter that there was a reason why the outcasts are hated. Said that without someone

Escaping The Caves

fighting in the caves, keeping the monsters there, there'd be a second Falling. And everyone would be lost. She was very adamant about how we had every right to hate those who would abandon such an important cause."

I opened my mouth, but John overrode me. "Her words, not mine."

After a brief pause, I closed my mouth.

"When Peter answered, he started to slur. Told Macy she was wrong on both accounts. Claimed everyone wouldn't be lost without the fighters in the caves. Said we had no right to hate people whose sanity had been slowly chipped away, bloodshed by bloodshed. That the outcasts deserved better than pity, but certainly not hate."

The idea of anyone pitying me made my skin crawl.

"Macy got offended by this. Wanted to know who would stop the monsters, if not for those already doing it. Asked Peter if he had some great weapon up his sleeve that no one knew about.

"Peter got to his feet then, almost overturned his chair in the process. Nope, he said, but someone does."

There were so many questions I wanted to ask, but the look on John's face told me to wait.

"Ruth laughed, but Macy, though loud and rude, is sharper than her tongue, and that's saying something. She narrowed her eyes, as if it would help her see the 'someone' that Peter talked about. Asked him if he'd have them believe that someone had a weapon that could take out the monsters for good. If there existed a weapon that would mean no more fighting, no more caves, no more outcasts."

Deep down, I knew there was no such weapon. But it didn't stop my heart from skipping a beat.

"Ruth told her friend not to listen to Peter's drunken chatter, but Macy said she wanted to hear this. Peter bowed and nearly toppled over. He told them he'd said all he intended to on the subject. But yes, that was correct. Said goodnight and tipped an imaginary hat at them, then tried to aim for the door."

I didn't know Peter, but I still had problems picturing him that drunk.

John's voice picked up speed. He could tell my mind was wandering. "But Macy wasn't satisfied. She grabbed hold of his shirt tail and turned him around. Wanted to know if what he claimed was true, why anyone in their right minds would keep such a weapon to themselves.

"Peter leaned closer. Said, that was the ting. That no one in their right minds would. But then again, that was politicians for you."

"Politicians? What the hell have they got to do with this?" I couldn't make sense of half of the story. It made me want to punch something.

John shook his head. Both of us were running low on patience. "Peter pulled out of Macy's grasp and aimed for the door. Wished us all a goodnight, and then did the drunken shuffle out of the diner.

"Macy and Ruth kept at it for another half an hour. Argued about which of them was the bigger fool, Ruth for not believing him or Macy for leaning towards doing so. Luckily, it wasn't just close to closing time anymore. It was well-past. After browning my nose for a bit, I was able to get them out of the place."

He sighed. "And that's all there is to tell about it."

Escaping The Caves

John sank back into the sofa cushions, drained a tall glass of water. I tried to process what he'd just told me, but any way I turned it, I wasn't able to make sense of it.

"So, let me get this straight. Something or someone has Peter believing that there exists a weapon that could wipe out the monsters entirely?"

John nodded. "Yep."

"But that whoever's in possession of this supposed weapon won't use it because of... what? Politics? To what end? This doesn't make any sense. What would anyone stand to profit from keeping the monsters in the caves?"

I got up, paced back and forth, but had to sit down again. My legs were rubberlike and it wasn't just from the running.

"Now that's the million-dollar question. What would any politician stand to gain from that? Hard to say, but if there's any truth to this, you can bet they have their reasons." John rubbed my back.

"But how would he have come by this knowledge? If it's true." I leaned into him without bothering to feel embarrassed by this display of affection in front of Sam. Besides, he seemed lost in his own world.

"You forget that he made a lot of powerful friends climbing that infamous ladder in the city. Someone might've let something slip at one point. This certainly isn't common knowledge. Peter would undoubtedly be in a lot of trouble if it became known he'd talked. If it's true," he added, but the tight set of his jaw told me he thought it was.

I straightened, looked at him. "And you forget that all of us will be in a lot of trouble if someone doesn't talk. We have to get word back to the caves. We need immediate backup if we're to stand any chance at all against the monsters. And we need to know more about this weapon."

John sighed. "You're going out there to see him now, aren't you? Jess, it's getting late. He was drunk when he told this story. He might not own up to having said anything at all."

"Trust me, he'll own up to me if there's anything to own up to. One way or another, we need to get to the bottom of this. And he's our first lead." I got up, hesitated next to Sam.

"Don't worry." John got up and stretched. "He gets that way sometimes, better just leave him be. I'll check in on him in a while."

I picked up my jacket. After my run, I was in desperate need of a shower, but with the next Falling possibly right over the next hill, personal hygiene would have to take a backseat. "Where are you going?"

"Have to pick up Eve. Marjorie refuses to come over here." John wrapped a blanket around his father's shoulders. Sam smiled at him, but returned to his own inner world without a word.

"Why? Is she still upset about that fight you had here?" I closed the door behind us.

John pulled me close, his arm a perfect fit around my waist. "Yeah, more like she's upset about you. Or us, I should say."

I raised my eyebrows. "Seriously? I thought she had a boyfriend?"

"Oh, she does. But she doesn't like anyone playing with her toys. Even her discarded ones," John said wryly.

"That woman..." I shook my head. "But no. I'm not going to start. If I do, I won't be able to stop. You deserve so much better than her."

"Good thing I've got you then." John stopped just around the corner from our house. The sun was setting. It painted the sky in a multitude of hues of red, yellow, pink and orange. There was a melancholy feel in the cooling air. It squeezed my heart. "Jess, no matter what happens, promise me you won't leave without saying goodbye first."

"I would never do that. John, I'm not going anywhere. Or, well, I have to, don't I? To fix this mess, if I can, but I'm not leaving you. I… I…" No matter how much I wanted to, those three words just wouldn't come.

John cupped my cheek and caressed it with his thumbs. The light illuminated his hair, making it seem ablaze. "Jess, I've known from the beginning that you weren't likely to settle down here with me. You don't strike me as the picket fence and two-point-five kids kind of girl."

He said it with a smile, but there was a sadness in his eyes that made my heart ache. My free hand went automatically to the scar on my lower belly. But this was hardly the time to discuss these things. If we were lucky, there might be later.

"I might be. One day." I pressed my lips to his to hide the stinging in my eyes.

"Yeah. One day." John kissed me back. He was thorough about it. "Now, go on. If you don't, I won't be able to let you go."

"All right," I said, a little out of breath. "I'll be back as soon as I've talked to Peter. Then we see where we go from there."

"Okay." John kissed me again. This time he held back what I really wanted.

"I won't leave you, John."

He smiled, but didn't reply. I didn't take my eyes off him before he was out of sight. Just before turning a corner, he looked back and waved.

Chapter 14

I walked Kelly home in the evening enough times to know the route to her house well by now. The sun was slowly sinking down behind the mountain range, as if tired after a long day. Kelly sat, rocking back and forth in an old rocking chair at the porch. She dozed. Her stomach round and strutting. It wouldn't be long now.

Kelly opened her eyes, roused by my steps on the gravel in front of the house. When she saw me, she smiled, slowly like the sinking sun. "Jess, what brings you here?" She looked at her watch. "Is something wrong?"

I didn't want to alarm her, but there wasn't really any time to beat around the bush either. "I'm afraid so. Kelly, I need to speak to your father. It's urgent."

Kelly labored to get out of the chair, but waved my offered assistance away. "I'm fine, really. Christ, I'm huge. Dad? What do you want with him?"

"I need to speak with him."

Kristin Talgø

"So I heard. What you failed to mention was why." Kelly steadied herself on the armrest of the chair.

I was about to answer, when Jane, Kelly's mother, came out on to the porch. My spirits plummeted further. The sense of urgency increased.

I won't waste either mine or your time by describing her unnecessarily. Suffice to say that, despite our small town in the outback, she still dressed to impress. Not a strand of hair escaped her neat bun at the back of her neck. Her make-up was perfectly in place. Just like the fake smile she presented to me.

"Hello, you must be Jess. I don't believe we've had the pleasure of being introduced yet. I'm Jane, Kelly's mother, as I'm sure you know." Her fingers grazed my hand. She looked as if she was tempted to wipe her hand on her trousers.

I nodded. The appropriate reply would've been to tell her it was nice to finally meet her. But I've always been a terrible liar.

"To what do we owe this unexpected pleasure?" Jane finally asked.

"Is your husband home? I really need to speak with him."

Jane covered up her surprise with another frosty smile. "Peter? What on Earth could you want with him?"

I suppressed an urge to simply shove the woman aside and look for Peter myself. "It's difficult to explain, and it really would be best if I could talk to him first. It's urgent."

Jane dropped the smile. "I'm sorry, but I really must insist. If you'd like to speak to my husband, I have a right to know what it's regarding."

Before I could ruin all of my chances to talk to Peter, he came out on the porch. He was the complete opposite of his wife. Scruffy, rumpled, with no pretenses left. He rubbed his eyes, what was left of his thinning hair standing out at odd angles.

"What's all the racket about? Can't a man take a nap in his own house without being disturbed? One hour. That's all I wanted. One lousy hour." His bloodshot eyes landed on me. "Jess. What the hell are you doing here?"

"Peter!" Jane's hollow cheeks flushed.

"It's okay, really." I found Peter's rudeness a welcome honesty after Jane's fake politeness.

"Well, I repeat, if slightly modified, what are you doing here?" Peter tucked in his shirt.

"I need to speak with you."

"About…"

"About what you told Macy and Ruth that night in John's diner."

Peter's expression had been grumpy but forthcoming. Now it shut down completely. I could almost hear the walls coming up. "I'm sure I don't know what you're talking about."

I stepped in front of him, blocking the entrance to the house. "I'm sure you do know."

Peter stiffened. "I was drunk that night. I'm not proud of it, but I was. If I said something that's caught your attention, I'm sorry to have wasted it."

I breathed deeply. "So, it's true then."

"What's true? Peter, what is going on?" Jane darted looks back and forth but none of us answered. Kelly had inched closer. Her hands cradled her stomach protectively.

"Of course it's not true!" Peter burst out, spittle flying from his lips. The skin underneath his stubble was so pale it'd gone almost grey.

"Then you admit you know what I'm talking about." I crossed my arms.

215

Peter clenched and unclenched his fists in rapid succession. "Jess, leave this one alone. I'm warning you. You do not want to stick your nose where it doesn't belong."

"I'm sorry to hear that, but I have no choice."

Peter flashed his teeth. Suddenly I could see the man who'd gone to such great lengths to get to the top where the powerful and ruthless ruled. That man was beaten, but he still existed. Good. I could use that.

"Oh, on the contrary. You do have a choice. Turn back now and we'll pretend this ill-advised meeting never happened. It was John, wasn't it? Goddamn that man. He shouldn't have told you." Peter smashed his fist into the railing on the porch.

Jane sat down in the rocking chair. "Peter, please tell me you didn't say anything you shouldn't have." Her hands shook as she smoothed her hair.

Peter rounded on her. "Of course I've said something I shouldn't have! This outcast wouldn't be standing here if I hadn't, now would she!"

The silence descending on us was suffocating.

"Outcast?" Jane tried to get to her feet, but failed. Some strands of hair had escaped her neat bun, probably for the first time since kindergarten.

"Oh, wake up, Jane! Are you really so self-centered that you don't recognize her from the train? Jesus, you really are, aren't you?" Peter looked at his wife with something close to contempt.

"But… but… but why haven't you said anything? Dear God, she's been walking around here for all these months. She lives under the same roof as a small, defenseless child and you never said a word!" Jane twisted the rings on her fingers. Round and round they went, just like her accusations.

Escaping The Caves

I was two seconds away from interrupting her, when Peter did. "Please be quiet, Jane." He never raised his voice, but the coldness in it shut her up.

"Do you really think that John doesn't know? Or that Sam doesn't suspect? The man's hardly two blocks down from complete dementia, and yet he understands what you don't. But considering what you know, I think it would be best if you kept this information to yourself. Things are going to get very ugly around here very fast. The last thing anyone needs is you adding fuel to the fire. Am I making myself clear? Jane?"

Jane looked at her husband as if seeing him for the first time. "Yes. We're clear." Her fingers still twisted her rings.

"Good. Now, Jess. I guess you better come inside. But before I tell you anything, I want to know what you know first." Peter looked me straight in the eye.

"Yes, sir."

"And avoid the sarcasm please. I'm in a foul enough mood already without it." He turned and walked into the house.

I followed him. Kelly looked uncertainly at her mother before she did the same. Jane stayed where she was, her rings going round and round.

The inside of the house was a schizophrenic mix between Peter and Jane. Part of the interior was, although old and worn, immaculate and clean, almost to the point of the neurotic. The rest was a discomforting mess of newspapers, coffee cups and the like. There wasn't a trace of Kelly in there. She kept to her room as much as possible when she was home. You didn't have to take more than one look at the place to see that this wasn't a place for an expecting mother.

I sat down on the edge of one of the sofas, the neurotic ones, Peter in one of the stained armchairs. Kelly opted for the only neutral chair in the house.

Peter and Kelly listened quietly to what I'd told John and Sam. It wouldn't do to scare Kelly in her current state, but if told to leave the room, she'd listen in on the conversation anyway. At least this way I'd be there to pick her off the floor if needed.

Just like John and Sam, they grew very pale and very quiet. When done, I got up and poured myself a drink of water from the kitchen. Neither Peter nor Kelly had moved an inch by the time I got back.

"Now, I've told you what I know. I'd appreciate it if you'd return the favor." I looked at Peter, but squeezed Kelly's hand. When I tried to pull back, she wouldn't let go.

To give Peter credit where credit was due, he didn't bother to question or analyze what I'd just told him. "What I told Macy and Ruth that night was true," Peter said. "The abridge version goes something like this. After the Falling, certain people—both those appointed and those who appointed themselves to gather up the pieces and start to assemble them again—have tried to recover the technology that became lost during the massacres.

"Other people, like your great-grandfather, took it upon themselves to live out their lives in exile, to defend humanity by keeping the monsters confided to the caves. This was, in the beginning, utterly vital and crucial to the continued survival of the human race."

"It still is vital and crucial," I said through gritted teeth. If it wasn't, then what had all those deaths been good for?

"Do you mind?"

I spread my hand in a go-right-ahead gesture.

"Thank you," Peter continued. "Most people, as well as everything that had been built over the past centuries, had

Escaping The Caves

slowly corroded and fallen with the expansion of the monsters. When humanity finally got the upper hand on them, someone had to make sure they didn't escape.

"This meant that your great-grandfather and the others who came with him were too busy building a community around the terrible duty they'd agreed to, to bother with what went on with the rest of the world. They left that to the ones who tried to rebuild the cities. The first warriors in the caves took their duties as seriously as the situation demanded. They trusted those left in the cities to do the same."

"And did they?" I couldn't help it. The question slipped out.

This time Peter didn't snap at me. He nodded. "They did. But the ones re-building society in the cities weren't as selfless as the men and women in the caves. Some, I believe, had honest intentions. They wanted to build a better and fairer world, based on learning from past mistakes and what they deemed would benefit most people.

"Others—like the grandfather of George Sampson, for instance—weren't so keen on sharing fairly with everyone. They saw a world in ruin, a world they could potentially shape to suit their own purposes. They saw a world ripe for the taking, just waiting to be seized. And seize it they did."

Ethan's face flitted across my mind. I rubbed my temples.

Peter looked at me, but didn't stop talking. "Part of shaping the world to their liking included unearthing the old technology, so to speak, even if that same technology nearly led to our complete destruction."

I dropped my hands into my lap. "What do you mean? You know where the monsters came from?"

Peter cracked his knuckles. "I know some, but only very little. It would only serve to confuse you more. I have no straightforward answers. All I know is that part of the most advanced technology was misused, and eventually led to the closest we've come to the apocalypse so far."

"I don't want straightforward answers," I said. "Only the truth. All of it."

Peter's face worked. "Fine. I'll tell you this, but only to shut you up so we can continue with the real story here. From what I've heard, the monsters were thought to be part of some vast, brutal war machine. Weapons of mass destruction were already developed, but the downside of those was that you ran the risk of obliterating not just your enemies, but your own country and allies as well."

I tried to picture a weapon that was more destructive than the monsters, but came up short.

"The idea of the monsters originated first as a hypothetical notion, a what-if. What if you could create an army of soldiers, all your own? A lean, mean killing machine, to lend a phrase. What if you could create warriors who were not only strong and fierce, but intensely loyal? Soldiers who would obey your every command, without hesitation. Without mercy and without guilt. These soldiers would risk their lives because it was what they'd been designed to do. And there would be no worrying about human loss, at least not on the winning side, the side of the monsters."

"An apt description for a weapon," I remarked. "The monsters."

Kelly's father smiled. It didn't reach his eyes. "They didn't call them the monsters to begin with. No one would ever create a weapon calling it by its rude and accurate purpose. I believe they called them S.W.I.F.T.s Soldier With Intentions of Friendly Termination."

Escaping The Caves

"Friendly termination? Are you kidding me?"

Peter shrugged "I'm sure they had all sorts of righteous reasons to justify their new weapon. There would be less human casualties. There'd be no need for human soldiers on our part. And once the mission had been accomplished, S.W.I.F.T.s would feel no need to rape and plunder like human soldiers."

I started at this. No soldier I knew of would want to hurt anyone after a shift in the caves. Then I thought of the look in some people's eyes, and wasn't so sure after all.

Peter cleared his throat. When he was sure I was listening, he continued.

"S.W.I.F.T.s would also be programmed to only take out the sanctioned targets, the enemies of war. This would greatly reduce the risk of civilian casualties."

"Programmed? I don't understand."

"S.W.I.F.T's, or—to hell with it, the monsters—were biodegradable robots. In plain English and grossly over-simplified, they were part machine, part animal tissue."

I tried to picture the monsters, but all I could see were a pair of red, glowing eyes.

Peter nodded. "You've seen the monsters for yourself. You're one of the few people I know who've had close encounters with them on numerous occasions and are still alive to tell the tale. They walk on two feet like humans. And I'm sorry to say, the intelligence which these beings were programmed with is alarmingly human as well. This means they're capable of adapting and calculating their moves."

"They're vicious, but far from stupid." I licked my lips. "That's what makes them so dangerous".

Peter eyed me. I stopped biting my fingernails. "You okay?"

I nodded.

"All right. What I'm about to say next is superfluous given the circumstances, but I'll say it anyway. The monsters had one gigantic flaw: the intelligence programmed within them. They were given a certain ability to think for themselves and draw conclusions based on facts. From what I've deduced, their programming overrode the sense of loyalty and respect for human life, which was supposed to be at the core of their being."

"Respect for human life? At the core of their being?"

Peter waved a hand at me, irritation creasing his brow. "The monsters saw that they could take orders from those who'd built them, those who considered themselves to be superiors, their masters, and get killed in the process. Or they could take out their masters and roam the world as they pleased."

"Obviously they chose the latter."

Peter sighed. "Where was I? Yes, your great-grandfather took up the lead of keeping the remaining monsters at bay."

Something nagged at me. "If the monsters were originally created by humans, how come they still exist?" "Good question. It is partly due to their extraordinary healing abilities. Those you don't kill, but only wound, will eventually heal on their own given the patience of time. I also believe they've learned the skills of repairing those who've been wounded beyond their built-in healing center. But even so, they should've been extinct by now. Unless someone has supplied the caves with more monsters. Which brings me back to the original story."

"Supplied the caves with more monsters? Who the hell would do that?"

"Jess…" Peter pinched the bridge of his nose. "Could I please tell you all of this without you interrupting me every two minutes?"

I bit back what I really wanted to tell him. "Sure."

"Wonderful. Now, those who took on the responsibility of rebuilding the cities considered gathering the lost technology among their main priorities. Outwardly they performed their selfless duties excellently. They provided for those who couldn't provide for themselves, they organized the rebuilding of houses, hospitals, schools etc.

"But behind the scenes, they pulled strings that would've been best left alone. Among the technology that they recovered was the technology that brought the monsters into existence in the first place."

"What? They didn't think the monsters did a good enough job killing off half the planet the first time around?"

Peter looked at me as if he couldn't understand how such an idiot like me had survived for so long. "While the monsters were still a constant threat and the fighters in the caves remained a crucial necessity to the survival of the human race, those in power in the cities were pretty much left to their own devices."

"What do you mean?"

"What I mean is, as long as things ran more-or-less smoothly, both in the cities and in the country, no one was going to question their nearly-unlimited power or wealth. People in general might not prosper, but they didn't starve either. But it soon became clear to the powerful men and women that as soon as the monsters were annihilated, their power wouldn't go unquestioned any longer.

"People would demand elections, free speech. They would question the gigantic disparity between how they lived their lives and how those in power did. Unless their demands were met, there would be riots and uprisings. And sooner or later, the power of the few would fall to the power of the people, like so many times throughout history."

This meant nothing to me. I didn't know anything about history and I didn't want to either. All I cared about was the future. To make sure there'd be a future.

"As long as the monsters remained a constant threat, none of this would be an issue. At the time of the Falling, people were completely caught off guard. Millions were destroyed by the weapons they'd designed themselves. At the onset of the attack the monsters had destroyed any weapon that could take them out, much like a fist swats a fly.

"This time around, the people in power knew how dangerous the monsters were and took necessary precautions against them. The monsters that were dispatched to the caves… I still don't know how they've been able to get them in without any of you knowing about it, but they weren't activated until they were far inside the caves. And those in power made sure they did possess functioning weapons that could destroy the monsters once and for all if the situation demanded it."

"What weapon? Peter, you haven't told me what I really want to know."

"Jess, I don't know. All I know is that the situation demands it now. Once again, the folly of man has set the monsters loose. And once again the monsters have proven themselves capable of taking advantage of that folly. But I'll be damned if I'm going to allow them to outwit us one more time."

"And how do you suggest we prevent that?"

Peter smiled. This time it did reach his eyes. "These bastards need taking out. And you, Jess, are going to help us do it."

Escaping The Caves

Peter sank into the cushions on his messy sofa. He drained a tall glass of iced tea. My mind was a beehive of whirling questions and protests. But what it all came down to in the end was this: someone was to blame for all of this and that someone was going to pay. Big time.

I didn't trust myself to respond straight away. The only reason I didn't hit something was because I sat on my hands. It didn't stop the rest of my body from shaking, though. I glanced at Kelly and could see Peter's story had much the same effect on her, although in the opposite way. Whereas I trembled all over, she sat stock still. Her pale skin and immovable face made her resemble a marble statue.

"Kelly, are you all right?" Peter leaned toward his daughter. He clasped her hand.

His touch roused her. She didn't meet his eyes and slipped her hand back into her lap, her hands cradling her stomach once more. Peter pretended not to be affected by this. But I could read the hurt in his eyes well enough.

"Am I all right? After what you just told us, how can you even ask me that? And what's more, how could you know all of this and not try to stop it? Shit, Dad, people are being slaughtered daily, and for what? So that some power-crazed elite in the capital can remain in control?" Kelly's voice didn't match her unmoving body anymore. There were two red hectic spots on her cheeks.

Peter rubbed his face. He seemed to age a year by the second. "If there was something I could've done, don't you think I would've done it? But do you seriously think I could've taken George Sampson and his allies on, all by myself?"

Kelly still wouldn't meet her father's eyes. "Maybe not, but you could've warned those fighting in the caves that they weren't just fighting against the monsters, but the monsters who built them too."

Peter sighed. "I could've... but..." He looked at me and something about it pricked.

"What? Why do I get the feeling that I'm not going to like what's coming next?"

Peter drummed his fingers on his skinny thighs. "Jess, think about what I just told you. Someone has been working for George Sampson, and his father before that, and has provided the caves with new monsters for decades. Ask yourself this, would it at all be possible to accomplish without the help from someone on the inside?"

Shocked to the core as I was, I hadn't thought it possible for Peter to land another blow powerful enough to rattle me. He proved me wrong. My jaw dropped open. It was only by immense self-discipline that he avoided a very close encounter with my fist.

"How can you even suggest such a thing? You have never been to the caves. I have! I grew up there, fought there, loved there and lost there. If you think anyone living around the caves would've ever assisted in prolonging the carnage, you are so out of your goddamn mind you're not even in the right county anymore!"

Spittle dotted Peter's face like a fine coat of rain. He calmly wiped it off. "Indeed. Why would anyone in the caves want to prolong the carnage? Unless they stood to benefit something from it, that is."

I was so furious I could barely speak. "Trust me, there's no one benefitting from anything around the caves. We live and die by the caves, fighting our way through every single day. There's no one around the caves profiting from it. The caves are nothing like the capital. If you'd ever set foot there, you would know that."

Peter listened to what I said. He contemplated each and every word. "So everyone, no matter their station or ranking, fights in the caves?"

A prickly sensation, graining at my nerves, intensified. There was a vague memory of Sam and John looking at me with something close to pity, but I couldn't hold on to it.

"Yes, everyone."

"Everyone, Jess?"

"Yes, everyone, except... Well, someone's got to be in charge. If that someone was to be changed as rapidly as people tend to die in the caves, there'd be chaos!"

Peter only continued to look at me. My hands ached to smother his knowing face into that smelly sofa of his. "But he fought his share before taking over as Commander. He fought longer and harder than anyone else. Whatever faults he has as a man, he deserves his post."

Peter didn't budge an inch. "I'm sure he did."

"And he's lost people he loved, just like everyone else. A wife and three daughters. There is no way in hell he would ever help anyone's twisted power play by filling up the caves with new monsters, no matter what he was promised." I didn't like the way my voice mimicked my body, twitching and jumping all over the place.

"Everyone has a price, Jess," Peter said, the kindness in his voice like a slap in the face.

"You don't know my father!" I shouted.

"Jess..." Kelly put a hand on my arm and I realized I was

towering over Peter.

I sat back down again. "You don't know my father."

"Maybe not. He's a good leader from what I've heard, but-"

"Have you ever heard him mentioned as an inside man in the caves?" I dug my nails into my palms.

Peter pursed his lips. "No, I haven't."

"Then you have no right to accuse him. None whatsoever." I fumbled around in my shirt pocket, searching for cigarettes.

Peter leaned forward. "Maybe not, but think about it, Jess. Someone has been filling up the caves with monsters, making sure you don't kill them all. How can anyone have done that without the aid of someone familiar with the caves? And if not your father, ask yourself this: how could someone on the inside sneak something like this below your father's radar? Do you think that's a possible scenario?"

No, I didn't think that a possible scenario. Nothing got past my father, and I mean nothing. But I'd rather be damned than to admit that to Peter. He might not see it that way, but it was just as unlikely that my father would've willingly ensured the continued fighting in the caves. I remembered his face when I told him I was leaving all too well.

Do you think any one of us wants to be here, Jess, any more than you do?

No, I didn't think so. I got up, slowly this time so not to alarm Kelly. "I don't know what a possible scenario is in this case, but I intend to find out. And you better make damn sure that you don't go spreading your thoughts about my father around."

Peter got up too. He was still shorter than me, though. "I'm not the only one thinking these thoughts."

Sam and John's faces popped up again. "Still, keep them to

Escaping The Caves

yourself until I get back. If you don't mind."

Peter shrugged. "Doesn't matter. I doubt anyone would listen if I told them."

I thought of Macy. "I think you'd find that some people are always willing to listen to idle gossip and speculation."

"I won't say a word." Peter crossed his heart, but the sarcastic smile never left his face. "If it turns out to be true, you'll never be able to protect him."

"I'll jump off that bridge if I have to." I put on my jacket.

Kelly gripped my arm, her green eyes huge, scared and confused. "Where are you going? You can't leave me! I need you here when the baby comes."

Gently, I pried her fingers off me, one by one. I squeezed them. "I have to warn my father and the others that the monsters have crossed the mountain range. They'll have to send troops out here to guard the mines until we're able to deal with them more permanently. You'll be sitting ducks if I don't."

"But you'll come back after that, right?" Tears stood in Kelly's eyes, threatening to overspill.

I swallowed. "After that I'll have to go to the capital. Someone is to blame for this mess, but more importantly, someone possesses a weapon powerful enough to take out the monsters once and for all. We'll never be safe if we don't. Even George Sampson won't be able to argue with that."

"But who's going to be there when I have the baby?" Kelly's wet cheeks glistened in the dim light. Her hands trembled in mine like a small bird.

"Rosie will be there when you have the baby." I hugged her close. "I'll be back as soon as I can."

"But I need you." Kelly refused to let me go. "You're the closest thing I've ever had to a sister. I need you now more than ever."

Her sobs almost broke what was left of my heart, but what choice did I have? If I didn't leave I'd condemn both her and her baby to a certain death, as well as everyone else in this town. That included John and Eve. And after them, there'd be other towns. It was a big world, after all.

"Kelly, I have to go. If I don't, we'll all die. I'm not trying to scare you, but I have to go. If I could stay, I would, for as long as you need me, but all our lives depend on me right now. Including your baby." I stroked her belly, something I'd never done before.

"I'll be back, as soon as I can. If you don't see me again, I'm dead. But I promise you that as long as I breathe, I'll find a way to come back again."

Kelly shoved my hands away and stepped back. "I know you have to go, I get that. I'm not that self-centered or stupid. But even if you come back after saving the world, you'll only come back so you can leave again. Even when you're not an outcast, you're always going to behave like one, aren't you? You'll never be happy to settle down in just one place. Not for long, anyway."

Her words hit me like a punch to the gut because they were true. I'd been chained to one place all my life, how could I resign myself to another stagnant existence? I wanted to travel. Needed to. My mom and youngest sister might still be out there. It was my secret hope that if I found them, I'd find my sanity again as well.

But I didn't say any of this to Kelly and Peter. I only pressed a kiss to Kelly's brow, and whispered, "Be brave." Then I left the house without looking back. No one stopped me.

Escaping The Caves

My own house was dark and quiet when I returned. Sam and Eve were safely shut away for the night. Light spilled through the gap underneath the door leading to the living room. John was still up.

He saw the look on my face and opened his arms. I slipped into his embrace. Closed my eyes and inhaled his clean, comforting scent. He rubbed my back, slow, soothing circles that sent ripples down my spine, despite our dire circumstances. I really wished I could afford to stay the night.

"There's a night train leaving at half past eleven. By the look on your face, I'm guessing you're going to be on it?" John asked, arms still around me.

"I have to warn the others. And you need trained soldiers to keep the monsters from leaving the mines until we know how to handle them on a more permanent basis." I rubbed my face against his shirt, memorizing the sound of his heartbeat, the heat of his skin through the fabric of his clothes.

"Will they believe you?" There was no malice in his voice, only concern, but the words chaffed my heart just the same.

I thought about it, but only for a moment. "Yes. Yes, they will. My father is many things, but a fool isn't one of them."

"You're not coming back here after that, are you?" He tried to hide it, but the hurt lurked just beneath the surface.

I sighed. "After I've dispatched a team of soldiers to come here and make sure you're safe, I've to go to the capital. Turns out Peter told the truth. There exists a weapon capable of destroying the monsters once and for all. And I, for one, intend to do just that."

John stopped rubbing my back. "What exactly did Peter tell

you?"

Mindful of the precious seconds slipping by, I told him the story as quickly as I could.

"Jess..." John straightened. "I know you don't want to hear this, but what if Peter was right? What if your father has been a part of this all along? How do you think he'll react when he finds out you're onto him?"

I was too tired and rattled by what I'd learnt to argue with John, especially when I would be long gone in less than two hours. "John, I'm going to tell you what I told Peter. There is no way that my father would ever have helped anyone bring more monsters into the caves. I don't care if he was offered the whole world and the moon in the bargain. There's a greater chance of him becoming an outcast first."

John studied my face. "All right. If you believe that, I do too. After all, he's your father. You know the man. I don't. But..."

"But what?" I took advantage of his pause and planted a lingering kiss on his lips.

He smiled distractedly. "But what about George Sampson? After all the lengths he's gone to in order to make sure the monsters keep coming and you keep fighting them, do you really think he's going to hand this weapon over to you? It'll be his downfall. He knows that."

I pushed the lock of hair out his eyes, the one that always kept falling into them. "I thought about that and in the end, yeah, I think he will. Not because he wants to, but because he's out of options. He made sure that weapon was created so that if the monsters got out of hand again, they could be eliminated. He might not care about all the lives wasted on keeping him in power, but he won't risk his own. Men like him never do."

"Maybe not, but men like him never give up on their power

just like that, either. Be careful, Jess. Promise me."

"I promise I'll be as careful as I can."

John smiled, shook his head. "Now, why doesn't that sound like the promise I want to hear?"

"I'll come back to you." I breathed against his lips after a long kiss, which, under different circumstances, definitely would've led to the shedding of clothes.

John sighed. "Don't make promises you don't intend to keep."

"I never do."

He looked at me, hard and long. "Okay. I'll believe you on that score as well. But when all of this is over... you're not planning on growing old here, are you?"

I swallowed the lump in my throat. This wasn't goodbye. Not yet. John was too good a man to let go of. I'd be nuts to walk away, but I might always be nuts if I stayed. "I don't know if I'm going to grow old at all, John. We'll deal with it when we get there, okay?"

He grabbed the back of my neck and pulled me toward him. It was a desperate kiss, almost violent, as if he hoped to mold me to him permanently. "I love you, Jess," he whispered. His voice was harsh, raw.

There was a painful clench where my heart should've been. "I love you too."

Nothing good would come out of me telling him that, but not doing it would be a lie. I did love him. His heart was bound to break, with mine in the bargain, but there had been something between us from the very first time we saw each other on that train, so long ago. I didn't know about love at first sight, but whatever it was, it was real.

"I'll come back to you." I repeated it like a spell. "I'll come

Kristin Talgø

back to you. I'll come back to you." Three times is the charm. Hopefully it would come true.

Chapter 15

I embarked the night train for my journey back to the caves at half past eleven on the dot. John stood at the platform, waving. I suspect he stood there for a long time after the train rounded the bend, watching.

I'll come back to you.

Don't make promises you don't intend to keep.

I glanced around my carriage, but there were only a handful of weary travelers occupying random rows. None of them looked my way. Even so, I slipped out a compact mirror given to me by Kelly several weeks ago. She'd thought I should make more of an effort with my appearance. I'd told her that if making an effort meant smearing my face with all kinds of goo, I could do without.

The scar, left by the wound I'd inflicted on myself, had healed nicely. A little too nicely. My old scars, my tribal ones betraying my past life in the caves, started to shine through. With time my rash and violent move would be washed away like so much rain washing away footprints in the sand.

Hopefully by then, it wouldn't matter. The monsters would be destroyed and the caves would become dark and empty once again. We'd all become outcasts, of sorts. I wondered if my father would be able to find his place in a world where there was no need for his knowledge and skills as Commander of the Caves.

I thought with time, patience and some useful occupation, he might. Kyle, aka the Machine, was a different matter altogether. He lived and breathed for his position as second-in-command. It wasn't just what he did, it was who he was. His whole identity was wrapped up in his role as the Machine. He'd be utterly lost without it. The thought gave me no pleasure.

The landscape drifted by, but with the darkness outside and the dim lighting in the carriage, it was all but impossible to get a proper look at the scenery. I snuggled into a sweater I'd borrowed from John. He'd worn it earlier in the day and his scent still lingered. I rested my head against the window and closed my eyes.

Three train changes later, and close to twenty-four hours after boarding, I finally stood outside my old community by the caves. After the cool and pleasant temperature in Havensfield, being back in the desert was like being trussed into an oven.

The tall, grey fences loomed over me. Two men stood guard by the gates and moved to greet me. I use the term 'greet me' very loosely in this context. They were both armed to the teeth. Their muscles bulged underneath sweat stained t-shirts. And they saw everything.

"Halt. What is your purpose here?" I didn't recognize the man speaking, his blonde hair and grey eyes unfamiliar. But the one next to him, the dark haired one with the bandanna, I recognized. And judging from the widening of his brown eyes, he most certainly recognized me.

He didn't cock his rifle, but tightened his grip on it. "You shouldn't have come back here, Jess. There's no place left for you here. You leave, you leave for good."

It'd been only one night, but I could still remember the silky feel of his hair. I'd been drunk, but not that drunk.

"I know that, Wes. But trust me, once you hear why I'm back here, you're gonna be awfully glad I did."

"Shit, you're the Commander's daughter. The one who left." The blonde man forgot he was supposed to be on guard and lowered his weapon. Neither Wes nor I paid him any attention.

"Don't take this personally, but I very much doubt there's anything you could tell us that would make up for you leaving in the first place." Wes' rifle was cocked and ready, but his finger rested well off the trigger.

"I need to speak to my father. It's urgent." I risked a step closer.

"You know I can't let you do that, Jess. You know the rules. Turn around now. I'm not happy about seeing you, but I'll be even less happy about shooting you."

"Would you really do that, Wes? Shoot me in cold blood? Just like that?" I stepped close until my chest bumped up against that tiny, deadly hole.

Wes' throat clicked as he swallowed. "Tell me why you're here then. One chance, Jess. No messing about. I won't like it, but I will shoot if I have to."

Would he? Probably not, but I kept my thoughts to myself.

Kristin Talgø

I'd really hoped to get in and tell Father first. This wasn't the kind of news I wanted spread around until Father had given the all-clear. But seeing the look in Wes' eyes, I revised my earlier assessment. I'd been gone from the caves for a long time. All those months ago, if I'd been him, I would've pulled the trigger too.

"I've been living in a small town, Havensfield, at the other end of the mountain range here. They made a mine and dug too deep. They blasted too far. The monsters have travelled from our end to the other." I didn't need to tell him help was required. Wes was a soldier in the caves. He knew what the monsters meant.

"I don't believe you," Wes said, but he'd gone chalk white underneath his tan.

"I don't need you to. I need you to take me to my father. He'll believe me." I rested my hand at the edge of his rifle, gently lowering it.

"Jess..." Wes warned, but I met no resistance.

"What if it's true? We can't take the chance of not taking her to the Commander." His blonde friend didn't bother to cover up the shaky edge of his voice.

Wes slung the rifle over a shoulder. His left eye twitched. A nervous giveaway which had ruined many a poker game for him. "All right. We'll take you to the Commander," he barred my entrance through the gate, "but if it turns out you've lied to me, I'll kill you myself."

I walked around him and spoke over my shoulder. "If it turns out I'm lying, I think you'll have to get in line."

Escaping The Caves

I walked through the community, but didn't see any familiar faces. It left me half grateful, half disappointed. Kyle was on every street corner, but it was all in my head. How would he react when he saw me? Would he believe me? It didn't matter one way or another, but his distrust would hurt. That much I knew.

This wasn't Havensfield. Most people kept their noses to themselves, but those who did glance our way saw nothing of interest and looked away.

Father's dusty office building looked the same as it had for as long as I remembered. Wes and his comrade in arms placed themselves on opposite sides of the door leading to the office.

"We'll wait." Wes didn't meet my eyes.

"If you think your presence is required here more than at the gate, then by all means, do as you please." I twisted the door knob. My heart had been rearranged and was now lodged in my throat. It beat so hard I could barely see.

"I do think so, yes." Wes raised his chin.

I didn't bother replying. Wes opened the door and shut it behind me. Just like the building it occupied, my father's office looked exactly the same. Father sat behind his desk, buried behind a mountain of files and papers. He didn't look up.

"The polite thing to do before barging into a man's personal office is to knock, or haven't you heard?" Father's lips twisted as he spoke. Otherwise his face remained locked in his usual frown.

"I'm sorry, I forgot myself. Do you want me to go back and knock again?" I kept my voice light, but it was pitched too high.

Father looked up so fast I was worried he'd throw his neck out. "Holy mother of God... Jess... What the... Is that really you?"

On legs that were suddenly made out of gelatin, I walked over to his desk. "Yeah, it is. I... I need to talk to you. I know this is a little out of the blue, and I'm probably breaking about fifty different rules being here, but I know something which you need to hear."

Father walked around his desk. He pulled a hand across his brow. I'd never once seen him shake like this. "Jess... I thought for sure you'd be dead by now. Or at the very least, thousands of miles from here. I never thought I'd see you again."

It might've been a trick of the light, but his eyes looked suddenly wet. He raised his hand. I steeled myself for the blow I thought would come. A blow I would've understood, but I nearly fainted when I felt his rough, callused hand cup my cheek.

"My darling Jess..." His voice broke and he pulled me into a hug.

If it hadn't been for my heart being uncomfortably locked in my throat, my jaw would've hung open. It took me a full ten seconds before I hesitantly put my arms around him. When was the last time he'd hugged me? I couldn't remember.

When he pulled back, his eyes looked once again dry and in control. He didn't let go of my hands. "Have you travelled for long? Are you thirsty? Come sit, no, take my chair, it's better. I kept telling your mother I didn't need an expensive chair like that, but she wouldn't hear of it. Damned glad now, of course, considering I'm all but chained to it these days. Sit, sit. I'll get you a glass of water. Or do you want lemonade? I've got both."

Father fumbled around for glasses, his hands still unsteady. I sat down, not sure what stunned me the most, that my father had hugged me, fussed around like an old aunt, or mentioned Mom.

Escaping The Caves

"Thank you." I accepted a glass of lemonade and drained it in one go.

"It's good, isn't it? I can't get enough of it in this heat. Damn near gave me a heat stroke the other day. Here, let me refill that for you." Dad poured from a pitcher Jen and I had painted for him way back in kindergarten.

I sipped more slowly this time, using the excuse to examine my father. His eyes were as steady and sure as ever, but his hair had gone completely grey since I left. There was a new and plentiful collection of crow's feet around his eyes. Worry lined his mouth and a frown marked his brow. I didn't know if it was due to me leaving or not, but whatever the case, he'd aged ten years in eight months.

"So…" Father had finally stopped fussing and sat down opposite me. His knees nearly touched mine. He tapped the rim of his glass and looked at me. "Can I ask you where you've been all this time? Or is that on a need to know basis and I don't fall into that category?"

"No, I'd say you definitely need to know. In fact, where I've been is what led me back here again." I took a large sip, but didn't drain the glass. Father would only get distracted by refilling it yet again.

"I guess I'm grateful for wherever it is you've been then, if it brought you back here." Father didn't look at me when he spoke, but his hands shook a little when he placed the glass on his desk.

I had no idea what had triggered this change in him, but I didn't much care. Right now he needed to remain his strong and steady self. Still, it was a relief to see that the stone mask he usually put on in the morning wasn't as impenetrable as I'd always thought. Hard to believe as it was, it seemed my father was only human after all.

"You might not be so grateful when you hear what I have to tell you. Or maybe you'll be even more so. Could go either way, I guess."

"You're not making any sense. Maybe you should start from the beginning." Father leaned forward, chin resting on knuckles. He looked at me, making small mental notes of everything I said and did. It was the way John looked at Eve.

My heart threatened to overspill into my throat again. I swallowed. "Sure. I'll take it from the very top then. From when I left here?"

My father only nodded and I began. I told him everything, leaving out nothing. My story started with the train, with Edith, the leering conductor, and meeting John and Eve for the first time. I told him about seeing Peter, Jane and Kelly, even if I was unaware of the significance they would play both in my life and in all of this. I told him about Ethan. About how he got me thrown off the train, then tracked me, tried to rape me and how I killed him.

How I found out about Jackson, never betraying how much it hurt to know my father had lied to me about that. Father had his reasons, just as I had mine for leaving. The story moved on to Bill, and recuperating at his house. How I'd been forced to move on from there as well. Forever the outcast, always on the move.

There was the trek through the desert. The attempt to destroy my tribal scars before entering Havensfield, tired beyond measure at the idea of being chased out of town once again.

I told him about my life there. The diner, about Sam and Eve, Marjorie and John. I didn't tell him that we'd taken up as a couple. But my father was good at reading between the lines and I gave him plenty go on.

And I told him about Kelly and her relationship with Ethan, and who Ethan's father was. This led me to Jane and Peter. I told him everything Peter had told me. And then I told him about the mines. About the monsters. About my suspicion of the supposed-earthquake that had triggered the rockslide in the caves, killing Jen and Trenton.

When I'd finished, I drained the rest of my lemonade. Father got me another, but there was no small talk or fumbling around this time. His movements were sure and business like.

"First thing's first. Do you think the monsters will have attacked Havensfield by the time we're able to dispatch a team?"

"Your guess is as good as mine. But no, I don't think so. The other monsters will only know that one was killed by a bullet. They won't know it was an outcast that killed him."

"Which means they don't know that we know." My father stroked his chin. "They'll probably bide their time for a little while longer. They'll know they've been discovered, but they might think the town will be so scared they'll flee, heedless of their responsibility of informing those in power."

"That would be my guess too," I said.

"But we're only guessing. These monsters are crafty and clever. We can't afford to take any chances. Excuse me for a moment." Father got up and opened his door. He beckoned Wes close. There was a hushed one-sided conversation with him, making sure the other guard was out of the loop. Once he'd finished, he clapped Wes on the back and closed the door.

"Lieutenant Wesley will gather two teams. Twenty in each. They'll leave in less than an hour. I've given him strict instructions not to attempt penetrating the caves, to only keep a close guard. No monster should be able to leave the mines, and those who do won't go far. They'll send back reports once they've scouted the area and know what's what."

"Good. At least they won't be unprotected for much longer." I straightened my shirt, then my hair, unable to look Father in the eye. "Anyone I know on those two teams?"

Father pretended not to see the flush in my cheeks. "Lieutenant Wesley will be leading team Alpha. Second Commander Kyle will lead team Bravo. I want those two teams to be well-equipped with the best men and women we have. We don't know how many monsters have travelled from our end to the other."

I cleared my throat. "Won't that leave the caves more vulnerable? I mean, we're going to need good and able leaders here as well."

"Indeed." Father found my gaze and held it. "But I think Kyle's presence is needed in Havensfield. Or, at the very least, not required here for the moment. He might cause more damage than good, however unintentional."

"You're keeping him from me." The accusation was out before I could stop it.

"He disowned you, Jess. The moment you left he wouldn't hear a word spoken of you. He didn't even consider himself a divorced man. In his eyes he'd never been married at all. Don't make the mistake of thinking that the time and distance between you have softened him up. On the contrary, I'd say he's become more of a machine than ever before."

"You don't know him…" Why did I defend him? I didn't love him anymore. In any case, I was pretty sure he'd never loved me. Maybe the truth hurt too much coming from Father.

"I know him better than you think. And far better than you,"

Escaping The Caves

Father said flatly. "Don't waste your time on any lingering sentimentality where he's concerned. You won't get any from him, that much I can tell you."

We sat there, facing each other, a silent stand-off between father and daughter. In the end, I was the one to capitulate. Father is many things, but not a man you should enter a staring contest with.

"All right. Let's leave the subject." For now, I thought, but didn't say.

"Let's." Father heard my thought loud and clear. "Now that we've dispatched two teams to Havensfield, we can cross that off our list. For the moment, the mines are covered. But it's only a matter of time before forty soldiers, however seasoned and well trained, won't be enough to hold the mines. Not even backup is going to be enough when it comes down to the real battle. There will be a war, and as long as guns and rifles are all that's standing between us and them, the monsters will win in the end."

"We need the weapon."

"We need the weapon," Father agreed. He smiled.

An especially cold, dark night in the desert, I could've sworn one of the coyotes sniffing about had smiled at me. A fierce, violent smile. It told me I could run, but could never hide. My father smiled like that right now.

"I think we should pay this George Sampson a visit, don't you?"

⸺

Father kept me in his office until the teams were well and truly off the perimeter. Considering what was at stake, he probably didn't want one of his daughters to cause a scene by having a public row with her faithless ex-husband. Kyle and I had been famous for our public rows, much to Father's disgust and my eternal shame.

When the hour was up, Father opened the door. The hallway outside his office was deserted. "I'll need to inform those who need informing. I want the rest of the community to continue as usual. Those caves remain guarded at all times, but I don't want anyone tracking any monsters until we get back. If there is a war to come, and if our journey to the capital turns out to be less fruitful than desired, we're going to need all the men and women we have. We can't afford to waste any lives until it's absolutely necessary."

I jogged to keep up with Father's long strides. "Who will you tell and how will you explain to the others that forty of our best fighters are missing?" What I really wanted to ask him was who he could trust.

"I'll tell only my most trusted what they need to know. The others... we'll tell them that Wes and Kyle have taken two separate teams out to make sure the monsters haven't slipped past our defenses. We used to do that back when my father was in charge."

People looked at me. Standing next to my father, there was no doubt about who I was.

"And what... what will you tell them about me?" I kept my eyes straight ahead. There was nothing I wanted to see in the eyes around me.

"The truth. I'll tell them that you've returned with vital information concerning the continued survival of our race. And in order to make use of that information, we have to travel to the capital. Anyone who has a problem with that can come and see me."

One look at the hard set of my father's jaw and the way muscles bulged through his shirt despite his age, I knew no one would. They would certainly have a problem with it, but just like their hurt and anger, they kept it to themselves. They had plenty of practice.

"But what about…" I lowered my voice. "What about the informer? I mean, someone here on the inside must've helped them out with the monsters. New ones got into the caves." My lips barely moved, but I felt as if the entire community could hear every word I spoke.

Clearly my father felt the same way. He held up a hand. "It's been taken care of." And that was all that was said on the subject.

My father worked smoothly and efficiently. Instructions were given and carried out without any questions. Unfailing loyalty had been drilled into each and every soldier from the first day in the cradle, and today it showed. If my father said I could be trusted, they trusted me. If my father considered my information worth pardoning my desertion, my offence was pardoned.

I had just enough time to say hello to Jo and Julia. Julia had given birth while I was gone. Another girl in the family. The baby was just as fiery of hair and temper as her mother. She bawled all through my short visit. My eardrums reverberated long after I'd left them, but Julia didn't bat an eyelash.

Jo almost burst into tears the moment I crossed the threshold. She got busy with a cup of tea to hide her emotions.

Kristin Talgø

Julia stared at me for a full minute. In the end, whatever showed in my face convinced her to forgive me.

She placed her crying child in the crib and pulled me into a rough hug. "You look better. Not quite right, not yet. But miles and miles better." Then she kissed me, quickly, but straight on the mouth.

I stood stock still while she picked up her girl, Susanna. Jo came and hugged me too, but I nearly forgot to hug her back. All through these months, the good, the bad and the wretched, I'd believed my family despised me. I'd always wanted their approval and never gotten it.

So when the rest of our community followed my father and me as we made our way to the gates, some pleased, some angry, some still hurt and confused, it didn't bother me what anyone might think.

I had the love and respect of those I loved and respected the most. It was all I needed. Julia was right. I wasn't quite right. Not yet. But I was getting closer.

Chapter 16

Apart from the startled glances, our journey to the capital was uneventful. If I'd travelled alone, I'm sure some idiot or another would've bothered me, but the look on my father's face discouraged anyone from approaching us. It annoys me that people continue to underestimate what women are capable of.

Ethan made that mistake. He wouldn't be making another.

Father's tribal scars stood out as clear as a pimple on otherwise-unblemished skin. If you looked closely at me, you could see my own marks peeping through the other scar. But even if our scars hadn't been on display for everyone to see, there was something about our movements, speech and looks that set people's alarm bells off. Something about our manner spoke of danger.

Besides, if we really were outcasts we behaved pretty strangely for people with warrants on them. Most outcasts kept well away from the public, keeping to themselves, trying to kick up as little fuss as possible. I would know.

Kristin Talgø

But my father and I travelled in broad daylight. We used the most direct route to the capital in order to avoid as many train changes as possible. This meant we travelled through the most populated areas by the most popular train routes. Not typical for someone on the run.

Despite taking the fastest route possible, it still took us a week before we reached our destination. We disembarked at the main station in the heart of the capital. It was a Thursday, around 2 P.M. A big display hung from the roof in the main entrance hall of the station.

The display flashed the day, date, year and outside temperature repeatedly in red letters. Underneath was a huge train schedule where you could find details about any train.

I craned my neck upward as Father and I made our way across the station. I couldn't believe how tall the ceiling was. The beams crisscrossed so high above it nearly took my breath away.

"Hey! Watch it!"

I bumped into a man with a briefcase, which connected painfully with my thigh. Before I had a chance to apologize, the man was gone in the crowd. I hurried to catch up with my father.

I'd thought the station had been packed with people, but stepping outside on the pavement made my jaw drop open.

There were people everywhere. It looked like at a human anthill. People in all shapes, sizes and colors swarmed around on the street, moving at a rapid, purposeful pace.

Even Father, usually composed and in control, was unsettled by the crowd. "Now what?" he said gruffly, covering up his unease.

"George Sampson. He's the one we want, right? And if he's

as powerful as Peter made him out to be, then people are bound to know about him. Maybe someone can direct us to him?"

I looked doubtfully at the people pressing around us. No one appeared especially helpful. Their eyes were all fixed on some point in the distance, their mouths turned downward.

Even in our community, with death lurking behind each new shift in the caves, there were smiles and laughter. We couldn't afford not to smile and laugh. You never knew when it was going to be your last.

"Well, I guess we better ask someone then." Father took a breath as if he was about to plunge into deep water. "Excuse me, sir? Ma'am, if I could just have a minute of your time? Miss?"

I would've thought that in a city with so many people, they were used to helping each other out, but no one so much as looked at my father. They all steered past him, a momentary obstacle in the regularity of their lives.

No one had noticed our scars, but looking at both my clothes and that of Father's, we looked less than pristine and just a few blocks down from disheveled. I glanced around at the street corners and saw other disheveled characters sitting there. They were huddled in filthy blankets with paper cups in front of them. Occasionally someone would toss a coin or two at them, but most just walked straight past. They didn't even seem to see them.

Father still struggled to get someone's attention. He became more and more flushed by every refusal.

"Dad?" I tugged at his shirt. "Look." I pointed at the beggars.

My father looked. His thin lips twisted. "Oh, that's nice. I've saved all of these lives by risking the lives of everyone I love and know every single day of my life, and these people treat us as if we're no better than a common beggar on the street! Even they deserve better than this."

Without waiting for my reply or consent, he walked over to one of the beggars, an older woman sitting on a wooden crate. Her grey hair made me think of a bird's nest.

My father spoke to her. He put a few coins into her trembling fingers. The woman looked at him and nodded. Father helped her off the makeshift chair and seated her on a blanket on the ground. He walked back to me and put the wooden crate down on the sidewalk.

"Dad?"

"If they won't listen to me voluntarily, I'll damn well make them." Father got up on the wooden crate. He cupped his hands around his mouth.

"People of the capital!" His voice rang out. It deafened the sound of the crowd, and almost silenced the roar of the constant traffic. "Heed my words and mark them well!"

People stopped in their tracks, but some continued onward. To them, he was just a crazy man on a crate. I had a feeling this wasn't the first time they'd seen one in this city.

My father didn't lose his stride, though. His voice didn't need any amplifiers to be heard. He had commanded troops of soldiers in the caves since eighteen. At the age of fifty-four, he had plenty of practice being heard.

"My name is John, Commander of the Caves." A ripple went through the crowd. More people halted in their tracks. "Don't make the mistake of thinking that I, or my daughter, are outcasts. We come to you still fulfilling our mission as soldiers in the caves and defenders of humanity."

I watched Father and prayed he wouldn't betray too much.

Escaping The Caves

But I should have known better than to worry. Father hadn't become Commander based on his battle skills alone. He had grace, charisma, and above all, a sense of when to hold back and when to push forward.

He paused long enough to make eye contact with some of the people surrounding us. More people stopped, curiosity getting the better of them.

"In order to continue fighting for our survival, we need to speak to a man called George Sampson."

A hush descended on the crowd. Even the cars and buses seemed to become muted. Father raked his gaze over them. He saw the apprehension on their upturned faces.

"You know him." This wasn't a question. "And you fear him." People shuffled their feet, but none moved away. "I still need to find him and I won't be able to do that unless one of you steps forward with the information I need."

The group gathered around him didn't speak, but one woman tried to inch her way out of the mess she'd gotten caught in. Father fixed on her in a heartbeat. "You there. Yes, you, the pretty brunette trying to detangle yourself from the crowd. Do you have children?"

The woman's eyes darted back and forth, but no one moved to let her pass. Reluctantly, she shook her head. Father nodded, unperturbed. "A father then? A mother? Brothers or sisters? Friends and colleagues you cherish? You must have someone, surely."

The woman shrugged. Her voice was surprisingly strong and steady. Defiant. "Doesn't everyone?"

Better women than her had cowered in front of Father when he was on the warpath. Despite the insolent look in her eyes, I couldn't help but admire her.

"Not everyone." He indicated the beggars on the street. "You're one of the lucky ones. But that's an injustice for another day. For the moment, we have more pressing matters to attend to. Matters which concern all of you, and everyone you know and care about."

"Why should we believe some grey-haired old man with three scars on his cheek?" a gangly man spoke up. "For all we know, you're just another lunatic in a city of many, pretending to be a soldier in the caves. You could've made those marks yourself," the man added sullenly.

Father's silent reproach and angry eyes shot his argument down. His peevish voice trailed off. His silence left a void that no one offered to fill.

"Take a good long, hard look at my daughter and I, and you'll know I'm telling you the truth. Our scars could've been faked, but we're not. We're true warriors of the caves and are asking for your help." He didn't let anyone break eye contact. One by one, they were forced to meet his gaze.

"I need George Sampson's whereabouts. Now, who's going to prove themselves brave enough to answer me?"

Silence. Then a boy, fourteen, fifteen at the most, raised his eyes. "He'll be in his office. Most likely." He chewed his bottom lip.

"How do I get there?" My father's voice brokered no argument. Still, he looked at the boy with a kindness and respect which was bestowed on only a few.

"I... I can take you there." The boy's freckled cheeks flushed. "If you'd like."

"Step forward, son, and tell me who I've the honor of meeting." My father stepped down from the crate and handed it back to the old woman with his thanks.

Escaping The Caves

When he came back, the red-haired boy had managed to break through the dispersing crowd. Some hastily moved away, others shot my father filthy glances.

"I'm Patrick." The boy hesitantly held out his hand to my father.

He wasn't disappointed. My father shook it, looking him straight in the eye. "Well, Patrick, pleased to make your acquaintance. Now, if you would be so kind? We're on a tight schedule and it's getting tighter still."

Patrick didn't waste a second. He led the way.

In the taxi, I had to concentrate on not letting my mouth drop open at every turn we took. This city was huge, but what was more, the buildings... I'd never seen buildings this tall. They stretched all the way up into the steel grey sky above.

Sure, there'd been buildings like this in some of the films I'd seen with John and Kelly, but I'd chalked it down to some artistic exaggeration. But this was no film. This was real life, as real as it got. For the first time ever, I allowed myself to believe that Peter's story about the weapon might be real.

If there existed people capable of creating buildings as tall as these, made of glass no less, and keep them from toppling over, then they might be able to create a weapon powerful enough to destroy the monsters.

I looked at Father, but he'd once again adopted his mask of stony silence. His face revealed nothing. But even he wasn't capable of preventing the widening of his eyes. Nothing in his life, no matter how extraordinary it'd been, had prepared him for a city like this. It was equally beautiful and terrible.

Patrick couldn't keep his eyes off us, though he tried his best. He glanced repeatedly at our scars, those three marks of courage, honor and integrity. In his excitement he forgot he was afraid of us.

"Sir?"

My father turned to him.

"What's it like in the caves? They've made dozens of films about them, but no one has ever actually spoken to a real warrior. At least, not that I've ever heard of." Patrick's color rose.

Father frowned. "Film? What's that?"

Now it was Patrick's turn to look surprised. "You don't have that around the caves?"

"Obviously not," Father commented drily.

"Sorry." Patrick turned almost beetroot red. "It's, ehm, it's like moving pictures, ehm–"

My father waved away his explanation, but smiled when he spoke. "Doesn't matter. Don't trouble yourself. I shouldn't have answered a question with a question in any case. What's it like in the caves? Well, Patrick, let's hope we find this George Sampson, otherwise you might just find out."

My father turned back to the window. When the kid looked at him, I only shook my head.

"Don't ask. It would take far too long to explain, and besides, you don't want to know. Not really. None of you do." I thought of all the people who hadn't stopped to listen to Father.

Patrick was about to say something else when the taxi stopped. We got out and Patrick helped my father give the driver the right amount of money. While they settled the bill, I craned my neck. George Sampson's office building was by far the tallest I'd seen, and that was saying something. All the way at the top, I could just make out two gigantic, gold embossed letters. GS. Whatever Sampson's other flaws might be, low self-esteem wasn't one of them.

Father took one look at the building from bottom to top, but didn't say anything. Patrick stood there hovering behind us.

Father shook his hand once more. "Thank you. You can be proud of yourself. You spoke up when no one else did. That took courage."

Patrick flushed so hard I worried he might have a stroke. "Tha-thank- thank you, sir. I'm glad I could help. I hope you find what you're looking for."

"So do we." Father gestured for me to follow him.

"Goodbye, Patrick. And again, thank you." I smiled before walking after Father.

I never saw him again. I hope life's been good to him.

Entering the foyer, both Father and I stopped in our tracks. Apart from being huge, it was so squeaky clean and bright, my father and I resembled a couple of dust bunnies in comparison. A large fountain dominated the center of the foyer. At the end, there was a long desk with four people behind it. All of them spoke into an earpiece of some sort. When one of them turned his head, it looked as if he was speaking to himself.

Other people milled about, all of them tall and good-looking. They all wore tight-fitted clothes, all looked equally busy, poised and arrogant, not a hair out of place. They would've passed any inspection by Jane with flying colors. It even looked like some of the men wore make-up. My father's lips turned down as he noticed this.

Kristin Talgø

Conversation halted as we made our way across the polished marble floor, and then stopped all together. It was as if someone gradually turned down the volume. In the descending silence, our footsteps echoed across the foyer.

The people behind the long desk didn't notice anything amiss at first. They were too absorbed in the conversations that took place in their heads to hear the silence. It was only when Father and I leaned over the desk, our dirty elbows smearing the glass surface, that the man in front of us looked up.

His amber eyes turned to amber saucers. They moved from our dusty heads to our dusty jackets, only to settle on the marks on our cheeks. His Adam's apple bobbed up and down. Twice.

"Excuse me, sir, but I don't think you should be here."

My father flashed his teeth and the man recoiled. "Is this the office building of George Sampson?"

"Yes, but-"

"Then I'm exactly where I should be. And so is my daughter."

I offered a smile of my own. The man tried to sink into the upholstery of his chair. His co-workers, another man and two women, watched the scene with avid interest. It was only when my father tuned his attention on them that they suddenly found the screens in front of them interesting again.

Father turned back to the cringing man in front of him. His lips looked as if they'd been stung by a bee. Father glanced from the swollen lips to the eyes surrounded by a thick, black line, but kept his opinions to himself.

"Would you be so kind as to let Mr. Sampson know he's got visitors?"

The man licked his abused-looking lips. I'd seen skeletons with more meat on them than him. Dressed all in black as he was, he looked like the Grim Reaper come to life. "Mr. Sampson doesn't allow unexpected visitors, but if you leave your number–"

"Do I look like a walking telephone to you?" Father leaned further across the desk and the man cowered into his chair. "You tell your boss that John, First Commander of the Caves, and his daughter, Lieutenant Jess, are here to see him. Now."

The man shot pleading glances at his co-workers, but they pretended to have been swallowed by the screens in front of them. He cursed under his breath and pushed a few buttons on the phone next to him.

"Yes, umm, Mr. Sampson, sir? Yes, this is Juan from reception. There is a man and woman here to see you. Yes, I know you were about to go. Yes, I know you always do so on Thursday afternoons, sir, but - Yes, of course I value my job.... No, sir.... Yes, sir. All right, sir. Goodbye, Si -"

Shakily, Juan put down the phone. "Mr. Sampson is otherwise engaged. Please, leave your number and he will contact you as soon as he–"

Juan's voice became strangled as Father grabbed hold of his turtleneck. He pulled him across the desk and didn't stop until they almost bumped noses. "Call him again."

"But–"

"Call. Him. Again."

Juan's lips worked. "I'll get fired for this."

"Tell you what. If you don't do as I say, getting fired will be the least of your problems. Understand? And if you think I'm unpleasant, then you haven't been properly introduced to my daughter."

Juan's panicked eyes looked at me. I lit a cigarette, taking pleasure in ignoring the no smoking sign. I met his eyes, flicked the lighter off and on, and blew smoke rings in his direction.

"She's killed and maimed more monsters than most people I know of, myself included. What do you think she'd do to a small guy such as yourself? Hmmm? Be smart, Juan. Call the man." Father released him. Juan tottered on his feet, before he fell onto the chair.

Juan pushed the same buttons again. His fingers missed the correct sequence on the first try. "Give it to me." Father indicated Juan's earpiece. Juan was all too happy about handing it over.

After a bit of fumbling, he got it right. My father winced. Apparently George Sampson had been kept waiting on the line. "Mr. Sampson? We haven't met, but I'm sure you've heard of me. I'm John, First Commander of the Caves. No, I'm not joking. I'm dead serious. And unless you let us talk to you, dead is what you're going to be. No. No threat. Just the truth.

"I'm going to stop you right there, Mr. Sampson, because you're pissing me off. And trust me when I say you won't like me when I'm pissed off. Remember your friend Peter? Peter Hamilton? Ring any bells? I believe your son Ethan had some close encounters, shall we say, with Peter's daughter Kelly."

My father's lips grew so thin and his jaw so tight, they looked ready to break. "Mr. Sampson. Unless you want me to force myself into your office - and it won't be a challenge, only a nuisance on my part - I suggest you shut your mouth and let my daughter and me through. We've got some very serious business to discuss. About a certain weapon that's in your possession. And about certain monsters you've left free to wander."

Father plucked out the earpiece and handed it to Juan. "He wants to talk to you."

Juan paled, but did as he was told. "Yes, sir? Yes, sir. Right away, sir." He pushed a button and the elevator at the end of the foyer opened up. "Please. Get out. Get in. Get up. I don't care, just get away from me." Juan didn't meet my father's eyes.

"Happy to oblige." My father rapped his knuckles on the desk. All four of the people jumped in their chairs.

Father smiled. "Come along, Jess. Let's not keep Mr. Bigshot waiting."

Music played inside the elevator. The lush red carpet on the floor wasn't as lush and red when we stepped out of it. The soles of our boots were cleaner, though.

We walked down the hall, just as clean and bright as the foyer below. At the end there sat an astoundingly pretty woman, around my age or a little younger, behind a desk similar to the one downstairs.

She looked up as we approached. Her blonde curls bounced as she moved her head. Unlike Juan and the others, she didn't look remotely scared or uncomfortable. On the contrary, she stared at my father in a way that made me acutely embarrassed.

"First Commander John, I presume?" She batted her eyelashes.

"Yes, ma'am."

The blonde's glossy smile faltered for a moment, then shone bright once again. "This way, sir. Mr. Sampson is waiting for you and... I'm sorry, what is your name again?" Her blue eyes barely deigned to look at me.

"Jess. I'm his daughter." I lit another cigarette.

"I'm sorry, but you really can't smoke that in here."

The blonde pointed at another no smoking sign.

Kristin Talgø

"That's enough, Melissa. Let them through, for God's sake." A deep, grumpy voice drifted out through the open door behind us.

Melissa sat her tiny bottom back down on her chair. She tried another round of batting eyelashes at my father. "If there's anything I can do, please don't hesitate to ask."

"For God's sake, Melissa, this isn't some action hero out of those braindead films you watch. Stop your chattering and let the man through." George Sampson hadn't raised his voice, but Melissa immediately shut up. She averted her eyes, all the color lost from her cheeks.

My father walked past her and said without stopping, "Thank you for your kind offer, Melissa. I'll be sure to let your boss know how helpful you were."

Melissa closed her eyes. I didn't feel as merciful as Father, and put out my cigarette in her empty water glass. Father and I looked at each other once and nodded.

And so we entered the lion's den.

Chapter 17

George Sampson sat behind a desk so huge it made those belonging to his employees look like they were intended for children. He rifled through a set of files, as though he hadn't just shouted for us to get in. Father and I walked over until we could lay our palms down on his desk if we wished.

Ethan's father took another few seconds to look over the papers before putting them back into their file. He cleared his throat and stapled long fingers. Only then did he raise his eyes to meet ours.

"First Commander John." He emphasized the title, making it sound as if Father had made it up. "You were pretty adamant on seeing me. I know things work a bit differently way out by the caves, but around these parts, we appreciate it if people make appointments before showing up. Also, we tend to frown upon people harassing our employees."

Father smiled. George Sampson didn't bat an eye. "I'll keep that in mind." Father matched Mr. Sampson's condescending tone. "But given the circumstances, I'm sure you can be a bit lenient where social niceties are concerned."

Mr. Sampson leaned back. There wasn't a wrinkle in sight on his crisp, white shirt. "Oh, yes? And what circumstances would that be?"

"May I?" Father indicated the two chairs in front of the desk.

"If you must." Mr. Sampson brushed a non-existing speck of dust off his jacket.

Father didn't respond, but gestured for me to sit down too. "I'll cut straight to the chase then, shall I?"

Mr. Sampson only raised his eyebrows.

"The monsters in the caves, many of which you've added over the years, have travelled from one end of the mountain to the other." My father kept his voice level, but his eyes could've cut through steel.

Mr. Sampson didn't respond for a long time. The clock that stood in the right corner of the office counted the seconds. When Father didn't elaborate, he held out his hands. "I'm sorry, which part of that short statement relates to me? If I've understood you correctly, you accuse me of supplying the caves with new monsters. Is that correct?"

Father gripped the armrest of his chair. "It is."

"I see. And so you hold me responsible for the monsters expanding their territory, is that it?"

"Yes." Father spoke through gritted teeth.

Mr. Sampson didn't make the mistake of smiling. I don't think his teeth would've remained so neat and intact if he had, but he did allow the corners to twitch.

"John, may I call you John? No? All right. First Commander John, I don't know who's been feeding you stories, but I can tell you this. They are not true. Do you understand? I have never supplied the caves with monsters. And if said monsters have travelled from one end to the other, that is unfortunate, to say the least, but I'm sure you and your soldiers will be able to deal with the situation in a way you see fit."

Father folded his hands on his lap and didn't say a word. Mr. Sampson breathed deeply. He locked his grey eyes on me. They matched the color of the sky outside.

"Miss, you understand, don't you? Clearly someone has played a cruel trick on you. I'm sorry for that, but I have important business to attend to. If there's nothing else, then I would be much obliged if you and your father would leave. Thank you."

He bent down to the files again. Neither my father nor I moved.

After two minutes of failing miserably at ignoring us out of the office, Mr. Sampson lost some of his cool.

He slammed the papers down on the desk and burst out, "For God's sake, will the two of you inbred outcasts get the hell out of my office! I give you exactly thirty seconds to get out. If those chairs aren't blessedly empty by then, I will call security. Is that clear?"

Father smoothed a crease in his pants. "Mr. Sampson, we kill monsters for a living. And seeing as you supervised the renewed creation of them, you know very well what they're capable of. That, in turn, should give you some clue as to what my daughter and I are capable of."

Mr. Sampson narrowed his eyes. "Is that a threat?"

"Merely a helpful tip. To call security would be a bad idea. They would all end up in the hospital and that would, I'm sure, create quite a bit of unwanted attention, am I right?" Father paused. "And after everything that happened with your son

Ethan, I'm sure you could do without another scandal involving employees of yours being hurt in your office."

Color surged to Mr. Sampson's face. He still held on to some of the papers. When he noticed that they shook, he put them down. "You know nothing of my son."

Father pursed his lips. "I know enough. But my daughter, Jess, she knows a great deal. First hand, too."

Just as fast as the color had risen in his cheeks, it left him. "You're lying."

"I might be many things, Mr. Sampson, but a liar isn't one of them."

Mr. Sampson looked like he'd bitten down on a lemon. "So, Jess, is that it? You know my son, do you? How did that come about?"

"No."

"No? Excuse me, but your father just assured me he isn't a liar, so either you're lying, or he is. In any case, I'm getting tired of these games."

"I don't know your son. I knew him. He's dead."

Mr. Sampson didn't move a muscle. "And you know this how?"

"I killed him."

The clock, the distant drone of traffic and the harsh breathing of Mr. Sampson were the only sounds in the office. "You do realize I could have you shot and killed for murder, right?"

I lit another cigarette and kicked off my boots. I curled my feet up under me. Mr. Sampson looked like he wanted to scream and throttle me, not necessarily in that order. "You could. But there would be a trial, wouldn't there? And seeing how your deceased son was a rapist and serial killer, I don't think anyone would blame me for killing him before he could kill me."

"Liars. You're all liars." Mr. Sampson's jowls quivered.

"Mr. Sampson, you were the first on the crime scene after your son raped and murdered your secretary, Amanda, here in your office, as a punishment for your lack of fatherly affection, I believe. You covered that up, but trust me, if my father and I decide to blow the whistle on all the other shit you've covered up… Let's just say, there's not enough dirt in the entire world to cover it up." I inhaled, satisfied by the beads of sweat that gathered on Mr. Sampson's brow.

My father pretended to inspect his nails. He hummed an old tune under his breath. Mr. Sampson pulled out a perfectly-folded handkerchief and patted his face with it. "I repeat, how did you come to know my son?"

I flicked some ash onto the carpet. "I met him on a train. Or rather, he saw me, recognized me for who I was and got me thrown off. He then guessed which town I'd reach first. He ambushed me after I'd fallen asleep."

Mr. Sampson twisted his unnaturally full lips. "I doubt a seasoned soldier such as you could've been ambushed by the flagpole of my son, asleep or not."

"Under normal circumstances he wouldn't have, but those weren't normal circumstances. I'd left my community by the caves and my life as a soldier there for reasons which are my own. Suffice to say that I was very tired at the time. Ethan took advantage of that. I wasn't the first outcast he'd come across."

"How do you mean?" Mr. Sampson kept clicking a pen.

"I mean that your son, while he took pleasure in causing you trouble, was smart enough to realize that he couldn't kill indiscriminatingly. The police would investigate, and eventually he would get caught. But outcasts, there's a warrant on us all year around. We won't be missed. If anyone caught him, he could say he only did his duty, ridding the world of a dangerous traitor."

I stubbed out my cigarette on Mr. Sampson's desk. My temples pounded. Every time I thought of Ethan, I thought of Jackson. And what Ethan had done to him. I cracked my knuckles.

Mr. Sampson winced. "You're saying my son was a pathological killer who preyed on outcasts and that's how you knew him?"

"More or less. I've heard plenty of stories about him, and you, from Kelly. Remember her? Kelly Hamilton? The fifteen-year-old your son knocked up?" The pounding in my head was worse.

This time Mr. Sampson did make a mistake. He snorted and made that disgusting flicking motion with his wrist.

"Jess..." Father grabbed my wrist. He forced me to sit down again.

Mr. Sampson shot me a cold smile. "That little whore? If she put out where my son could put in, then she had it coming. I've got nothing else to say on that matter."

"That's fine. Because I've got plenty. Your son was following Kelly and her parents when he got distracted by me. He knew she was pregnant. As I'm sure you did too. It must've been pretty convenient that they got out of the city when they did."

"It was." Mr. Sampson had once again stapled his fingers.

"When Kelly heard that Amanda had been killed, she couldn't get out of the city fast enough. She's giving birth to your grandchild any day now, might already have done so. Don't you care about that in the slightest?"

He didn't miss a beat. "No. All that little bitch did was cause trouble. Just like her parents." Mr. Sampson nearly spit out the words.

My father got suddenly interested in the conversation again. "Her parents? Peter and Jane. How could someone like them cause trouble for someone like you?"

"Don't patronize me, John. You know what they knew and you know it's not the kind of thing a man like me wants people to know." The truth about his son seemed to have made him forget his mask of ignorance on the subject of the monsters.

"Peter…" Mr. Sampson shook his head. "His wife and him, they got above their station in life. None of them belonged in the social circles they attached themselves too. New money. There wasn't that much money to go around. But Jane was determined to hold on to their new social status, even if it bankrupted her husband."

Mr. Sampson turned his cold eyes on me. "Even if my son hadn't knocked up their daughter, it was only a question of time before they had to get out of the city in any case. That's the only reason why I tolerated them. Peter listened in on conversations he had no right to be around. Besides, I figured that even if he should be so foolish as to share things he'd do best to forget, who'd believe him? There's no evidence to back it up."

"I'm afraid that's not true," I said, "there's two pieces of evidence sitting right here."

"Yeah." Mr. Sampson bared his teeth. "And who do you think the public will believe? Two outcasts, or George Sampson, the benefactor of not just this city, but all the others on the east coast?"

My father sat up straighter. "I'm not an outcast."

"Weeell, that depends how you look at it, doesn't it? You

Kristin Talgø

might claim you've only left temporarily to sort out this unfortunate business, but if I were to claim that in fact you've left your post as First Commander of the caves with the sole purpose of creating havoc and disturbances in the cities? I repeat, who do you think people would believe?"

Mr. Sampson leaned back in his chair.

"They'd probably believe you," Father coincided. "At first. But when the monsters cross the border of your precious capital, they might rethink their trust in you."

The smile slid off Mr. Sampson's face. I could almost hear it drop on the floor, along with his leverage. "You will contain them. You've got no choice. As much as you despise me, you'd never permit the slaughter of innocents in order to get to me. Just like Peter and Jane, you forget your station, John. I don't just control the cities, I control you. And your daughter. I control everyone and everything. Anyone who's foolish enough to question my authority will soon learn just how much of a bastard I can be."

My father didn't bother to match Mr. Sampson's tone. Nor did he lean forward in his chair like his opponent. "And you, George, will soon learn how much of a bastard I can be, if you're foolish enough to persist in this. The monsters have crossed the mountain range from the caves to the mines on the other side, just outside of a small town called Havensfield. My daughter killed one, but there are plenty more where that one came from.

"You're saying my soldiers and I will contain it. I'm saying we cannot contain it. Thanks to you and your continuous supplies, there's too many of them. The time to settle your bill as arrived, George. You've got the weapons to destroy the monsters. You give me the means to activate it, or the monsters will not just destroy your cities, they will destroy *you*."

Mr. Sampson's whole face twitched. He smoothed down his thinning grey hair with one liver-spotted hand. "And why should I take your word for it? You hate me. I've got no reason to trust you."

My father smiled. "If you don't, you're welcome to take a walk around both the caves and the mines, and have a look for yourself. Perhaps the monsters will recognize you and spare you. Do you think that's likely, George? I don't, but then again, what do I know? I'm just an inbred outcast from the outback, aren't I?"

Mr. Sampson crumpled up the paper he'd been holding. "So, what you suggest is that I release the weapon to you, and you destroy the monsters once and for all? Have I got that right?"

"Yes."

"All right."

"All right?" My father sounded as disbelieving as I felt. "Just like that? You'll give up your weapon to us? No more arguments?"

Mr. Sampson spread his hands. "No more arguments. I know when I'm beaten, but just because I've lost this battle, doesn't mean I'll lose the war."

I dug my nails into the palm of my hands, but in the end, I couldn't help myself. "What do you mean by that?"

Mr. Sampson turned to me, again with the stapled fingers. Man, I never wanted to punch a man so badly in my life. And that included Kyle. "Jess, you and your father seem to be laboring under the illusion that once the monsters are no more, my power, and the control I have over these cities and the people in them, will crumple and die just like them."

"It will." My father spoke with a surety I envied. "Once the monsters aren't a constant threat anymore, people will start to question your authority. They won't stand for the injustice of a few exploiting all the resources while the many struggle to make ends meet."

"Won't they? John, no one is starving."

Father snorted. "Tell that to the beggars in the streets."

Mr. Sampson flicked his wrist. "Please. No one, least of all the majority of the public, cares about them. There has always been and always will be someone at the bottom of the food chain. Just as there has always been and always will be someone at the top. I'm at the top, John. And I'm not backing down."

My father kept his voice level. "You might not have a choice. When push comes to shove, the majority of the public might care more than you think. And they might just topple you over."

Mr. Sampson shrugged. "Let them try. You'll have your way, you and your daughter. I'll give you the weapon and you can destroy the monsters. Then what? Have you asked yourself this? None of you will be a soldier anymore. Where does that leave you? Sure, you can build yourself a nice little cottage in the countryside, plant roses, pick your nose.

"Your daughter has the hips of a breeder, maybe she can squeeze out a few grandchildren for you. But at the end of the day, do any of you think that will be enough? Right now you're vital to the survival of mankind, but once that's taken care of… You won't have a higher purpose anymore. You'll be nothing. Just like everyone else."

My father got up. I was all too grateful to do the same. To breathe the same air as this man made me feel polluted. "We'll take our chances."

Mr. Sampson remained seated. "How noble of you. One last thing though. Once the threat has been eliminated, you do

Escaping The Caves

realize there will be civil unrest? I will not back down from my position. Those who oppose me will suffer the consequences. One way or another, monsters or not, innocents will die. Are you prepared to live with that?"

"I'll take my chances," Father repeated. "If I don't, millions will die by the claws of the monsters. You're just a man, George. Even if you think otherwise."

With that, my father turned on his heel and left the office. I wanted to go after him, but there was the handover of the weapon to deal with. Mr. Sampson followed my train of thought, and said, "I'll arrange for the weapon to be delivered to you. Would you prefer it to be shipped to the caves or the mines? Or maybe both? There are two of them. I can have one arrive at each destination."

"How do I know I can trust you?"

Mr. Sampson laughed. "I can't be a hundred percent sure that you and your father didn't exaggerate the danger, and you can't be a hundred percent sure that I don't exaggerate my willingness to cooperate. Like your father said, you'll have to take your chances."

I nodded and turned to leave, but something prompted me to turn back. Mr. Sampson still looked at me. Still smiled as if he knew exactly what I wanted to ask him. "Yes, Jess?"

"The insider. The one who's been helping you and your accomplices to ship in the monsters? Who is it?" I said it fast and quick to hide the tremble in my voice.

Mr. Sampson's smile broadened. "Oh, I think you already know that."

The shaking started from the top of my head, working down to the soles of my feet. I left before I could ask any more questions I didn't want to know the answer to. Mr. Sampson's

Kristin Talgø

smile stayed with me the whole time.

My father waited for me outside the building. He sat on the curb and smoked. People pushed past us. No one paid us the least bit of attention. Just the way I liked it.

"Did he give you the details?" My father narrowed his eyes.

"Yes. There are two weapons. He'll have one shipped to the caves, the other to the mines." I tried to light a cigarette of my own.

Father lit it for me. "What did he say to you, Jess?"

I inhaled and avoided his cool blue eyes. "I asked him who the informer was. He said I already knew."

Father nodded. "We don't know for sure."

I laughed, but it was more a bark bordering on a sob. "Maybe not, but you suspected him enough to send him away from the caves."

My father sighed. He rubbed his cheek stubble. "I know no more about this than you do, Jess. I sent him to the mines because it would make it all but impossible for him to slip away without raising the alert. He's stuck now. Whether he's innocent in this or not, he'll have to wait for us to catch up with him and find out. And I will get to the truth. Whether it was him or someone else, I will get my hands on that insider."

I threw my half-smoked cigarette away. It only worsened my nausea. "I still don't understand how they were able to do it in the first place. Smuggle the monsters in there without one of us noticing."

Father held out his hand. He pulled me up. "Neither do I. But once the monsters have been destroyed, I'm not sure it matters anymore. What matters is that the monsters are wiped out and the insider is held accountable for his actions."

"What will you do to him?" My sunglasses went on despite the overcast sky. I needed some shelter from the violence in my father.

Father watched me put the shades on. "Don't ask questions you already know the answer too. Come on, we have a train to catch."

Chapter 18

We spent most of the time on the first train arguing about which one of us should travel to the caves and who should go to the mines. Though my father never said it in so many words, it was clear that he didn't want me to go to Havensfield as long as Kyle was there. I had no desire to see Kyle, but I wanted to see John and Eve again. There was a knot in my stomach that wouldn't relax until my own eyes had confirmed they were safe and sound. To ship me back to the caves would be tantamount to sending me into exile.

Father only grumbled at this. He didn't want to come straight out and state his reasons for why he didn't want me to go back to the mines, and his argument fell short. He could've overruled me, both as my father and superior, but he knew it was pointless. I'd always called my own shots, and neither he nor anyone else had ever been able to tell me what to do. I was able to adhere to other people's wishes if they were better founded than my own.

Kristin Talgø

In this case there wasn't any reason for me not to go back to the mines, other than that my father didn't want me to.

I wasn't quite able to figure out if he didn't trust me around Kyle, Kyle around me, or some combination of the two. But my father knew when to pick his battles. It became obvious less than two hours out of the capital that this wasn't a battle worth fighting. At least, not if he wanted to win.

"Fine." Father turned to the window, his jaw set in that tight line I knew so well. "You go back to Havensfield and ensure Sampson makes good on his promise. I'll do the same with the caves."

I nodded, but then realized he couldn't see it. "All right." I waited a few minutes to see if Father would ease up a little. His jaw remained tightly locked. "What will happen afterwards? If all goes well?"

Father didn't answer right away and I thought he'd decided to freeze me out for the rest of the train ride.

"Honestly, I don't know. We'll have to organize a new community. A new town, I suppose, for those who wish to stay. We'll have to find new trades for people, new occupations…"

He drifted off for a moment, searching the moving horizon. Rain had begun to splatter the windows, distorting the view. "Anyone who wishes to leave, to create a new life for themselves and their families elsewhere are, of course, free to do so." He wrinkled his nose. "I wouldn't recommend the capital, though."

I leaned my head against the back of the seat. "Sampson isn't going to let go of his power so easily."

Father snorted. "I think they're going to have to wrestle it from his cold, dead fingers."

We sat in silence for a while. The train moved through the

country. "Do you think there'll be civil war?"

Father opened his eyes. He'd been dozing. "No, not a full-blown civil war. I certainly hope not. But civil unrest… oh, yes. And plenty of it. Riots. Chaos. Casualties. Propaganda. Imprisonment. Torture. No, Sampson and his followers won't give up easily."

People would die. But people were already dying, had died in the most brutal ways for decades, thanks to Sampson and his likes.

My father looked at me closely. "We're doing the right thing, Jess. If the years ahead get rough and you ever doubt that, remember their faces and you'll know it was the right thing to do."

I didn't have to ask him whose faces he meant. They were still with me, every second of every minute of every day. But they didn't terrify me the way they used to. Jen, Trenton, friend upon friend upon countless friend. Jackson, my mom and Jenna, even if they weren't dead. I really hoped they weren't.

"What?"

I stopped chewing my lip. It always gave me away. "I just wondered…"

"Yes?"

It was like sticking my hand into a nest of wasps. And this was the closest Father and I had ever been. "Do you ever think about them?"

I didn't need to specify who I meant. Father locked down immediately. When five minutes had passed and he still hadn't turned to look at me, I closed my eyes. At least he hadn't started shouting.

"Every day."

I opened my eyes.

"I think about them every day." Father took off his jacket. He twisted it in his hands, the fabric torn at the worn seams. "Jenna was only three years old when Amy took her and left. If I saw her today, I'm not sure I would recognize her. My own daughter."

"I thought about that too. If I'd recognize them if I ever saw them again. Jenna would be… how old now?"

"Twenty-three, second Tuesday next month," Father responded promptly.

I didn't dare to look at him. I fiddled with my half-empty packet of cigarettes. There was a huge no-smoking sign at the front of the carriage. "Did Mom… did she ever talk about leaving?"

Father sighed. "All the time after she found out she was pregnant with Jenna. I never took her seriously. I was First Commander. I couldn't leave. Even if I'd taken her seriously and packed up our life, where would we've gone? We'd be outcasts. What kind of life is that to offer your children? Certain death."

"The caves meant certain death too." I tore the lid off.

Father put his jacket aside. "At least there is honor in that. As outcasts, we would've been hunted. Despised everywhere. We would never have been safe, could never have trusted anyone. You know what it's like. Would you have wanted me to make that choice for you? You were only eight then, Jess. What do you think your life would've been like growing up an outcast?"

It was a serious question and I thought it over as such. What did I think my life would've been like growing up an outcast? Better? Worse? The only certainty was that there was none. "I don't know. There's no way to tell, is there? I could idolize it.

Escaping The Caves

Picture the seven of us living peaceful, happy lives by the sea. Never have to endure so much death and pain. But maybe it would've been like you feared. Suspicion and persecution everywhere we turned. We might not have been alive at all right now."

My father hesitated, then took my hand. It was twice the size of mine. Warm and rough. "Believe me when I say that I thought about it time and time again after Amy and Jenna disappeared. I've turned it over so many times in my mind that I thought I'd go insane. And when Jen died... If leaving could've saved her, I would've risked everything by doing so. My honor means nothing compared to the lives of my children."

I tightened my grip on his hand. "You did the right thing, Dad."

He didn't turn to look at me, but his voice was unusually hoarse when he spoke. "Do you really think so?"

"I do. You did what you thought was right both for yourself as the leader of the caves and for your family. None of your options came with any guarantees. You made the one you thought was best. Just like Mom. It's all anyone can ever do."

My father nodded. "I hope they found happiness. I know the chances aren't that great, but I really do. When all of this is over and the term outcast is meaningless, perhaps..."

I smiled. "Yeah, perhaps."

A week after we left the capital, I was back in Havensfield. Two weeks of travelling and I hardly spent two hours in the capital. From the little I'd seen, I hadn't missed out on anything. People like Sampson might think it grand and worth their time, but I wasn't one of them.

I walked off the platform and inhaled the scent of the pine trees. The sun hid behind a thin veil of clouds, but the day was warm and pleasant. My father had taken a different route three days ago, heading back to the caves. He'd hugged me, fiercely, before he let me go. He hadn't said goodbye, merely picked up his small bag and headed toward his train. Half-way there, he turned around. He cupped his hands around his mouth to be heard. "I'll see you soon. And, Jess?"

"Yes?" I'd called back.

"Don't say anything. I'll deal with him."

My stomach had churned, my body instantly shaky.

"Promise me, Jess." Father shouted so loudly several people turned to look at us.

"I promise."

Father nodded and continued on his way.

Now I headed toward John's diner, bitterly regretting that promise. I'd keep it. I never made a promise I didn't intend to keep, especially one made to my father, but still. How was I supposed to look at him and pretend not to know? Would he be able to tell even if I held my tongue? I stopped chewing my lip. I had to stop that.

It was midday and the town was peaceful, as always. At least there was no risk of me running into him here, he'd be too busy making sure the mines were guarded at all times.

When John's diner came into view, joy surged through me. I could see John take orders, smile and clap people on the back. I didn't see Eve, but it was a weekday so she was probably in preschool.

I had to force myself to walk the rest of the way and not run. After a few meters, I broke into a light jog. I couldn't wait to see

Escaping The Caves

the look on John's face when he saw me. To finally be able to put my arms around him, to kiss him and feel his hands once again trail patterns down my back. I gave up my good intentions, and ran anyway.

The bell above the door jingled as I burst in. The whole diner fell silent and looked at me. There was a sudden and definite change in the atmosphere. In less than three seconds the chatty, relaxed lunch hour turned somber. Loaded even.

John put down the coffeepot he held, spilling some on one of the tables. I took a step forward, suddenly uncertain. My mind had imagined many different expressions on his face when we saw each other again, but not one as guarded as this.

"John?"

My voice seemed to break whatever had come over him. He smiled, relief all over him, and I did what I'd imagined for two weeks. I threw myself into his arms, not giving a damn that this would feed the town a whole month's worth of gossip.

"I missed you so much." John kissed my hair, neck, eyes, lips.

I laughed. "So I can tell. Or do you greet everyone who comes into the diner like this?"

"No, he certainly doesn't."

John's arms stiffened around me. My breath caught. That voice... So many months and yet that voice was as familiar to me as my own. John looked over my shoulder. His eyes darkened. I turned around, but kept my hand firmly around John's.

And there he was. Close to nine whole months and here he was. I took a deep breath. "Hello, Kyle."

"Hello, Jess." Half a smile played at his lips. He was just as tall, dark and annoyingly handsome as ever. Khaki pants and black boots. A white t-shirt strained across his chest. I had to give him this, with all his physical training, he had a body that would look good in just about anything.

His hair was tied back, just the way I liked it. It brought out his cheekbones, brown eyes and full lips. There was an unpleasant sensation in the vicinity of my heart and I squashed it. Something must've registered on my face though, because that half-smile turned into a real one. "Long time, no see."

"Yeah, well, you didn't seem very eager to see me again once I became an outcast." My voice wasn't quite steady. John's hand tightened on mine, adding to my guilt. He'd misinterpreted the reason for my tremble. After all this time, after everything Kyle had done to me and everything we'd been through, even with John next to me, and he still had that effect on me. I hated him for it.

Kyle's smile faded. "Can you blame me for that? You might've come back to fulfill your duty as a soldier, but that day you were a traitor. You betrayed us all. You betrayed me."

I let go of John's hand and took a step forward. "Is that really how you see it? Or is it just convenient to spin it like that?"

Kyle's eyes narrowed. "I mean," I continued. "It makes it easy for you, doesn't it? I left, leaving you free to point the blame at me. You don't have to own up to anything, because I was the one to leave."

Kyle clicked his tongue and flicked his wrist. I ground my teeth. I knew it would be a big mistake to slap him in front of all these people. "Don't make this about us, Jess. This is about you

Escaping The Caves

leaving everyone and everything you'd sworn to uphold. You can't put that on me."

"You never asked me why I left, though. Never bothered to try and understand my reasons for leaving." I dug my nails into my hands.

Just like all those times before, it was impossible to know what he was thinking. "I would've. If you'd talked to me, I would've listened."

"Would you? You never listen. Not really."

Kyle raised his chin. "Let's not do this here." He nodded toward his team; they sat with their lunches forgotten in front of them. I didn't need to look around to know that everyone else in the diner was avidly listened to our conversation.

He opened the door. "Let's go for a walk."

"Jess." John put a hand on my arm. "Are you sure? I mean, will you be okay?"

No jealousy, only concern. "Yeah, I'll be fine. Don't worry. It's just something I need to do, you know, to…"

"I get it. Just… don't be too long? Eve will be home in about two hours and she's missed you like crazy."

I smiled and kissed him. "I've missed you like crazy too."

"I need to be back at the mines soon. If you want to do this, let's go." Kyle let the door slam shut behind him.

I gave John one last look, and followed.

Kyle was already a good way down the street, but I didn't hurry to catch up with him. He'd like that. Me running after him. I'd be damned if I'd give him the satisfaction. He was one of the bravest soldiers I knew, but I'd met beautiful women who were far less vain than him. To be desired was like a drug, addictive, pleasing and destructive all at the same time.

At the corner of the street, Kyle stopped and waited for me. We headed toward the forest and the trail toward the mines. "I hate it when you do that," Kyle said through clenched teeth.

I started. "What?"

"Talking to me like that in front of others."

I thought of all the times he'd argued with me in front of far more people than that, scant regard for my mortification. "I didn't try to embarrass you," was all I said. All the elements for a full-blown fight was there, but I tried to head it off for as long as possible.

Kyle nodded curtly.

We walked in silence for a while. I sneaked glances at Kyle out of the corner of my eye. He moved easily. His muscles flexed with every movement. *I don't even really like you. Yet you have this strange hold of me. Why is that?*

Kyle caught me looking. "You don't look too bad," he said, "for someone who's been an outcast for close to nine months."

I shrugged. "I've been here in Havensfield for five of them. They let me shower."

"They didn't know you were an outcast, did they?" Kyle stepped over a fallen tree.

I ignored his outstretched hand. "No. Only a few."

Kyle kept his eyes fixed on the trail. "And they didn't have a problem with that?"

"Do you think John would've taken me in, let me work and live with his family, if he had?"

"Guess not. He sure didn't seem very troubled by your status as an outcast."

"Why do you care?"

Escaping The Caves

Kyle didn't respond. It was cool beneath the trees, chilly almost. The trail was soft. It must've rained last night.

"Is it just your pride that cares?" I needed to know. It was always a bad idea to ask questions you didn't want to know the answer to, but I needed to know all the same.

Kyle raised his eyebrows. "How do you mean?"

"That I'm with John. Is it only your pride that makes you care? I don't suppose you've lived the life of a monk since I left. You were never that loyal even when we were together."

Kyle's jaw hardened. "Don't go there, Jess. Don't go bringing up the past. It's got nothing to do with this."

"It's got everything to do with this!"

A flock of birds took flight at my raised voice. He'd never admitted that there had been other women, but he'd never denied it, either.

"Why did you do it, Kyle? Why marry me if you didn't even love me? Was it my father? Did you think it would be advantageous to marry the First Commander's daughter? You became Second in Command two years later, after all." The words tasted bitter in my mouth. They made me feel bitter.

"Marrying you had nothing to do with me becoming Second in Command!" Kyle shouted. He walked faster. "If you have so little faith in me, at least have some in your Father. He's got too much integrity to fall to nepotism."

"I'm good at what I do, Jess. Very fucking good. You can question everything else about me, but not that. Never that. Do you hear me?" He grabbed my wrist.

I lifted my face up to see him clearly. "Then why did you marry me? Why did you stay married to me?"

He almost tossed me aside. "I made a choice. And unlike you, once I do, I stick to it."

"But you never loved me." I hated how pathetic that sounded, but he was supposed to have been my husband.

No matter how many times I turned it over in my head, I kept coming back to that. And I didn't know how to move past it. I was supposed to have been the one person he couldn't do without. Despite all the evidence, I couldn't wrap my head around how little I'd meant to him. Especially when he'd meant everything to me. It was hurtful and humiliating beyond words.

Kyle didn't answer me. He merely kept up his rapid pace through the forest. I didn't bother to keep up, my feet were too heavy. Once he realized I fell behind, he stopped, but didn't turn around. I came up next to him. We stood there and looked at the twisting trail. The mines weren't far away now. Our time alone was almost up.

Just when I'd given up hope that he'd offer any explanation, he spoke. "Just because someone doesn't love you the way you want to be loved, doesn't mean they don't love you."

I sought out his eyes until he was forced to look at me. "If you'd loved me, you wouldn't have–"

"You don't get to define what love should be like! Or you can, but you have to accept that someone else, that I might have a different way of looking at it. Love is different for everyone."

I swallowed. "Maybe. But the way I see it, love should be something extraordinary. If you're fortunate enough to find it, you treasure it." The bitter aftertaste wouldn't leave me.

Kyle rubbed a hand over his face. "Everyone makes mistakes, Jess. You've done it. I've done it. But we learn from those mistakes and we move on."

I turned on him. "What are you saying? That we should've fought harder for us? Tried to salvage what we could? You gave up on me without a fight, Kyle. To me, that doesn't speak of love."

Kyle shook his head. "We're never going to agree on this. The damage's done."

"Yeah. It certainly is." I tried to calm down. He could be telling the truth. Or maybe he was just spinning stories the way he'd always done. He knew exactly what I wanted to hear, and he knew how to turn what was right in front of me into something else. How to make me doubt my own eyes and ears. He made it difficult to trust my own senses.

Or maybe I was unfair. Maybe he was honest, for once. The fact was, I couldn't tell anymore. He was so good at distorting the truth, making a lie look believable. If he suddenly played with open cards, I'd have no idea.

I didn't trust him. And without trust we had nothing. I'd promised my father I'd let him take care of it, and I intended to keep that promise.

"Fine. Let's just drop it. We're through. We have been for a long time. Once this is over, we never have to see each other again."

Kyle nodded. "The mines are just up there. You should come and have a look. I'll brief you on what's been going on."

I let him take the lead, needing to put some space between us. I watched his strong back and legs, and wondered if I would've been this drawn to him if he'd been less physically attractive. Maybe I was just a foolish and shallow woman, who confused desire with love.

Whatever the case, he wasn't - never had been and never would be - the man I wanted. The man and marriage I grieved for didn't exist. I'd been holding onto something that was only real for as long as I believed it was. But it was as insubstantial and transparent as a puff of smoke.

Kristin Talgø

We crested the hill and the mines came into view. Wes' team were evenly stationed around and above the entrance. Some were missing. Most likely they scouted the area, to make sure there weren't any rogue monsters about.

Apart from the armed soldiers and the foreboding mines, the scenery was idyllic. Tall, green spruces and a clear, blue sky. A few plump clouds sailed by. A curious squirrel stopped half-way up one of the tree trunks and sniffed the air before it continued. Two swallows swooped overhead, adding their calls to the other birds further inside the forest.

I let out my breath. No monsters close by today. "Have any of them been spotted?" I asked Kyle. We walked over to Wes.

"No, nothing that we've picked up. And believe me, we would've picked it up." Kyle nodded at some of the men and women.

No monsters. I wasn't sure if I found that comforting or alarming. Either they'd gone into hiding or they planned something big. In either case, I wanted Sampson's weapon in my possession sooner rather than later.

We stopped in front of Wes, who held out his hand. "I believe I owe you an apology."

I looked into his brown eyes and wondered when he'd gotten the ugly scar above the left one. Could've been any number of times, he hadn't become a Captain being a coward. "You owe me nothing," I said, referring to more than what had passed between us the day I returned to the caves.

Wes nodded. We were all good at reading between the lines. "Even so. I'm sorry I doubted you. You were always one of the

Escaping The Caves

best, Jess. I'm glad to have you back."

I smiled and tried not to think about what that scar might've looked like before it healed. From the looks of it, Wes was lucky not to have lost the eye. I should've remembered when he'd gotten it, but it escaped me. I shook my head. It was hardly relevant.

"Anything the matter?" Kyle frowned. He was probably afraid I still talked to the ghosts in my head.

"Nothing more than you already know. Why don't we step aside for a moment, and I can brief you on the trip."

I gestured for Kyle and Wes to follow me.

We didn't walk far, just enough so the others couldn't overhear us. They were well trained. Not one of them strayed from their post to enquire after news. Not even so much as a glance in our direction.

I summarized the trip and left out nothing.

"Sampson will ship one weapon to the caves where my father is waiting, and one here. If he's true to his word - as I think he will be, given what's at stake - the weapon should be here in less than a week. Maybe sooner."

Kyle nodded. "Until then we continue as we've already done for the past two weeks. The monsters have stayed in hiding so far. Let's just hope they stay that way just a little longer."

I looked at the dark entrance of the mines, thinking about its darker inhabitants. "From your lips to God's ears."

Kyle cocked an eyebrow. "Since when do you believe in God, Jess?"

I made a small gesture and he stopped talking. "Wes? Are you all right?"

For a moment, Wes didn't seem to hear me. Then he shook himself as if waking from a dream. Or a nightmare maybe, judging from his pale skin. "Yeah, yeah, I'm fine. Just been a long morning, that's all."

Kyle put a hand on his shoulder just as he turned away. "Hey, are you sure you're all right? Was there something about what Jess told us that's got you worried? Is there something we've missed?"

Kyle's worried eyes searched the face of his friend and colleague.

Wes bore it for a moment before looking away. "Nah, man. I was just... This Sampson guy, he doesn't necessarily sound like the trustworthy type. I mean, if he doesn't come through on his promise to deliver the weapons... Then we're, what's the technical term?" He rubbed his jaw and laughed. "Oh, yeah. Fucked."

Kyle's frown deepened. Before he could put his foot in it by saying something cynical and unfeeling, I stepped in. "We'll be fine, Wes. True, I don't trust Sampson any further than I could throw him, which is to say not at all, but in this case, I think he'll pull through. He doesn't have a choice, does he? He might not care about the lives of innocents, but he does care about his own."

I put a hand on Wes' arm. For a second it looked like he wanted to flinch. He smiled. If I hadn't known him since I was seven, I might've believed it to be a real one. "Of course. I'm sorry. I'm acting very unprofessional here."

Kyle snorted, but seeing the look on my face he passed it off as a cough.

"I'll make the rounds. Make sure everything is as it should be. It'll take my mind off things. Get it back in the game." He patted me on the back, but didn't meet my eyes as he left.

Kyle pursed his lip as he looked after Wes. "What was that

all about?"

"No idea."

"I can't believe I'm about to say this, but if I'm not very much mistaken, and I hope I am, Wes just lied to us. Wes, of all people!"

"Shhh! Keep your voice down."

Kyle's face twitched. He hated to be shushed. Especially by his wife - now ex-wife. "What was that about?" he repeated.

"I'm not sure…"

"I've known Wes for as long as you have - longer, actually - and he has never, not once, turned pale and scared while someone told him the lay of the land. He's one of the strongest and bravest men I know. Even if we were forced to take on a whole mountain full of monsters, he wouldn't turn to jelly." Kyle slammed his fist into a tree, startling a couple of birds.

"Then what's got him so spooked?"

Kyle straightened. "You tell me."

"I don't know any more about this than you do."

"Are you sure about that?"

I forced myself to stand my ground, even if I could see the pores on Kyle's face. My back was up against a tree. Apart from literally dodging him, I wasn't going anywhere. "I've told you everything I know."

Kyle stared at me. My breath quickened. Did he have to stand so close? After what seemed an eternity, he broke eye contact. He rubbed his hands across his face. I looked up and noticed how red his eyes were.

"Have you slept at all since you got here?"

Kyle smiled. "Not much. Trying to hold off an apocalypse. I can sleep when I'm dead."

I winced. "Don't say that."

"Sorry. When I'm old then. Better?"

"A bit." I returned his smile. It felt good not be angry with him. That kind of resentful anger got very heavy after a while. It'd been weighing me down and I had no desire to carry it around anymore.

Some of his hair had escaped its ponytail. I tugged it back behind his ear. He caught my wrist, pressed his lips to the tender spot above the veins. His eyes held mine. This was madness. We hadn't seen each other for so long, we'd both moved on. Some of the time we didn't even like each other. We were the most dysfunctional couple I could think of, and yet... No. We didn't love each other anymore. Did we?

I held my breath, half-afraid he'd kiss me, half-wanting him too. I'm ashamed to admit that John never even crossed my mind just then.

Unfortunately, I never found out. Just as he leaned closer, Kyle's team returned to relieve the team on duty.

I cleared my throat. "I should get back. I'll... I'll see you later."

"Jess." Kyle held my arm. My heart skipped a beat. It was enough to make me hate him all over again. "What is it you're not telling me about Wes?"

I ignored the unpleasant plummeting sensation in my gut. Told myself it wasn't disappointment. I withdrew my arm from him. "Nothing."

"Don't lie to me, Jess. Whatever else you do, don't do that."

I contemplated just walking away from him. God knows he'd done it more than enough times to me, but it felt too good not to be on the outs with him again. I didn't want to risk breaking that fragile truce. "I told you everything. Even that Sampson must've had someone on the inside helping him."

"Yes?"

I looked at him.

"Jesus Christ, Jess, you can't suspect Wes! For fuck's sake, he saved your life! Three times, if I remember correctly."

"I know he has."

"Then how can you—"

"Look, I'm not even supposed to discuss this with you. I made Father a promise and I'm getting dangerously close to breaking it."

Kyle's eyes narrowed. "Why? What reason does your father have for not wanting you to discuss this with me? I'm Second in Command, Jess. I've as much right to discuss a possible traitor as you do."

Suddenly the mines appeared positively welcoming. Anything to get away from Kyle. He knew me too well. It was only a matter of time before he put the pieces together.

"Oh shit." Kyle's face fell.

My father was going to kill me.

"Kyle…"

"Are you fucking kidding me?" This time the other soldiers forgot their training. Several heads swiveled in our direction. "After everything I've done… For you, for him, for our community… And he suspects… You suspect… me."

Kyle sat down like a kid too tired to stand up any longer.

I made sure the others once again minded their own business and sat down next to him. I didn't try to touch him. "It had to have been someone high up in ranks to be able to pull this off without my father or anyone else noticing."

"What have I ever done to make you distrust me like this?"

My eyebrows arched. "Do you really want me to answer that? Cause if so, we're gonna be here a while."

Kyle clicked his tongue. "Don't start with me. Not now."

"Then don't ask me questions you don't want to know the answer to."

He seemed about to say something he'd regret later, but held his tongue. Kyle picked up a cone and tossed it into the forest. "I'm not a traitor, Jess. I'm not the insider."

I sighed. "If you were, would you tell me?"

"Probably not."

I shrugged.

Kyle turned to me. He pulled my chin around so I was forced to look at him. "Then tell me this. What do I stand to gain from having our friends and family killed? Tell me that, at least."

I tried to pull away, but he held on. His fingers dug into my chin. "It's your life. To be a soldier in the caves. Second in Command. Everything you are, everything you believe is rooted in that role. The authority, the power that gives you... do you really think you'll find that again once the monsters have been destroyed? Can you picture yourself living any other kind of life?"

Kyle loosened his grip, but didn't release me. "And you believe me capable of witnessing those closest to me being killed in order to maintain that role?"

My silence was answer enough.

Slowly, he dropped his hand. "I didn't know you thought so little of me." He said it as if he was commenting on the weather, but his voice shook.

"Kyle." I clamped my hand down on his shoulder. He didn't get to run away from this. "I don't. But after everything we've been through, can you honestly blame me for questioning you?"

Kyle shook me off. "I'll keep an eye on Wes until your father gets here. He can deal with him then. He can deal with me then."

"Kyle…" I got to my feet, but he was already too far away for me to catch him without causing a scene. I stopped, disgusted with myself. After all this time, after everything I'd learnt, seeing us so clearly from a distance, I was still running after him. Trying to get him to listen.

When I returned to the diner, John had already closed. I went around and let myself in the backdoor like I'd done so many times before. There was a sick, uncomfortable feeling in my stomach. I found John along with Eve and Sam. They sat in the living room and played a game of cards. Their obvious delight at seeing me again worsened the uneasy feeling. John was the only one whose eyes didn't fully meet mine.

Sam and Eve were too preoccupied with my re-telling of my so-called adventure in the capital. I avoided the details of the meeting with Sampson, not that it required much evasiveness on my part. Both Sam and Eve were chiefly interested in knowing what the big city had looked like, smelled like, how the people had been, etc.

Not wanting to disappoint them, I painted them as exciting and rosy a picture as possible. I focused and enhanced its strong points and avoided its faults. Such as the exhaust fumes, the starving people on the grimy streets, and all the others who simply walked past without sparing them so much as a glance.

The evening passed without interruption or confrontation. If it hadn't been for the sense of something unspoken between John and me, it would've been like any other evening. Dinner filled with conversation that consisted of much nonsense between Eve and Sam. I read to Eve before bedtime and tucked her in. All common, but enjoyable domestic delights. There was a heavy sadness weighing down my heart and I told myself there was no accounting for it.

After the oldest and youngest member of the family had gone to bed, I ventured to put my arms around John as he dried the dishes. He didn't pull away, but he didn't lean into my embrace either.

"You should visit Kelly." He placed a clean and dry plate on the counter.

"I intend to." I buried my face between his shoulder blades. His back moved as he continued to dry another.

"You should see her tonight. It's still early enough to visit." The second plate scraped against the first one.

"I'm sure she can wait a little longer. I haven't seen you for two weeks."

"She had a son about a week ago. I think she would like it if you didn't put off seeing her now that you're back." John put the plates away.

"Why didn't you say so sooner?"

John shrugged. "You were off in a bit of a hurry. Besides, I'm telling you now. And like I said, there's still time for you to visit tonight." He attacked the glasses and turned his back on me.

I watched him work and considered if I should address the elephant in the room, but thought better of it. It would undoubtedly lead to an argument and questions I didn't know if I had the answers to. "I'll only be a short while."

John nodded. "Take your time." He didn't turn around to watch me go, nor did he respond to my kiss on his cheek.

Escaping The Caves

Kelly sat out on the front porch as I walked up the driveway. She looked up and smiled as she saw me, but it was a tired smile. Happy, but tired.

"You came back." She pulled the blanket closer around her son.

"I always keep my promises." I sat down on the chair next to her.

"You're among the few who do, then," Kelly said, still smiling. She looked incapable of doing anything else whenever she looked at her son. Her eyes seemed permanently locked on him. She tried to lift them to meet mine, but they were immediately drawn back to the soft bundle in her arms.

"He's beautiful, Kelly," I said, and meant it. He was.

The baby lay snuggly in the crook of her arms and enjoyed the warmth of his mother, the soft breeze on his tiny nose. His eyes were closed, his blue-tinted eyelids fluttered as he dreamt. I marveled at his perfection. His unblemished skin, his pink lips and his tiny fingernails.

"He is, isn't he?" Kelly sighed.

"I came as soon as I could." I put my index finger close to her son's. They closed around it. He was surprisingly strong for someone so little.

"I knew you would." Kelly kissed the blonde fuzz at the top of her baby's head. She looked even younger than before. The birth seemed to have taken a lot out of her. But there was a new sense of maturity about her as well.

"Have you thought of a name?" I was getting caught up in the kid's magnetic field. It was impossible to take my eyes off him.

"Yes." I heard the smile in Kelly's voice.

"And?"

"I've named him Jess. After you."

The surprise jolted my eyes back to her. "Are you serious?"

"Of course. Why wouldn't I be? You've helped me far more than you realize over the past months, and I wanted my son to have a name that means something to me. You mean something to me. A lot, actually. And Jess can be used both for girls and boys. So, I've named him Jess." Kelly finished with a firm nod.

I was so stunned and touched I had to swallow several times before I trusted myself to speak. "Thank you," I croaked. "You've... you mean a lot to me too." I kept my eyes on the other Jess, sleeping peacefully next to me.

"I know. I also know you're not very good at expressing your feelings, so you don't have to look so panicked." Kelly stroked Jess' brow and nose. He shifted, but didn't wake up.

"But I didn't do anything. I was a mess. Still am, in many ways," I said, thinking of Kyle and John.

"It's not what you did as much as who you are," Kelly said.

Unable to find the ability to express what her words meant to me, I just nodded. After a moment of silence, only interrupted by the soft snoring of baby Jess, Kelly said, "I hear your ex-husband is part of the team guarding the mines."

I started and pulled my finger out of Jess' grasp. "How did you know that?"

"John came over, the day after I had Jess. We talked and he mentioned it." Kelly's voice remained neutral, but her son started to twitch.

"I see. Yeah, he's Second in Command and seeing as my father supervises the caves, he was sent here." I pulled a loose thread on my jacket.

Kelly shushed her son. "Have you seen him?"

"Yeah." I cleared my throat. "I saw him today. We had a talk."

"A good one?"

"Depends on how you look at it, I guess. It started out bad, enjoyed a brief rising curve, and then ended worse." I pulled the tread loose and curled it around my fingers.

"He's never going to change, Jess."

I met her gaze, which for the first time wasn't directed at her son. "You've never met him."

"No. But from the little you've told me, I don't think he's the kind of man who changes his ways. Maybe for a short time, but not permanently." Her eyes strayed once more to the sleeping child.

I bit back a sharp retort. What did she know? She was sixteen, for God's sake. Just because she'd become a mother, it didn't automatically grant her any more knowledge on the matter of men and their likelihood to change their ways.

"How did the birth go?" I changed the subject.

Kelly snorted, but didn't press me. "It went well, I suppose. Fucking painful of course, but everything went according to plan. The kid got out, as you can see. We're both declared strong and fit."

"I'm happy to hear that. You did well, Kelly." I took another look at her son. "Very well."

"Maybe, but the real test starts now. I haven't had a full night's sleep since he got here, and I don't suspect I'll have one for quite some time." Kelly wrinkled her nose, but her eyes never lost that glow.

"How are your parents?" How did they react, was what I

really asked.

"They're very well, actually. Went totally ga-ga once they saw Jess. Dad started to cry, and I almost had to wrestle with Mom to make her give him back." Kelly shook her head.

I laughed. "Good. That's very good. You'll be well taken care of. Both of you."

"Yeah, I think we will. For the first time since I became pregnant, I'm happy about it. He's the best thing that's ever happened to me and ever will," Kelly said.

I was both delighted and envious of her calm, sure sense of where she belonged. There wasn't a doubt in her mind that her place was beside Jess. No matter what she did or where she went, she had that little boy to keep her anchored to the right things in life. She hadn't just gotten a son. She'd been given a little compass to help her navigate through life. Keep her aim true and straight.

That melancholic feeling settled deeper in my gut. I breathed deeply. "Are your parents home?"

Kelly almost raised her eyes. "No. They went out to stretch their legs and get some air. They've hardly left me and Jess alone for a moment." Kelly rolled her eyes, but it was obvious her parents cared and the attention meant a lot to her.

"Just wanted to tell them about the trip and what came out of it." I looked at my watch. The visit had already lasted longer than I'd intended. My gut was filled with an irrational fear that every second I spent away from John was a second where he drifted further away from me, as if we were stranded in two different boats caught up in two different currents.

"Tell me then. If they're not back by the time you've finished, I'll pass the story on to them. You must be very tired." Kelly avoided mentioning John.

"Sure." I told her everything. Once I'd finished, Kelly wanted only to know one thing.

"When this is all over, will you leave?"

I sighed. "Honestly? I don't know. I really don't know yet."

Kelly searched my face. "All right. I won't press you for an answer you don't have. But promise me one thing?"

"Of course. Anything."

"If you leave, it's because you want to or need to, or maybe both, but not because your ex-husband wants you to." Kelly spoke quickly, afraid I would interrupt her.

"Kelly, trust me, my ex-husband couldn't care less if I stay or go, as long as wherever I go, it's somewhere far away from him," I said. I didn't like how desolated that made me feel.

"I wouldn't be so sure of that."

"Yeah? Don't take this the wrong way, but what could you possibly know about that?"

Kelly shrugged. "Just something about the look on John's face."

That leaden feeling intensified. "John's just afraid of losing me. But if he does, it's got nothing to do with Kyle. My ex-husband is just an easy target for him to direct his anger at."

"If you say so."

I reminded myself that Kelly cradled her one-week-old son. It was best if I left before my tongue got the better of me. "I'll come by tomorrow." I kissed both of their cheeks.

Before the curve in the road hid them from my view, I looked back. They still sat and slept in the same position. The sky could've fallen down and Kelly would've nonetheless had eyes only for her son. Not even on the coldest night in the desert as an outcast, had I felt so completely alone.

Chapter 19

Sampson came through on his promise. The weapon, which turned out be a missile with a powerful explosive at its core, was flown in the day after I returned to Havensfield. I'd heard of airplanes, but never actually seen one. Apparently it was the kind of technological progress Sampson preferred to keep to himself, away from the public. Whatever reason he had for this, I bet it wasn't for the greater good.

The pilot and another man, in a hurry to get away, placed the missile next to the mines and flew away. Clearly, he didn't want to be around if this thing went off before being placed within the heart of the mountain. Problem was that this heart was infested with monsters that wouldn't look too kindly on being blown to extinction.

"So, how should we do this?" Kyle paced back and forth in front of the missile. It was quite big, but there were handles on each side of it. We'd be able to get it inside the mines.

"It's quite simply, really. In theory." I looked at the gleaming metal in front of me. Who would've thought such a plain-looking object could be so deadly?

"And what's that theory?" Wes spoke from his place on a rock.

After his strange reaction the day I returned, he was almost back to his normal self. But his eyes remained distracted. At least he hadn't run away, though it did little to lessen my suspicion toward him.

Kyle wouldn't look at me. He treated me with cold civility, but I was more worried about John than him. The latter had feigned sleep when I got home from Kelly. After that, there hadn't been much time or opportunity to clear the air. It remained loaded and unresolved.

"Jess?" Kyle looked in my direction, bringing me back to the present.

"Right. Needless to say, we're only going to get one chance to do this right." I indicated the missile in front of us. "This one needs to be placed deep within the mines. My father will make sure the same is done in the caves. There's a timer on it, which we can set so we'll have enough time to get the hell out of here before it goes off. Once it's launched, it will travel a certain distance, then explode."

"And the same will happen on the other side of the mountain range." Kyle nodded. "The combined explosion on both sides should kill most of the monsters, but those that survive by some freak chance, will be crushed by the avalanche the explosions trigger. It should do it."

"It should, doesn't mean it will." Wes wiped his lips. Whether he was nervous about it being effective or not was unclear to me.

"If some of them aren't killed within the mountain, they'll be

Escaping The Caves

forced to come crawling out from underneath the rocks. And we'll be the welcome party." Kyle bared his teeth.

"There's just one problem though." I looked at the two men.

Kyle turned to me for the first time since our argument. "The monsters aren't going to let us just walk out of there. And that's providing they let us get far enough inside to put the missile in place." I took off my jacket.

The day was getting warmer, not to mention that the idea of ending my days in those mines made me hot and bothered. And not in a good way.

"We'll take one team in with us. Hopefully the members will cause enough of a distraction to allow us to get the missile in place. That's our main priority. Once that's done, the chips can fall where they may. If we get out, we're lucky. If we don't..." He didn't need to finish the sentence.

Whether or not we got out of those mines alive was immaterial. Our job was to get the missile placed and loaded. Everything after that was of no concern.

"If we don't make it out, the other team can sweep through the remains and take out any monsters that are still alive. But I don't think that's likely." Kyle eyed the weapon in front of him.

"Something tells me this is more powerful than it looks."

"In the end, this mission is pretty much like any other we've ever had in the caves. We go out, do our job and then do our best to get out in one piece." I thought of John and Eve. Kelly and her son. I'd really like to see them again once this was over. But if it wasn't in the cards, at least I knew they'd be safe.

"We'll do it tomorrow. It'll give us time to prepare and plan it all properly. Those of us who have people to say goodbye to can do that. We'll reconvene here as daylight breaks." Kyle looked at Wes. "You've been very quiet. Do you have anything to add?"

Wes started. "What? No, no. Sounds like as good a plan as any. If we live, we live. If not, at least the rest of mankind will be safe. Or as safe as it has ever been. Sooner or later, I'm sure they'll come up with another way of massacring each other for the sake of power and wealth. They always do. Makes me wonder what we're doing it for. In the end…"

Kyle narrowed his eyes, but didn't comment. I pictured Eve and baby Jess, and couldn't hold my tongue. "We do it for all those innocent lives you've witnessed since you got here. All of those and millions more. We might not be able to prevent the future generations from destroying each other, but we can save this one. And the one after us. That should be more than enough reason." I spoke more sharply than intended

Wes got up. "Of course. I'm sorry. I didn't mean to sound unfeeling. Been sleeping badly lately. Don't worry." He saw the look on Kyle's face. "You can count on me. I'll do my best and I'll have your back tomorrow. Just like the good, old days, huh?"

He patted Kyle's back as he walked away and gave me a half a smile. If anyone of us got out tomorrow, I didn't think he would be one of them. He'd do his job, but something told me he didn't want to survive the mission. He'd want it to be his last, to be remembered as a soldier. I thought of what Father would do to him when he found out who the real insider was, and I couldn't blame him.

Kyle glanced at me. I could tell he was thinking along the same lines. "You'll spend the day in town, I guess?"

I nodded. "You?"

He shrugged. "I'll be here. I've lived my whole life as a soldier. If I die tomorrow, I won't regret dying as one either."

I closed my eyes against the sun, giving me an excuse not to look at him. "What if you do survive, though? What will you do with your new-found freedom?"

"Now that's a more difficult question. I don't know. I'll figure it out, with time."

Something in his voice made me open my eyes. "And you? Will you go or will you stay?"

An image of the ocean I'd never seen rose to mind. It'd kept me going all through the desert, all those never-ending days and nights tormented by the ghosts. If I left Havensfield, I wondered how long it would take before they returned.

"If I live through tomorrow, I'll let you know." I smiled.

Kyle looked at me for a moment. "All right. I'll see you tomorrow. Don't forget to set the alarm."

He walked back to the other soldiers, leaving me free to do as I pleased. We'd faced death together countless times before. We'd never been ones for sentimental goodbyes. We weren't about to start now.

I walked back to town and took great care to notice my surroundings. To inhale the fresh, warm scent of the forest and memorize the sound of the birds singing in the trees. How the sun dappled the ground through the foliage above. I was alive and happy. If I died tomorrow, at least I'd know what that felt like.

If it was the last day on this earth for me, I didn't waste my time daydreaming of far off places and people I'd never meet. I spent it with Kelly and little Jess, marveling at the child's beauty and perfection. Peter treated me with a new kindness and respect. Even Jane acted less like a doll and more like a human

Kristin Talgø

being.

I played football with Eve and listened to her haltingly read one of her favorite books to me, tucking her hair behind her ear as she sat on my lap. Her skinny, strong body soothed the ache in my heart.

Sam didn't call me Brenda once that day. He bickered with me about the smallest things, but brought me lunch and touched my arm at every opportunity he got.

Even John seemed to have forgotten about his initial hurt. He closed the diner for the day and spent practically every second of it next to me. His hand constantly touched me, to reassure himself I was still there.

That night we spent clinging tightly to one another. We didn't say goodbye, but I tasted salt on his lips. If we could've crawled beneath each other's skin, I think we would've.

It was an extraordinary thing to love someone and be loved like that. I filed the experience and sensations away, knowing they'd be the ones I'd fall back on if my life ended in the mines. He'd saved me when I first got to Havensfield, kept me strong and true, and he helped me stay that way to the very end. There were some things in life which even death could not touch.

Just before dawn broke the next day, I got out of bed, dressed in silence and kissed John, careful not to wake him up. If he had, I'm not sure I could've brought myself to do what needed to be done.

Kyle, Wes and the rest of the team were already in place when I got there. The other team would wait at a safe distance from the mines. Whether they would witness us emerge from them remained to be seen.

Kyle looked at me. "Ready?"

"As ready as I'm ever going to be." I accepted the rifles he held out and strapped them crisscross on my back. My old, faithful gun was in its usual holster at my waist.

"Good. Everyone knows what to do. Or do I need to repeat myself?" Kyle swept his eyes over his team. No one spoke.

"All right." He turned to me. "Wes and I will carry the missile. The others will spread out two and two in front and behind us. We won't have much room to maneuver in here. I want you, Jess, to stay close to me. Whatever else happens, this missile gets in place and loaded, okay?"

"Yes, sir."

Kyle's lips twitched. He wrapped his hand into my hair and held me by the back of my neck. When I stiffened, he tightened his grip.

He winked. "For old time's sake." The kiss was brief, but warm.

He gave Wes the signal and they lifted the missile at the same time. Then we entered the mines and our most important mission to date.

Chapter 20

Only guided by the lights on our weapons, it was a hazardous journey through the dark. The thin road led deep into the mines before the shaft with a rickety looking elevator came into view. The elevator would only take ten people at the time. We sent the other team down first in case the monsters were closer than we thought.

My guess was they would be hiding deep within the mines. They'd want to us cut off from as many escape routes as possible before attacking. I had no doubt the monsters knew we were coming. We might not have seen them, but that didn't mean they hadn't been able to get a whiff of our plans. Most likely they didn't know the full extent and the details, but they knew we were coming.

Well, we'd know soon enough.

Once the all-clear had been sent up, we went down. The hinges on the elevator screeched. The noise clawed at my high-strung nerves. No one said a word. Slowly, it descended into the mountain. I had a fleeting, but terrifying moment of claustrophobia when I thought of the powerful mass of rock that surrounded us on all sides.

I still remembered the sound of the mountain coming down on us, the sound of Jen and Trenton lost to me forever. One look at Kyle told me his mind travelled along similar lines.

The elevator came to a shuddering stop and we exited. Five soldiers spread out in front of us. I did as Kyle had asked and stayed close to him. I strained both my ears and eyes for any unwelcome noises or appearances. The rest of the team spread out around us. Their boots moved soundlessly in the dark cavern.

Every instinct was on red-alert, but no one attacked us. We passed, undisturbed, through the mines, inching closer to where we wanted to place the missile for maximum damage. The lack of attack should've pleased me, but instead it had the opposite effect.

My skin hummed with the unnerving silence. It pressed down on me, invading my ears in a way no amount of harsh noise could've done. It was like the day I'd stumbled upon the monster at the mines. I hadn't seen it until it chose to leap, but I'd known it was there nonetheless. The whole forest had known something was amiss. The proverbial calm before the storm.

"Stay close. It won't be long now," Kyle whispered. The sound crawled over the walls. It seemed to travel through the entire mountain.

I nodded once, not wanting to waste my breath. He was right. It wouldn't be long now and I'd need all the breath I had. Kyle stopped. He and Wes lowered the missile to the ground as carefully as if they handled a newborn infant. I swept both my

Escaping The Caves

gaze and weapon around the area. Nothing moved.

Kyle followed the instructions he'd been given by the man accompanying the pilot, and set the timer on the missile. Forty-five minutes. We had less than an hour before it went off. There would be an equally-powerful weapon flying in from the other side. It had taken us about thirty minutes to reach our destination. And we moved at a rapid, uninterrupted pace. It left us with only fifteen minutes to spare.

I turned to Kyle and nodded. He pressed the final button. The timer flashed red. Countdown had started. Kyle straightened and raised his weapon. I'd been paying close attention to what he'd been doing. Only now did I notice that everyone else was busy eying our exit route. Or more precisely, the walls and ceiling in that direction.

I glanced up and my stomach dropped, just like the unsteady elevator, one shuddering jerk at a time. The walls and ceiling crawled with monsters. Their black, pupil-less eyes gleamed in the sharp glow from our lamps. Most of them only stared at us, their bodies tense and ready. But some cocked their heads to the side and bared teeth. They smiled.

The cold intelligence reflected in those insect-like slits sent icy fingers trailing down my spine.

On some soundless signal, they attacked all at once, but Kyle was too skilled not to have anticipated them. He gave a signal of his own, half a second before they did. For all I know, it was what saved my life.

After that, everything became blurry. In the midst of battle there is no room for details. Light, darkness, screams and blood all blend together until they're hardly distinguishable from one another. There was no time to see who fell and who was able to fight their way through the wave of monsters that crashed down on us. Their numbers were great, but there weren't as many as I'd feared. My fingers moved with a speed of their own, emptying my weapon, re-loading it and repeating the sequence over and over again.

I never lost sight of Kyle. Despite of the ensuing confusion, we stayed close to each other. For the time being, pain didn't exist. I felt my clothes stick to me, both from perspiration and blood, but my muscles moved with ease.

By some miracle we, along with five others, made it back to the elevator. Kyle pushed me in, but moved to close the doors before he got in himself. "Wait!" I clamped down on his arm, slick with blood.

Almost annoyed, he shook me off. "There's no time, Jess. Someone has to hold them off. Otherwise none of us get out of here alive."

"No!" Desperation clogged my throat. I might not be meant for him, but there was no way I'd lose him like this, after everything we'd been through. "I won't let you."

Kyle leaned close, but didn't kiss me. "You haven't got a choice." Over his shoulder, I saw monster upon monster run at an uncanny speed along the walls and floors. They moved like a black, unified mass of deadly spiders.

I was about to scream with frustration when someone behind Kyle shoved him. Kyle grunted. We were both pushed into the elevator. The grate closed in front us. "Wes! Wait, don't do this!" Kyle shook the grate, but Wes had locked it together with one of his rifles.

He slammed a torn, bleeding fist against the button and the elevator started up. His clothes were mangled, barely holding on in some places. A flap of skin from his forehead hung into his right eye, obscuring it from view. But the left one blazed with determination. "I have to, Kyle. You know I do. I owe it to you. All of you."

Kyle lowered his hands from the grate. Realization filled his face. "Why?" He had to scream to be heard above the cacophony of the monsters closing in.

Wes shrugged. "It was all I knew. If you have to tell people, at least tell them I died honorably defending the human race, just like I always have. I never broke my oath!"

His voice cracked on the last word, too abused from shouting to hold on any longer. Kyle raised his hand in a salute. Wes returned it, before he turned to meet his death. He was able to kill just enough of the monsters to allow the elevator to reach daylight again.

The elevator stopped just short of the opening. The monsters had probably disengaged it and would come crawling up the wires any moment. Kyle opened the top of the elevator. One by one, we climbed out of it. We used our last bit of strength and cut the wires. The elevator plummeted down the shaft. Whatever had attempted to use it as a ladder would get an unpleasant surprise.

"GO!" Kyle shoved me and the rest of his team in front of him, herding us out of the mines.

We didn't waste any time. We had less than a minute before everything around us turned to dust. Legs pumping, we sped along the tracks, only too happy to leave the mines and its inhabitants behind.

We'd just made it to the edge of the forest outside of the mines when the earth beneath our feet shuddered. It threw us to the ground. There was no loud explosion - the missile was too deep underground for that - but we felt the power of it all the same. I looked up and saw the mines cave in. The entrance shuddered and crumbled. It exhaled a huge cloud of dust and smoke.

The rumbling ground lasted longer than anticipated. Less than ten seconds after the first explosion, we felt another. My father had been successful. Whether he'd been as lucky with his escape as us remained to be seen.

I swallowed. My eyes stung, dust and grit clung to my wet eyelashes. Kyle reached for me and I squeezed his hand. I didn't care if it hurt my wounds. We watched the smoke clear and felt the earth settle. The other team moved out from their hiding places and searched for any survivors who might creep through the cracks in the ground.

None came. It wasn't likely that any would. I considered how the combined force of the missiles had affected us above ground, and couldn't even begin to imagine what the scene below must be like. There would be no more caves or mines within this mountain again. It was a wonder the mountain range was still standing. I'd seen multiple avalanches all along it as far as I could see from here, but the mountain itself remained intact. As long as the monsters that dwelled beneath it were destroyed, I had no problem with that.

Shakily, Kyle and I got to our feet. We leaned on the unharmed team which had remained above ground, and made our way back to town. After decades of living under the threat of the monsters, they were no more. I suspected I'd feel the relief and joy of it once the shock settled. Right then, I felt nothing but a strange, empty calm.

Escaping The Caves

"I wish you'd wait a little longer before going." John tucked a stray hair behind my ear. "Your father survived. He won't go anywhere. I'm sure he would understand if you waited a bit before travelling. You're still healing."

We stood on the platform at the train station. We'd received word from an accomplice of Sampson that my father's mission had proved as successful as ours, and that he'd lived to tell the tale.

The image of the ocean grew stronger and more vivid in my mind every passing day, but I needed to see my family again before I left. I'd travel through Havensfield on my way back again. This was probably why John hadn't offered much of an argument. I'd come back once more. He'd most likely placed his hopes on being able to convince me to stay then. His hopes could last a while longer.

I didn't have the heart to shatter them yet. There was even a part of me that hoped I would change my mind, though I knew better.

"I'm fine." I kissed him. "I didn't suffer any major damage. Trust me, once you've had your guts hanging out, a few scratches doesn't do much to rattle you."

John winced. "I wish you wouldn't say things like that. I'd rather picture you in one piece."

"Sorry." The whistle on the train blew and I flung my rucksack onto the train. "I've got to go, but I'll be back before you know it."

"You better be." He smiled.

"You know I will." One last kiss and then I had to fling myself onto the train as it picked up speed. By the time I reached a window, the platform and John were out of sight. Kyle read a newspaper, pretending he hadn't watched our goodbye.

⁂

"What will you do?" I walked next to my father through our community. It would, in time, be turned into a small town. At least, if my father had his way. He usually did.

"I'll stay here. Anyone who wants to stay is welcome to do so. There'll be no shortage of occupations when we rebuild this place. Sampson is even financing it. He seems to think he can hold off trouble for a while if he only keeps most of the ex-soldiers busy here. Or 'cavemen', as he calls us."

"Will you tell them?"

"About Sampson supplying the caves with monsters? What for? I'll admit I won't be sorry when he falls from grace and power, but I've no desire to feed fuel to a fire that I believe is inevitable. If my services as a soldier are needed for the people, when the time comes, I'll get my revenge on Sampson. I'm in no hurry." My father spoke with the conviction of a man who would see justice, one way or another. Sampson might live well into his eighties, but sooner or later my father would end him.

We nodded at people as we moved through our budding town. People still looked a little shell-shocked, but there was an almost giddy relief in their behavior. On my request, doctors who specialized in trauma had been offered positions here, and several had accepted.

Apparently, working with ex-soldiers from the caves proved to be highly interesting for people in such positions. There had even been more applicants than we imagined.

Escaping The Caves

People here were still very skeptical of seeking help. We had lived by a strict doctrine for years: anyone who broke down wasn't fit to wear the scars on their cheeks. But as we now had ample opportunity and all the time in the world for nervous break-downs, that would change.

I knew better than anyone that sometimes if you wanted to re-build your life, you had to tear it down first. It wasn't possible to build a house on crumbling concrete and rotten wood. I hadn't spoken to anyone yet, but I knew sooner or later I wouldn't have a choice. The ghosts would have their say.

In any case, doctors who wished to work here didn't need to worry about being out of a job anytime soon. With what everyone in this community had been through, there'd be enough emotional and mental traumas to satisfy doctors for years to come.

"I'm glad you didn't tell anyone about Wes." I lowered my voice.

Father's lips thinned. Wes' betrayal had hurt him deeply, but not as deeply as it would've had it been Kyle. "There is no reason why anyone should learn of his shame, or why his family should suffer the disgrace of his poor judgment and choices. What is done is done. At least this way his secret will stay buried with him."

"Thank you."

My father nodded and changed the subject. "When will you leave?"

I looked at the time. "In three hours. I want to see Jo and Julia before I go, say goodbye to my nieces. But I'll find you before the train leaves."

"Will you come back here again? At some point?" Father kept his eyes on the road.

Kristin Talgø

I kissed his cheek. "Yes."

He colored, but smiled. "Good. And... if you... see them... I'd like to know."

"You'll be one of the first."

"And your friend, this John, what will he think about you leaving to travel to the west?"

My stomach twisted into a knot. "He won't like it. But he won't stop me."

"He loves you."

"Yes. He does."

Father stopped at a corner. He knew the direction I was headed. "And you? Who do you love?"

"I love you."

Father snorted. "That's not what I meant."

"I'll be fine."

"I'm sure you will. I'll see you later." Father let me go, even if he must've known what I would find. Sometimes we need to see things with our own eyes before we believe what we already know. Sometimes pain is the only road to freedom.

⁎ ⁎

Everything was the same. The gate that lead to his small house, which was really only a room in the shape of a house. The tap set into one of the walls and the bucket beneath it. How many times hadn't I showered there? How many times hadn't Kyle and I showered there together, our bodies wet and slippery with soap?

I shivered and opened the door. Kyle wasn't in, but his room wasn't empty. In bed, reading a book, just like I used to, in the same position as I had countless times before, sat another

Escaping The Caves

woman. She looked up, a question in her brown eyes. I didn't recognize her.

If she'd been naked, I doubt I could've been more shocked. There was something about the familiarity in her position, the intimacy of someone relaxing at home, which told me she'd been around for a long time. To sleep with someone was one thing. I knew all too well sex could be used as a way of taking your mind off uncomfortable things, but it didn't need to mean that much.

This was different. It was letting someone into his home, not just when he was around, but even when he was out. That meant trusting someone, wanting her to be there when he returned. This was choosing someone. It hurt a lot more than I thought it would.

Call me slow, but in the matters of the heart, we're not rational creatures. Our mind might know the truth, but if our heart is set on a different direction, it will cling to any crumbs offered.

There were no crumbs left now. The table had been swept clean. I turned and left.

Kyle came walking towards me half-way down the street. When he saw my face, he knew where I'd been. His jaw tightened. No doubt he expected some emotional outburst, some embarrassingly public scene of accusations and hurtful remarks.

I slowed down, but didn't stop as I passed him. "I came to say goodbye, but you weren't in. I wish you all the best."

Kyle turned toward me, but didn't move to stop me. "Thank you. Safe journey. I hope you find what you're looking for."

I looked over my shoulder. "So do I. Maybe we'll see each other again someday."

Kyle walked backward so he could see me. "Maybe. Goodbye, Jess."

I turned my eyes to the front. "Goodbye, Kyle." Those were the only words left to say. Everything else had either been said or done. There was nothing left to hold on to. And so I let him go.

I haven't looked back since.

"Will I ever see you again?"

How many people had asked me that? I still didn't know the answer.

"I hope so." I stroked John's cheek, thinking of the first time I saw him, that fated day on the train. Despite being an outcast, he'd never treated me with anything but kindness and respect. And eventually, love.

Despite what John might think, I knew how fortunate I was to have been loved by a man like him. Sadly, it didn't make it any more right to stay.

"I hope you know what you're giving up." John couldn't help the note of bitterness that crept into his voice.

His pain hurt me more than my own did, and the latter hurt plenty. "I do. But I need to do this, John. There are places I need to go and people I need to see. If I stay here with you, I won't be able to do that."

"Jess, I would never keep you from doing what is important to you, I just..." He gripped the back of my head. Our brows touched. "Love you so much."

I didn't bother to hide my tears. "I love you too. But if I stay, I won't remain the woman you love. I'll turn into someone else.

Escaping The Caves

And I don't think you'd love her so much. I certainly wouldn't."

John smiled through his tears. "I'd love you no matter what you were like. But I wouldn't want your unhappiness on my conscience. Do I think you're a fool for walking away from what we have? Yeah, I do. But I know better than to try and talk you out of something. I guess you just have to realize, in your own time, that what we have, Jess... That doesn't come around too often."

I nodded, determined not to show him how much his words scared me. The pain of losing him would be remarkable, but I knew that if I stayed we'd lose each other anyway, in a far worse way. I kissed him, deeply and thoroughly, hoping to convey my feelings.

"Sometimes when you love someone, the best way of showing them is by letting them go."

John laughed. The edge to it cut me to the bone. "And if we're meant to be, you'll come back to me?"

I forced myself to meet his eyes. "Yes."

"But you can't promise me that."

"No."

"I won't wait forever, Jess. Not even for you."

"I wouldn't want you to."

His voice and hands shook when he pulled me into one last embrace. "I love you. Remember that."

I buried my face in his neck. I wanted to live out the rest of my days there. To say goodbye to Sam and Eve had been hard. This was torture.

"And I love you. Don't forget."

Almost roughly, he helped me onto the train. He didn't stay to watch it leave this time. I didn't blame him. I didn't want him to see me like this either.

Epilogue

The waves crash onto the shore. The sand turns dark where it is touched. I sit far enough on the beach to avoid getting soaked, but close enough so the water laps at my toes. How long have I travelled for? I stopped counting the days a few months back. It didn't seem important. For the moment, I'm content to live in the present. The future will get here soon enough and the past will always be there. It follows me wherever I go. Whether I choose to dwell on it or not is entirely up to me. I can only move forward. The past, even such as mine, is becoming just that. The past.

The sun sets. It closes in on the horizon, colors everything in a pink, orange hue. There have been rumors going around about trouble brewing in the east. In the cities and the capital especially. It doesn't concern me. At least not yet. I'll help out if it becomes necessary. I miss my father and should very much like to see him again.

But I would like to be able to let him know how they are

first. If they are still alive. A lone seagull cries. I look up. The sky is so vast, but it soothes my soul all the same. If they are still out there, I will find them. One step at the time. Sooner or later my feet will take me to them.

There's no more need to hide. On the contrary, I'm met with respect and cheer wherever I go. I don't want to take advantage of anyone, but people's generosity where food and a bed for the night is concerned, is much appreciated. Wherever my help is needed, it's given.

The ghosts haven't found their peace yet, but they don't scare me anymore. I've accepted them. Perhaps they'll be my companions for the rest of my life. I listen to them, but I won't let them dictate my life anymore. Won't let them create boundaries or limits for me. They're a part of me, but I still have a life to live. One I'm very grateful for.

The cold seawater is soothing against my warm skin. I will stay here for a while I think. John is still a constant ache in my heart. Whether or not fate will bring us together again remains unclear to me. If we decide our own fate, then I haven't decided yet. I love him enough to trust that if it's meant to be we'll find our way back to each other again. When the time is right.

For now, I want to just sit here. To enjoy the sunset and the ocean. I've got no company but my own, and right now that's enough. There's more travelling ahead of me, and hopefully there always will be.

But I'm done running.

Kristin Talgø is a Norwegian science fiction and fantasy writer. For as long as she can remember, she has loved to read and write stories. She wrote her first story at the age of seven, continued through her teens, but didn't start taking it seriously until she was nineteen.

The main reason why she writes is because it makes her very happy. In the summer of 2010, she attended a Creative Writing Course at the University of Edinburgh. When no one here ridiculed her neither for wanting to be a writer nor for writing science fiction and fantasy, she came out of the closet as a writer and hasn't looked back since.

Ever since she was a kid, she's been drawn to the kind of books that pulls her into strange, mysterious, alternate realities. As long as a story grabs her, she can read just about anything. But science fiction and fantasy will always have a special place in her heart, and so it has become the genre she in which she writes.

She also has a bachelor degree in Social Work. During this degree, she discovered she was severely challenged as an academic writer, and she went straight back to being a creative one. But at least she got to live in Ghana for a time, got married and had a daughter. While she's no longer married, she still has her daughter. And so all things told, she considers her time well spent.

She is currently studying journalism in Oslo, Norway. While she's never going to be a hard-core news journalist, the stress of it alone would kill her, she enjoys feature and would like to dabble in literary journalism.